THE WORKS OF LIANG YUCHUN

梁遇春

著译全集

·九卷·

李力夫 商昌宝 主编

海峡出版发行集团 | 福建教育出版社

本卷总目

Some Best English Poems
英国诗歌选 …………………………………………… 1

Madrigal
情歌 …………………………………………………… 453

Some Best English Poems
英国诗歌选

(英汉对照)

梁遇春　译注

"自修英文丛刊"之一，上海北新书局，1930年6月付排，1930年8月初版

CONTENTS
目　　次

序言　谈英国诗歌 ·· 17

Old English Ballads

The Call
呼唤 ··· 52

Barbara Allen's Cruelty
Barbara Allen 的残忍 ·· 52

O Gin My Love Were You Red Rose
若使我的爱人是那朵红蔷薇 ···································· 56

The Twa Corbies
两个乌鸦 ··· 60

The Douglas Tragedy
Douglas 家的悲剧 ·· 64

The Sixteen Century（The Elizabethan Age）

Sir Walter Raleigh（1552—1618）

The Silent Lover

静默的爱人 …………………………………… 76

Edmund Spenser（1552—1599）

（缺目）………………………………………… 78

Sir Philip Sidney（1554—1586）

To the Moon

呈月亮 ………………………………………… 80

William Shakespeare（1564—1616）

Sonnets

十四行诗 ……………………………………… 82

Man's Ingratitude

人的忘恩 ……………………………………… 96

（缺目）………………………………………… 98

A Sea Dirge

海葬的挽歌 …………………………………… 100

Ariel's Song

Ariel 的小歌 …………………………………… 100

Thomas Campion（1567—1619）

（缺目）………………………………………… 102

（缺目）………………………………………… 104

Ben Jonson(1573—1637)

To Celia
呈 Celia ·· 106

John Donne(1573—1631)

（缺目）·· 108
（缺目）·· 108

The Seventeenth Century

Robert Herrick(1591—1674)

To the Virgins, to Make Much of Time
呈少女们，劝她们看重青春 ············· 112

To Anthea, Who May Command Him Anything
呈 Anthea, 她能叫他干任何事情 ·········· 114

To Daffodils
呈水仙 ·· 116

Edmund Waller(1606—1687)

（缺目）·· 120

John Milton(1608—1674)

To Mr. Lawrence
呈 Lawrence 先生 ································· 122

On His Blindness
他自己的失明 ······································ 124

Richard Lovelace(1618—1658)

To Lucasta, Going to the Wars
出征前呈 Lucasta ·· 126

John Dryden(1631—1700)

(缺目) ·· 128

The Eighteenth Century

Alexander Pope(1688—1744)

The Quiet Life
恬静的生涯 ·· 132

Henry Carey(1693—1743)

Sally in Our Alley
我们巷里的 Sally ·· 134

Thomas Gray(1716—1771)

On a Favorite Cat, Drowned in a Tub of Goldfishes
一个人们钟爱的猫儿泅死金鱼缸里 ····························· 142

Oliver Goldsmith(1728—1774)

(缺目) ·· 148

William Blake(1757—1827)

Introduction to "Songs of Innocence"
《天真的歌》的序诗 ·· 148

Love's Secret
爱情的秘密 ·· 152

Auguries of Innocence
"天真"的推测 ·················· 154

Robert Burns(1759—1796)

To a Mouse
呈耗子 ························· 154

John Anderson
John Anderson ················ 162

A Red, Red Rose
一朵红红的玫瑰花 ············· 164

The Nineteenth Century

William Wordsworth(1770—1850)

Lucy
Lucy ·························· 168

Lines Written in Early Spring
早春偶成 ······················ 180
(缺目) ························ 184

The Solitary Reaper
寂寞的刈禾人 ·················· 184
(缺目) ························ 188

The Inner Vision
心中的幻影 ···················· 190

To Sleep
呈睡神 …………………………………………… 192

Samuel Taylor Coleridge(1772—1834)

Love
爱 ……………………………………………… 194

Walter Savage Landor(1775—1864)

Ianthe
Ianthe ………………………………………… 206
Why
此何故耶 ……………………………………… 206
The Maid's Lament
小女的哀语 …………………………………… 208
Finis
尾声 …………………………………………… 210
Death
死 ……………………………………………… 210

Thomas Moore(1779—1852)

（缺目） ……………………………………… 212

George Noel Gordon, Lord Byron(1788—1824)

（缺目） ……………………………………… 214
All for Love
一切全是为爱情 ……………………………… 218
（缺目） ……………………………………… 220

To Thomas Moore
呈 Thomas Moore ································· 222

Percy Bysshe Shelley(1792—1822)

Stanzas Written in Dejection near Naples
Naples 湾畔愁中书怀 ······················· 226

Ode to the West Wind
西风歌 ·· 230

The Indian Serenade
印度的良夜之歌 ······························· 238

Love's Philosophy
爱的哲学 ·· 240

To a Skylark
云雀歌 ··· 242

The World's Wanderers
世界的漂泊者 ···································· 254

A Lament
哀歌 ·· 256

John Keats(1795—1821)

Ode to a Nightingale
夜莺歌 ··· 258

Ode on a Grecian Urn
希腊古瓶歌 ······································· 266

La Belle Dame sans Merci
没有慈心的美丽姑娘 ················· 272
On the Grasshopper and Cricket
蚱蜢同蟋蟀 ······················ 278

Thomas Hood(1798—1845)

The Bridge of Sighs
悲叹之桥 ························ 280

The Victorian Age

Elizabeth Barrett Browning(1806—1861)

The Mask
假面具 ·························· 292
Grief
悲哀 ···························· 296
（缺目）························· 298

Edward Fitzgerald(1809—1849)

The Three Arrows
三条箭 ·························· 300
（缺目）························· 302

Alfred Tennyson, Lord Tennyson(1809—1892)

The Miller's Daughter
磨坊主人的女儿 ··················· 304

Edward Gray

Edward Gray ·········· 306

The Eagle

鹰鸟 ·········· 310

A Farewell

别矣 ·········· 312

（缺目）·········· 314

（缺目）·········· 314

（缺目）·········· 318

（缺目）·········· 320

Crossing the Bar

渡过沙洲 ·········· 322

Robert Browning（1812—1889）

（缺目）·········· 324

Meeting at Night

夜会 ·········· 324

Home-Thoughts, from Abroad

在国外时的乡愁 ·········· 326

Home-Thoughts, from the Sea

海中乡思 ·········· 328

Life in a Love

整整一生花在向一女人求婚里面 ·········· 330

Apparitions
出现 ……………………………………………… 332
Epilogue
尾声 ……………………………………………… 334

Matthew Arnold(1822—1888)

Self-Dependence
自助 ……………………………………………… 336
Requiescat
安灵祈祷 ………………………………………… 340

Dante Gabriel Rossetti(1828—1882)

Sudden Light
顿悟 ……………………………………………… 344
Three Shadows
三影 ……………………………………………… 346

Christina Rossetti(1830—1894)

(缺目) …………………………………………… 348
Remember
忆 ………………………………………………… 350
Up-Hill
上山 ……………………………………………… 352
Last Prayer
最后的祷告 ……………………………………… 354

William Morris(1834—1896)

（缺目） ··· 356

Error and Loss

错误同丧失 ·· 356

Algernon Charles Swinburne(1837—1909)

The Garden of Proserpine

Proserpine 的园地 ····································· 360

Modern Poetry

Austin Dobson(1840—1921)

The Child-Musician

稚年的音乐家 ··· 372

Robert Bridges(1844—   )

Winter Nightfall

冬天的薄暮 ·· 374

Nightingales

夜莺 ·· 378

Elegy

挽歌 ·· 380

William Ernest Henley(1849—1903)

Unconquerable

刚强不屈 ··· 384

（缺目） ··· 386

The Blackbird
乌鸦 ……………………………………………… 388
The Passing
去世 ……………………………………………… 388

Robert Louis Stevenson(1850—1894)

Rain
雨 ………………………………………………… 392
The Wind
风 ………………………………………………… 392
Young Night Thought
小孩子晚上的梦想 …………………………… 394

Alice Meynell(1850—1923)

The Shepherdess
牧羊女郎 ……………………………………… 396
At Night
夜间 …………………………………………… 398

Francis Thompson(1857—1907)

Daisy
雏菊 …………………………………………… 400

William Watson(1858—　)

Invention
发明 …………………………………………… 408

Leavetaking
告别 ·· 408
Alfred Edward Housman(1859—)
（缺目）·· 410
Arthur Symons(1865—)
Love in Dreams
梦里的爱情 ·· 412
Rain on the Down
沙堤上的雨 ·· 414
William Butler Yeats(1865—)
The Lake Isle of Innisfree
湖中的小岛 Innisfree ·· 416
Ernest Dowson(1867—1900)
（缺目）·· 418
A. E. (George William Russell)(1867—)
Frolic
行乐 ·· 418
Stephen Phillips(1868—1915)
（缺目）·· 420
New "De Profundis"
新时代的悲哀 ··· 422
William Henry Davies(1870—)
The Moon
月 ·· 426

15

Leisure
闲暇 ·· 428
Truly Great
真正的伟大 ·· 430

Walter de la Mare(1873—)

The Stranger
生人 ·· 434
An Epitaph
墓铭 ·· 436
Silver
银色 ·· 438

Wilfrid Wilson Gibson(1878—)

The Messages
遗言 ·· 440

John Masefield(1878—)

Sea-Fever
航海的热狂 ··· 442
The Seekers
探寻者 ·· 444

James Stephens(1882—)

Hate
恨 ··· 448

序言 谈英国诗歌[1]

英国古民歌

英国古民歌是中世纪里民间所开的文艺之花。那时他们过着共同的生活,大家具有共同的情绪,所以能够合起来,编出单纯真挚的民歌。后来文化进步,印刷术也发明了,生活是一天一天地更趋于复杂,人人各有自己的环境,彼此的隔膜一层层地深下去,大家自然不能够再合伙来唱出牵情的调子了。也可以说,普通人的生活同诗情是越离越远了。新的民歌既然无

---

[1] 本篇序言,原以"谈英国诗歌"为题,最初发表于1930年7月16日《现代文学》第1卷第1期。《英国诗歌选》1930年8月初版时无此序言,1931年4月再版时收入。此篇据1931年4月版整理。——编者注

从产生，旧的民歌又渐渐归于湮没，若使没有 Thomas Percy （1729—1811），司各脱（Sir Walter Scott，1771—1832），同 Francis James Child（1825—1896）这般独具只眼的人们，孜孜兀兀地来收集，将村夫农妇口里所唱的记下来，这许多可喜的民歌真要绝迹于人间了。

民歌既是大家合伙做出来的，所以它的第一特色是没有个性。它不去表现个人的兴感，到〔倒〕是将全社会的情绪曝露出来。民歌的第二特色是简单，它里面的思想，情绪，词句，韵律和结构全是最朴素无华的，因此更显出它的新鲜气概同壮健风格。民歌的好处也就在这点。哥德说过："民歌之所以有价值者，全借着它们是直接从'自然'得到原动力的。"创造民歌的人们天真地不加雕斫〔琢〕地讴歌出他们共同的情感，这些作品既是自然而然地从他们的心里深处流露出来，所以能够自然而然地深注到听者的心里。华兹华斯（Wordsworth）说道："一切好诗都是强烈的情感的自然洋溢，"民歌的好处恰是在这点。后来虽然有许多大诗人，像司各脱，华兹华斯，济慈，丁尼生，罗赛谛，吉百龄等，非常激赏古民歌，自己做出很有价值的歌谣来，但是这些新歌谣总不能像古民歌那么纯朴浑厚，他们也因此更能了解民歌的价值。

最普通的民歌集子是 Percy：*The Reliques of Ancient English Poetry* 同 Everyman's Library 里面 Brimley Johnson 所选的 *A*〔*The*〕*Book of British Ballads*。若使要一本搜集无遗，考证精详的本子，那就不能不推 *Child's English and Scottish Popular Ballads*（5 vols）

为第一了。剑桥大学出版部印有节本（*Student's Cambridge Edition*），然而也是有七百多页，字又是印得很小的。这部书的确是想研究歌谣者所必备的。

伊利莎白时代的诗歌

这真是一件奇怪的事情，英国文学的极盛时代多半是当女皇执政的时候。伊利莎白女皇看到英国戏剧的成熟，同英国抒情诗吐萼扬华，开得满园春色，安女皇朝英国散文演进成为一种玲珑的文学工具，维多利亚女皇朝，英国那几位最伟大的小说家都正在写下他们不朽的杰作。这三朝里尤以伊利莎白时代最为动人心魄。那时文艺复兴的思潮震荡了全欧，人们大梦方醒地望着这个"世界的发现和人的发现"，大家都怀有无限的热狂和希望，个个人都觉得身里充满着跃跃欲试的生命力。英国那时又值隆盛之世，百姓过着太平的日子，没有什么苦闷，老是笑嘻嘻地听听慷慨激昂的骑士故事和荒诞不经的海客瀛谈，看看演戏，赛会，假面剧种种的玩意儿。他们一面还吸收罗马的古典学问和意大利，西班牙，法国的文化，酒馆里的主顾常拿文学批评来做高谈阔论的题目，朝野一同显出一派新气象来，人民生活的内容可说是丰富极了。在这块肥沃的土壤上就开出了万千朵临风招展的抒情诗小花，那一种斗艳怒发的盛况是英国诗坛上空前绝后的巨观。这个时代的抒情诗有两个特色，它们的情调具有天然的甜蜜同新鲜，好像乡下的山歌，丝毫没有做作的痕迹，却是这么可口，这么清新，真可说是天真流露的作品，好似我们的《古诗十九首》。那一种简朴不俗的口吻，后人虽然非常欣赏，却绝不能做到，这也许是因为此后时代精神同大自然是背道而驰，到我们这般尝着世纪末悲哀的人们，对于它们更只有含着无穷惆怅的赞美了。当时一位大诗人Sidney说道，"瞧你自己的心写出来罢"（"Look in thy heart and write"），这句直爽的话可做当时诗人的考语，他们都是童心尚在的可爱人们。他们的第二特色是根据这个特色而来的，因为他们情感纯挚，所以他们的思想也是直率挺拔，会深刻地印在我们心里，他们的诗里存有壮健的意味，这也许是出于他们那种简单的入世的人生观，也许是因为他们都是忙人，不像后来文学家那样雕琢字句，沾沾自喜，化为一个没有心肝的无聊文匠，一些洒脱的气概也没有，自然只能写出柔弱不振，四平八稳的句子了。

　　Sir Walter Raleigh（1552？—1618）——他是伊利莎白朝一个权臣，他又是一个探险家，一个战士，一切骑士的精神他全备有了。据说蕃薯同烟草都是他介绍到英国的。他后来被詹姆士第一杀死，为的是要市西班牙皇帝的欢心。他临刑的前一夜还做一首滑稽诗，这种如虹的意气的确是那时候的风尚。他不是一个有名的诗人，然而他有几首诗是非常可爱的。

　　史本塞（Spenser，1552？—1599）——他年轻的时候很穷，在剑桥度苦学生的生活。后来做了许久的官，最终死的时候却又是很穷，Ben Jonson还说他是饿死的，这也许是为着要说得动听点罢。他最伟大的著作是《仙后》（*Fairy Queen*）。他的诗浸在幻想的境界里。他是幻觉的，不是善于观察自然同人性的诗人。但是他的诗情是这么缥缈，他诗的音调又是这么铿锵，人们都把他叫做"诗人们的诗人"（The poet's poet）。

Sidney（1554—1606）[1]——这个豪爽英迈的青年是史本塞的好朋友，他在战场上忍着口干将一杯难得的水给身旁的兵士去喝，这件事是谁也知道的。他著作的范围极广，批评同创作两方面，都有相当的成就，可惜才过三十岁就死了。

莎士比亚（Shakespeare，1564—1616）——有人说他是世界最伟大的文学家，这大概不是过誉罢。他对于人性有极深切的了解，他看出人性的丑恶同美善。他不单写出人间世一切的色相，而且画出人们黄金的幻梦，所以他既是写实作家，又是浪漫作家。他对于任何种的人都有同情和原谅，所以他所描写的是真正的人性，一点儿偏见也不杂在里面，他心里本来是给温情占满，毫无偏见的余地了。他使用文字真可说是神工鬼斧，他毫不费力地用美丽的句子将他那微妙的意思传出来，文字和意思在他手里达到平均的发展，恰到好处，两不为害。据说他对于自己的作品不大重视，发财后，在家乡过舒服的日子，绝不问他著作的存亡，自己也不去把它们收集起来，这的确具有大文学家的风度。他的短诗神采飘逸，天衣无缝，不愧仙品之称。

---

1 据后文，Sidney 卒年应为1586年。——编者注

Campion（？—1619）[1]——是一位有名的医生，他的诗几乎全是为乐谱做的，音调甜蜜可喜。但是他却有一个主张，以为诗歌应当是无韵的，这类错误是诗人充作批评家时所常犯的。他的批评学说不久就被人们忘却了，而他的诗歌却与天地同存，这也可见出乎感情的东西的力量是超过出于理智的，因为那是个人性格更深的，更基本的表现。

Ben Jonson（1573？—1637）——他是这个浪漫时代里的古典主义诗人，他反对史本塞，以为不该乱用风花雪月的字眼，他心中理想的是表现得恰到好处，强弱均匀，一丝不漏的玲珑作品。他自己的小诗是具有男性的壮健和女性的秀雅的。这两个性质好似相反，其实相成，精练的句子常使人觉得秀色照人，拖泥带水的东西却绝说不上柔美。

Donne（1573—1631）——他也是史本塞诗派的反动者，他弃掉普通所谓的文字同诗的题目，专从枯索平凡的现实里去找诗料。他能把臭虫说得非常有趣动听，这样子不用诗的情调遮住现实，却将现实加以诗化，是很近于近代人和现实肉搏的精神，所以他是近代人所喜欢的。他不单是热情沸腾，而且思想玄妙，能够挟着热情一道儿奔驰。他被约翰生称为玄学的诗人，他的诗里每个意象，每个显明的思想后面都隐隐地现出人生同宇宙的最终神秘的闪光，使人们想入非非，所以玄学诗人于他倒是个好名称。

---

[1] 据后文，Campion生年为1567年。——编者注

十七世纪诗歌

Ben Jonson 同 John Donne 既是一反伊利莎白时代作风的诗人,他们自然而然地另开一种诗派,Jonson 的古典主义,和 Donne 的用古怪的幻想溶入诗里都成为第二代诗人的风气。当时诗人专取一个很小的题目,堆砌上许多惊人的比喻,用严密的构造将四五佳句紧凑成一首完整的短诗。他们失去伊利莎白时代雄伟壮丽的魄力,因为文艺复兴的高潮已经退下去了,他们不能喷出火焰,只能结些晶晶的露珠。虽然没有什么了不得的地方,但是在这类小慧可人的好玩的诗里,他们不失为达到完善境界的聪明人了。但是这些情诗太斫琢了,弄得后来只剩个形式,里面没有什么真情。恳挚动人的情歌暂时不再现于文坛了,一直等到十八世纪的勃莱克(Blake),彭斯(Burns)这般〔班〕人出来,我们才又有一巢新的歌鸟,唱出牵情的相思曲。

Herrick(1591—1674)——他和 Donne 一样,也是一个牧师。他的抒情诗音调非常悦耳,好似清溪的歌声。他唱着鲜花,茅亭,采桂,畅饮,暮春和盛夜的好景,新婚的夫妇和他们的喜筵,以及天堂的欢娱。他是那时代写短诗人们里的最大诗人,他的诗里存有永生的青春和不醒的幻梦。

Walter(1605—1687)——这位十七世纪里享有盛名的恋歌作家的特色是甜蜜。他在诗的形式上有个大贡献,他把古代诗人的对句诗体裁(heroic couplet)改良一下,就变为当时新诗最普通的形式,在诗坛上占有一百五十年的势力。

Lovelace（1618—1658）——他是个风度翩翩的美少年，才华又佳，所以当时人们都爱他。不幸得很，他因为忠于王事被反对党囚闭起来，他的爱人，Lucy Sacheverell——"Lucasta"——又以为他已经死了，就跟别人结婚。他后来穷愁潦倒得不堪，怪可怜地死了。

这个时期里最大的诗人当然要推那《失乐园》的作者——米尔顿（Milton，1608—1674）。他在十七世纪的位置，正像莎士比亚在伊利莎白时代一样。他用最美的形式把清教徒严正克己，虔信朴实的精神完全表现出来。他曾说过，"诗人自己应当是一首诗"（The Poet must be himself a Poem）。他那高尚沉雄的人格正像一首慷慨伟大的诗歌。他生在文学批评开始洗涤英国诗坛的时候，他自己对于古典文学又有很深的研究，所以他的诗没有伊利莎白时代诗人那种放肆同胡闹，可是他的想像力是不弱于他们的。他虽然没有他们的流利自然，可是他有一种更微妙的风格，对于自然也描写得更深刻，诗的结构也更见谨严，最可佩服的是他那种宏大的风韵，苍老劲道，绝不是别人所能效颦的。无论咏什么题材，用什么格式，他总是具有狮子搏兔那样的从容态度，所以他能将一种新的生命贯注到一切形式里去。他的杰作《失乐园》是谁也知道的，尤以开头两卷最为伟大。有人说好像两条大黄金柱子。他的十四行诗在文学史有很重要的位置，以前诗人做十四行诗多半是一写就几十首衔接着，内容又脱不了言情说爱，米尔顿却指出给我们看，十四行诗是偶成的诗最合宜的形式。米尔顿的十四行诗内容是很复杂的，有的是歌夜莺，有的是叹自己年华的消逝，有的是反抗强暴的呼声，有的是赠朋友的温语。因此给华兹华斯这般善于做十四行诗的人们开了一条大路。

他在大学毕业后在家闲居六年，专攻古典文学，后来投到政治的漩涡里去，做Cromwell的秘书。他那伟大的人格在政治生活里也是同样地可钦敬的。他工作太勤，不久就成为盲人了。查理二世复辟后，这位盲诗人隐居着写下他的杰作，寂寞地死了。

米尔顿是旧时代最后一位的大诗人，是无限好的夕阳。他和伊利莎白时代的诗人同样地歌咏着人生的热情，现在却来了一个新的风气了。理性同幻想变做诗歌的唯一题目。他们虽然也在做情歌，但却不是由狂热里进出来的火花，而是理智镕炉锻冶成的。这般〔班〕新时代的人们受了法国当时古典主义的文学批评的影响，老是讲究剪裁，干净，精巧，无疵，明了，这些方面。他们的诗是冷冰冰的，不过这类结晶的东西也有它的亮光，也有它的美处，也很值得吟味一番，并且约束住了前时代草率放纵的毛病，在训练方面来说，的确是很有益的。

Dryden（1631—1700）——是这新时代诗坛上的唯一的权威者。他是讽刺诗的能手，最善于做俏皮的句子。他的目的是想达到强壮有力的思索，微妙精确的形式。文雅无疵的辞句和完美流利的韵律，这几点他全都成功了。有人说他缺乏同情和热忱，这是有点冤枉的。他不是没有强烈的情感，只看这本集子里他这首纯挚的情歌就知道。他所以好似无情，那是因为他生在批评时代，理智时代，只有他的理智得到完全的自由发展。所以他不单是个诗人，并且是一位大批评家。人们总跳不出时代，就说他带些冷酷，那也是可以原谅的。

十八世纪诗歌

（一）古典主义

有些批评家把诗人分做两类："自然"的诗人（the poet of Nature）和"技巧"的诗人（the poet of Art）。前一类是史本塞，莎士比亚，米尔顿这般具有灵感的诗人。他们靠着自己的美丽的心境，伟大的气魄，和强烈的热情，来领会"自然"里美丽，伟大同强烈的意味，他们真可说是和"自然"的灵魂有个神秘的感通。他们既是用想像力将"自然"和盘托出，凡是禀有天性的人们对于他们的作品当然会起共鸣，而感到一种神游八极，与万物一体的喜悦。他们从"自然"走到读者的心里，使读者觉得他们的诗歌都是读者自己心坎里所蕴有的说不出来的真情。至于那班"技巧"的诗人就大异其趣了。他们是懂得世俗上人情的聪明人，善于观察社会里的微末色相，喜欢完整的艺术品，人工烘染过的自然景致，以及人生里微温的柔情。总之他们最怕过火，不敢任意奔驰，他们的目的在于合理的安闲生活，他们不求什么奇观，不想表示个人的性格，只是聚精会神来琢磨出玲珑的字句。他们不讲生活内容的丰富，却想创造温文尔雅的生活。他们是俗世的俗人，没有什么狂梦地执着现实。但是他们在诗的技术上面的确是费了苦心。那种斩钉截铁，短小精悍的诗句在诗匠的工夫方面是很值得赞美的。这类作品好像在一块小象牙上刻下一篇笔划清楚，字小于蚁的《滕王阁序》。没有一个爱好艺术的人不会不啧啧称美，虽然内中没有多少人生的奥妙和高超的理想。这是假古典主义的妙处，Pope（1688—1744）就是这时代的骄子。他比Dryden更进一步，他诗里绝没有Dryden所不免的粗糙成分，也许是因为Dryden的心比他的还更具有力气的缘故罢。Pope的长处是扮出一个毫无偏见和私心的人，对于事情下个似乎公正的判词（他有名的长诗《批评论》属这一类），或者用最刻薄的口气，把他所厌恶的人物加以微妙的痛骂（他的讽刺诗属这一类），或者将安闲的生活和人生里通常家庭朋友的情愫用最雅致的辞句描绘得楚楚可人（他的"书信诗"和我们这集子里的诗属于这一类），或者用一种滑稽口气将小事铺张地叙述得令人不禁不断地微笑。他真可说是一位最伟大的具有一切小聪明的诗人。在这类以趣味见长的诗里，他可以称王。他是个残疾的人，癖〔脾〕气很坏，这也许因为他具有慧眼罢。他才二十四岁就得到福禄特尔（Voltaire）的称赞，认为"当时全欧的最大诗人"。他一生除却做诗外没有别的什么大事情，不到六十岁就到Westminster Abbey和过去的诗人做永久的伴侣了。

（二）过渡时代

伊利莎白时代末年的诗歌任情写去，草率粗糙的地方极多，因此失去了自然的美。古典主义起来纠正这个毛病，立下许多规则，他们的诗，虽然完整匀称，却太矫揉做作了，也绝不是自然流露的作品。到了十八世纪下半期有一般〔班〕诗人出来，他们是崇拜史本塞，沙士比亚的，他们是注重热情，想像力同大自然的，他们是感情主义（sentimentalism）者，他们觉得"自然"就是"上帝"，那么人的本性当然是善良的了。爱人类变为人们最重要的道德，爱自然做了他们宗教的信条，只要人们能够返到自然境界里去，天国会顿然现在人间。他们既然怀了这么一种天真的信仰，热溢地做出诗来，他们的诗虽不如莎翁同时那些诗人的天马行空，也都还有一种恬然自适的风姿，远胜过假古典主义底下小诗人们的死板板的句子。他们多少总受些古典主义的影响。所以他们的作品仍然保留有严整完善的构造，这是古典主义惟一的遗产。

诗的作风变了，诗的题目当然也是一样地换个方向了。前半期的诗人将所有的才华全化在去描摹刻划上等社会种种的形相和发出尖酸刻薄的热嘲冷讽，他们绝不去管这天青地碧的大自然，充其量也不过拿来做个背境，凑凑热闹罢了。现在感情主义这团火把这冷酷的讥讽溶得无影无踪。人们离开那虚伪的社交，投身到大自然的怀中去了。起先还是不敢恣情地享受自然的美，却好像学步的婴儿，胆小地慢慢前进；也可说是因为闭在暗室里太久了，反受不了阳光的照耀，所以一面还用手遮着眉头，只从手指缝里偷向外望。到后来在自然里跳跃飞奔，和自然拈花微笑，就铺好往浪漫主义的路了。那时既已发现了自然，自然里飞鸟鸣虫，游鱼走兽也变为他们所喜欢的东西了，他们常用无限的同情和慈悲来替它们写照。这种歌咏动物的心情此后在诗坛上老占有很大的势力。同时他们对于尚在自然怀中的儿童也起了羡慕和惊奇。他们既弃了绅士淑女们来赞美野外风光，当然对于乡下人的生活会感到浓厚的趣味，他们将村夫野老农妇和乡里小姑娘的朴素的生活和真挚的心境用简明的辞句描绘，那种熙熙攘攘的气象真仿佛乐园现于人间。但是他们还能看出穷人的辛酸，洒下同情的眼泪。他们一知道了去鉴赏平民生活的苦乐，就走进歌谣文学这丛落英缤纷的树林。他们忽然知道，天下绝妙的诗歌是俯拾即是的，只须把晒日黄的老村妇口里唱的古歌谣记下，就是一首纯出天籁的诗，前面谈英国歌谣时所说的 Percy 是这时候搜集歌谣的大家。总之，这是个过渡的时期，我们由不毛的瘠土将走到花笑叶舞的园中，渐入佳处了。

Henry Carey（1693？—1743）——是 Halifax 公爵的私生子，他写了几本笑剧。他最有名的诗是，"Sally in Our Alley" 这首歌谣。

Gray（1716—1771）——这位害羞的，恬退的，神经锐敏的诗人是生性愁闷，善于说出自己胸中郁着幽情的人。他旅行外国时写回给他母亲和二三知交的书信都非常可喜，我们现在读那些信，仿佛有一个流连于意大利山光水色中的愁人现在我们的眼前。他眈〔耽〕于冥想，深有所感于人事的变迁。他那首《墓畔哀歌》（"Elegy Written in a Country Churchyard"）是这类抚今追昔文学里的杰作。但是他也瞧出人间世里的滑稽情调，有时用他那奇妙的幻想，做出蕴有无限回甘意味的诙谐诗。他的好友说："Gray除开滑稽文学外什么东西都很费劲；滑稽是他天生的，特有的心情。"我们这里所选的是一个好例子。他一生没有什么大事情，晚年做牛津大学近代史和近代文学的教授，可是他没有上过一次讲堂；他的诗不多，却都具有很高的价值。

高尔斯密士（Goldsmith，1728—1774）——这位诗人脾气极好，心地极仁慈，自己做人却胡涂到万分。他在大学里当苦学生，后来想做牧师。但是他的衣服太艳丽了，因此落选。他买好舱位预备渡重洋到美国去垦荒，可是当船离开英国时，他正逛得高兴，就忘记按时上船了，只好又回到家乡去。他转过念头来去学法律，又没有学好，最后到爱丁堡医科学校里念书。野性难驯，在那里玩了两年，他忽然想到大陆去，名义自然是去继续学医。他在荷兰得到一个莫名其妙的学位，然后漫游大陆，靠他的吹箫本领来糊口。一年后回到祖国，当然还是一贫如洗的。他回来后干许多无聊的事，当小学里的助教师，当书店里受雇的作家。他还挂过招牌当医生，但是门可罗雀，他后来病死是他把自己医坏了，那么那般〔班〕不来就诊的人们真有先知之明。他此后的生涯是化在著作，躲债，（他老是欠债，不管他挣了多少钱）和干慷慨的事情之中。他死时还有许多未清的债。但是他性情的和蔼，品行的纯洁，思想的高尚是凡跟他接近的人们所异口同声地赞美的。他终身行事老像个小孩，具有小孩的任性和小孩的天真。他是英国文学史中最可爱的人物的一个。

他写有一篇小说《威克斐牧师传》(*Vicar of Wakefield*)——

许多小品文字，最有名的是 The Citizen of the World，那是假托一个侨居英国的中国人写给住在北京的老师的许多书信，里面有描状英国当时社会情形，非常有趣。他还写有两本喜剧《诡姻缘》（"She Stoops to Conquer"）同 "The Good-Natured Man"。他有两篇长诗《荒村》（"The Deserted Village"）同 "The Traveller"。他相信古典主义，但是他那爱自然，爱人类的天性和冷冰冰的古典主义实在是水火不相容的，所以他的诗形式上不管多么古典派的，内容始终是新的精神——感情主义。他无论在那种作品里都十分显明地流露他的性格，他那仁者之心是溢于言表，这点也是这新时代的精神。

　　勃莱克（Blake，1757—1827）——近代许多批评家认他为第一个说出十九世纪浪漫派的思想的人，因为他是第一个用想像的能力将我们从现实里解放出来。他的想像力能使他现出万千色相，一会儿是天真烂漫的小孩，唱出蕴有极美童心的短歌，一会儿化为世故老人，看到世界里一切阴险和权谋，一会儿与自然为侣地领略大地的风光，一会儿看穿宇宙极深奥的神秘。他最可惊的天才是在能用极简单的字句，几乎一大半都是单音字的，将这许多意思传递出来。并且因为他用的是最易明了的短字，这些意思也更深刻印在我们的心里。当他唱山羊，小花，春天和催眠歌时，他用的字句是这么简单，真好似一个牙牙学语的小孩倚在慈母膝下时说的痴语。他那种意思极分明的辞句说到神秘时，我们加倍地感到那真是宇宙里最深的神秘，是剥蕉般找到人生的核心的作品，因为他的文字正好似一块透明的玻璃，我们得到和神秘直目相视了。那班用莫名其妙的字眼来说神秘的人们说的不是神秘，到〔倒〕是表现自己思想能力的薄弱。要这样子说得明白万分，而里面的神秘却终是一个不可解的神秘，这才是真正的神秘诗人。他八岁时就常在白天里看见天使，他一生里和灵的世界总是相通消息的。他又是个善于镂板的人，他用铜板画来做他诗集的插图，这种铜板雕刻是他所发明的，他那些画也正和他的诗一样，具有空前绝后的美。可惜他死后，一位朋友说这类淫巧的技术是魔鬼指使的，把他的心血都付之一炬，只剩一点儿下来，做我们赞美同怅惘的材料。他和 Donne 一样都是现代人所乐道的诗人。

彭斯（Burns，1759—1796）——若使我们要找一个真正的出自田间的平民诗人，那么不能不推这位贪酒好色的农夫彭斯了。他从十四岁一直到廿四岁老在他父亲的田里耕作，*To a Mouse* 就是他耕田时的一点感触。他的诗集发表后誉满全国，他的生活也更放荡，才三十七岁就因身体摧残太甚而死了。从十七世纪以来，热烈的恋歌已绝响于文坛许久了，彭斯的情诗却能承接伊利莎白时代一往情深的情调，重燃起抒情诗的火焰。他不单是能写出激越的词句，他几乎每句出口的诗都带了这感奋的色彩。那时正需要这么一个情感极浓的人来拨开理智的雾障，彭斯拿乡下人的诚恳，冲破当时诗歌里种种的虚伪同束缚。他还介绍给我们他对于自然那种亲切同谙熟的态度，浑朴动人的苏格兰土语，以及许多新的材料，如乡下的佳节盛会，爱动物的心情，地方色彩以及快乐入世，嘻嘻哈哈的人物。爱情，悲情，诙谐，大自然，总之凡是可以激动人心的东西都在他的诗里找出。他这个多情多感的心灵抛弃了一切古典主义的桎梏，放口地用他家乡的土语唱歌，到这时候，我们已走进波涛汹涌的浪漫时代了。

十九世纪诗歌

（一）浪漫派时代

返于自然的呼声，我们在前几位诗人的诗里已经隐约地听到了，现在却是自觉地说出。人们因为感到自然的伟大，就觉得最近于自然的乡间生活是理想的生活，天天受自然的陶冶，和自然的精神息息相通，溶在自然里面的乡下人是理想的人物。他们对于人们天生的热情和性格也起了尊敬，觉得这也是自然的一部分。他们认为我们在大自然里是平等的，同是大自然这位母亲的儿子，所以一切国界，种界，阶级界，贫富界，在他们眼里都是无谓的区分。我们同样地具有人性的尊严，越是平凡的生活，与自然越是接近。他们又看出自然里有无限的神秘，自然是神的化身，因此他们都是偏于泛神论的。总之，他们所歌咏的是当我们与自然，与神奇，或者与平凡生活的哀乐接触时所得的牵情的经验。他们这种新鲜的题材已经够值得我们的欣赏了。

他们的文字的富丽，音律的复杂，叙述里所含的力量和烈火，情感的温柔和浓厚，看到人们灵魂深处和大自然深意的识见，一种更广大同更有智慧的仁慈心，都是极可惊人，差不多是任何时代也赶不上的。他们这样子凭着想像力来对于一切做更深一层的观察，的确另辟了一块新的境地。在这块新花园里野花芳草任意灿烂地开着，绝不受古典主义种种的藩篱。他们的诗句乘一时诗兴而抑扬顿挫，不去讲死板板的和谐，结果倒产生一种更微妙的音乐。他们真可说是抓到诗的神髓了。自由是他们一切行动的理想目的，他们的确把诗歌解放了，使诗的精神得到自由的发展。这算是英国诗坛上的极盛的时代。

华兹华斯（Wordsworth，1770—1850）——这位湖畔诗人的幼年是在清秀的湖边过去的，当他是个小孩子时，就喜欢那里明媚的风景，后来也就死在这寂寞的地方。法国革命爆发的时候，他跑到法国参加活动，还有一段浪漫的恋爱，生了一个私生子。他的亲戚断绝他经济的来源，他只好回到英国来，这使他免得跟那般〔班〕革命党同上断头台去。他有一位患肺病的朋友死后留下给他九百金镑，他就靠着这笔款到乡下去，度个清贫的生涯。

当法国革命变为拿破仑专制的局面，他很痛心，失望于一切了。这时他的妹妹Dorothy同他的好友Coleridge带他回到诗的园地里去。他们渐渐形成一个理想，那是用睁开的眼睛和敏捷的想像力去观察自然和人。他对于"自然"所取的态度和他以前的诗人是完全不同的。他认为自然是个活的东西，具有一个灵魂。这个灵魂浸润到花草山水里去，使它们各具有灵魂。我们的心和自然的灵魂本来有个预先安排好了的和谐，所以自然能够把她的思想传给我们，我们也能深切地去体贴，等到最后自然和我们化为一气了。他这样子将自然人格化，他对于自然正像对于朋友或者姊妹那样爱着。这是他对于自然那种亲切的观察，同热情的描写的来源。

他这个崇拜"自然"的宗教有力量来锻炼同安慰人生。他看出简朴生活的可敬，英雄的功业不能打动他的心，他所最赞美的倒是近乎白痴的乡下人和看出自然的神秘的小孩子。他谈着人事时总是这样独具只眼，人生从他的诗里放出一道又清醒又严肃的光辉。

他主张感情要经过一度恬然心境的洗涤后才能入诗，所以他不常做情诗，怕的是情歌的热烈口气会违背了这个原则。但是他那几首情诗是极可爱的，真可惜不曾多做几首。

辜勒律己（Coleridge，1772—1834）——华兹华斯的天才是在于将诗的精神贯注到简明的真理里去，辜勒律己的长处却是使本来有诗意的东西会具有现实的力量，使人们不得不信。他的诗多半是关于缥缈神奇的事情，然而里面的个个意象都这么有生气，我们却觉得这些幻想是比捉摸得住的东西还要更真实些。他使我们在空中楼阁时好像是足踏实地的。这样子他提高了我们的心境，我们能够容纳荒诞的幻想了，不再像从前那么心地偏狭，老执着眼睛看得见的事物。他是个辩才无碍的哲学家，凡是跟他谈话过的人们都震惊于他的娓娓动听的辞令，据说他能将最玄妙的理论说得非常分明。他又是个识见精确的批评家。有人说他是英国惟一的批评家，他能说出各门文学的精义，他那锐敏的眼光看出作品里的艺术生命，绝不像当时断章取义，肆口漫骂的批评家。他虽然有这么多的天才，可是他的诗篇不多，这一半是因为他对于法国革命的失望，他的身体不康健和他的吃鸦片习惯，一半也是出于他天性里的意志薄弱，缺乏执行的能力，和不能耐劳。所以他自己的成就不多——这些一点儿的杰作却是极有魔力的诗歌——而他激发别人的文学天才的功劳是非常大的，华兹华斯就是一个好例子。他的杰作也是当他和华兹华斯同住在一起互相勉励那一年里做成的。此后他和华兹华斯兄妹到德国去，回国后他们同骚西（Southey，他的妻子是骚西妻子的姊妹）同卜居于湖滨。他此时因为生病染上鸦片瘾，这做了他终身的恶魔。他把妻子交给骚西去供给，自己就在英国和大陆游荡一生。华兹华斯说道，"当时别人虽然写有奇异的作品，辜勒律已是他所知道的惟一的奇异的人物"。

　　Landor（1775—1864）——他是浪漫派里得到古典文学的真精神的诗人。他将浪漫的空气和古典文学的完整，文雅同节制合在一起。他的短诗很有希腊短诗（Epigram）的风味，恐怕只有 Ben Jonson 能够和他相比。他诗里的气魄是任何人都赶不上的，好像盘空的苍松，或者大海的波峰。他一生遭遇多半是不如意，喜欢同人家打官司。他一份很大的家产就在法庭里化去一半，还有一半他挥霍得干净。老年时他的儿子不肯供给他的生活费，若是没有白朗宁的殷勤款待，他将受到饥饿的苦痛了。他的诗还不如他的散文那么有名，那也是镕浪漫派的斑烂〔斓〕色调和古典派的优雅均匀于一炉的作品。他替后来散文家辟一条途径，可说是最早的散文革命家。

Moore（1779—1852）——他和Landor刚是相反，他没有什么学问，他的诗的惟一长处是流利可歌。肤浅是他最大的毛病，但是自伊利莎白时代以来，很少诗人的抒情诗有像他的那样宜于乐谱。在这个偏重光怪陆离的美和玄妙的思索的时代，有这么一个平易的歌者，唱出悦耳的歌声，很可以一休息我们紧张太过的神经，也未始不是一件好事。

拜伦（Byron，1788—1824）——他的父亲是一个有名的无赖，他的母亲是一个愚蠢的女人，他这个男爵是从他的叔祖，一个坏爵士，世袭来的。他十九岁出有一部诗集，被当时批评家痛骂一阵，二十四岁他出版他的 *Childe Harold* 的前两部，据他自己说，睡一晚上，第二早起来就已成名了。他后来娶一位Milbanke女士，刚刚一年就离婚了，有人说是出于Byron行为的卑劣。到底实情如何现在还是一段公案。总之，他为英国社会所不容，于1816〈年〉春天离英国，就永不生还了。他在南欧流荡了七八年，最后助希腊独立，还没有成功他就死了。拜伦在外国的荣誉远胜过本国人历来对于他的批评。法，德，意，俄，西班牙新浪漫文学全受他直接或间接的影响。歌德，泰纳，以及许多大文学家对于他都是万分倾倒，几乎认为英国最大的诗人。他介绍许多新的意境，新的观念到英诗里去。但是他最大的长处是他那种烈火般的力气，使他的诗含有无限的生气，无论那个读者都会受感动。他是个嫉俗愤世的人，尤其恨传统的观念，他所渴望的是自由，是这个组织严整的社会里所不能得到的自由。他的诗因此充满了社会革命的呐喊声音,他的作风是直截痛快,慷慨激昂的。我们读时还隐约地看出一个眉飞色舞的英雄独自凄凉地悲歌。但是他的诗有一个致命的毛病,那是他的情感常是不诚恳的,使读者觉得这些无非信口唱着的好听句子,并不是从心里流出的。所以许多人对于他的诗怀一种不能压下的厌恶,装腔作势的确是他的大弱点,所以不管他的诗是多么气雄万夫,我们总觉得有些美中不足。

雪莱(Shelley,1792—1822)——拜伦和雪莱人们常常合在一起批评,他们的确都是爱自由的诗人,破除社会习俗的健将,同是为当时规矩的绅士淑女们所侧目的。他们个人方面也是好朋友,然而他们的性格却有天壤之分。拜伦是自私自利,常带着十八世纪诗人尖酸刻薄的作风,并且常作厌世之言,摆出那种看透了人生一切,在旁边说风凉话的冷酷态度,使有些读者对他觉得心寒。雪莱却是慷慨得叫人惊奇,他始终保持着他的童心,好像是住在缥缈世界里的神仙。然而他对于人间世的事情,却不胜其愤激,那一种勇往直前的乐观精神是这么可亲可敬,他的诗的确可以提高我们的心情。总之,拜伦是以理智精锐见长的,雪莱却是想像的化身。

他是一个最会做梦,最善于描摹梦的情调的浪漫作家,他的长诗全是带有梦的色彩的,"Prometheus Unbound"是用戏剧的形式来写梦,"The Witch of Atlas"是用叙事的体材〔裁〕来写梦,"Epipsychidion"可说是纯粹精神恋爱(所谓柏拉图式的恋爱,Platonic Love)的梦。梦是浪漫派作家最喜欢的东西,作

《一个吃鸦片人的忏悔录》的 De Quincey 就是整个人浸在梦的情绪里的人。雪莱既然是逍遥在梦的国土，所以他的诗是最有诗意的，是纯净诗的结晶，如果我们要知道什么叫做诗，我们只要细读一下雪莱的短诗，立刻会了解什么是诗。他的诗正如虹霓一样的光芒四射，也是同样的不沾尘土，同样的神秘不可测，那种微妙轻灵是读者只能感到，而说不出的。他将人心更微妙的地方这么深切地领悟了，他甚至于常用抽象的东西来形容目前的风光，而使我们对于自然得到深一层的了解。他和华兹华斯一样认为自然是活的，但是华兹华斯只把自然看做是思索的源泉，雪莱却将自然当做爱的表现了。至于他音调的销魂，描写的有生气，那虽然是末节，也是许多诗人所赶不上的。

他出身贵族，年青的时候，在大学做一篇《无神论的必然》，被学校开除了。他娶一位年青的姑娘，后来离婚了，又和 Godwin 的女儿结婚。他一生行事多半是随着冲动，所以有些可以指摘的地方，但是他的心老是洁白的。他后来因为坐小艇漫游，葬身于波涛之中。据说他最喜欢放纸船，到壮年还是如此，他这缥渺的生涯真可说是池中一条浮荡着的纸船，是一条未登彼岸就翻船的纸船。

济慈（Keats，1795—1821）——这位诗人本来是学医的，后来看出自己的诗才，就专心做诗，不幸才二十多岁就害肺病死了。他是接浪漫派的心传，开了维多利亚时代作风的诗人。他不像前面两位那样热心于当时的社会情形和政治状态。他的心都寄托在希腊和中古时代，他歌咏他们的神话和传说，他直觉地体贴出他们的生活和精神,所以一个不通古典文学的人说出古代的情调时,能令许多渊博的学者心折。他富有希腊人爱美的习气,美是他一生惟一的追求。他从光荣的过去历史里去找出许多美的材料和色彩,这做了后来诗人的模范。在他眼里诗情是最重要的,他到处寻讨诗情,他自己创造了许多新的诗情。他是为美而去求美的,是真正的爱美者,不像许多诗人专拿美来做宣传主张的工具。有人说他与人离得太远了,这也许是因为他才二十五岁就去世了,所以他的诗还没有达到完全的发展。但是拿他所成就的来论,他在他着力的那方面的确已很成熟了。他说出他喜欢的东西的美而是跑到那东西心里,好似是那东西自己在那里说话似的。他的辞藻极艳丽,可是一点也没有堆砌的毛病,这是因为他个个字都是从热烈的情感里迸出,天下绝没有惨淡无光的火花。他不单赞美普通人所认为美的东西,而且从许多愁闷不堪的境地里也能找出美的鲜花来,这是他的新贡献。

Hood(1799—1845)[1]——他是一个处在极苦的环境里而自得其乐的人。他善用双关语做滑稽诗,又是凄凉辛酸的诗的能手。他能用诗情贯注到人道主义里去,他常用巧妙轻盈的句子来写极刺心的事件,因此更显出内中的悲惨。爱伦坡(E. A. Poe)对于他的《缝衣曲》("Song of the Shirt")同《叹息之桥》非常激赏,说这首诗的韵律和这疯狂的题目恰好相合。他

---

1 据后文,Hood的生年应为1798年。——编者注

和济慈一样也是死于肺病的。

(二) 维多利亚时代

维多利亚时代是社会改革，平民主义盛行和科学发达，进化论出世的时期。所以那时的人心是被种种复杂的思想所扰乱，人们对于政治，科学，宗教各方面都有须要改弦更张的趋向，诗人自然是更灵敏地反映出这个纷纭错杂和人生鹄的之追求。因此他们的诗不如浪漫派时代那么鼓着浩然之气，痛快淋漓地说出缥缈的幻梦。他们要了解这顽铁也似的现实，想用思想来调剂这个现实。他们不望着天空低吟高歌，却是看到地上的无穷纷乱，拿诗情来对付现实。因此他们的态度比前时代更慎重，他们的口气更认真，他们具有一种严肃的气象。当时的学者对于宗教，人类和宇宙的起原既有深刻的研究，普通人的宇宙观和人生观免不了为之动摇，这时代里最伟大的诗人丁尼生和白朗宁就着力于从这些已破的残垒里建起一座信仰的宫殿。他们用深沉的情感，来发挥人和神的关系，和悲哀同永生的关系。他们浓厚地染上玄学的色彩，但是他们先从男人同女人的性格看出人生的真谛，他们借人们的身世来表现玄妙的神秘。人生始终是他们的题材，他们却是从人生里去找出一个人生观，后面现出一个玄学的影子。不是先有个宇宙论，然后再演绎出一个人生哲学。所以他们的诗不流于理障，不是哲学的散文，却是充满人生意义的杰作。然而人们不久也厌倦于这样子去探讨一切事物的究竟了，于是现出精神的不安，怅惘和失望，有的逃于专赖意志力的自己忍痛的 Stoic 派思想，有的向美的国土里一息疲累的心儿，安诺德（Arnold）就是前一种人，罗赛谛（Rossettis）兄妹，Morris，史文朋（Swinburne），是第二种人。这般从美得到安慰的人物是神往于中古时代传说的浪漫情调，和万缘俱寂的宗教生涯。他们还向希腊罗马和意大利的但丁去找灵感，总之凡是可以引人暂忘人间世的苦闷烦恼的意思，他们都用那曼声轻圆，凄迷婉转的音调描摹下来。浪漫派时期是始于狂风怒涛，终于济慈的沉醉于美这个酒杯里，维多利亚时代同样地始于虔诚真挚，终于睡在美这个摇篮里，天下的事物永远是兜着一样的圈子跑，所差的是圈子不同而已。我们现在也正在另一个圈子里兜着哩。

白朗宁夫人（Mrs. Browning，1806—1861）——她年轻时候，是一个喜欢读书同做诗的姑娘。但是她身体太弱，三十多岁时她的兄弟死了，她受了很大的刺戟〔激〕，过了六年寂寞静默的病室生活，她的诗里满眼清泪的神情大概是受这种生活的影响。她四十岁时和Browning一见倾心，违了她顽梗父亲的意思，跟这位少年诗人偷跑了。她的诗最大的毛病是音节不谐，但是她的情感却丰富得够使人忘记了这个弱点。她最有名的诗是"Sonnets from the Portuguese"，那是叙述她和白朗宁恋爱时她内心的波涛。

Eizerold[1]（1809—1883）——他是个性情温厚，和蔼可亲的

---

1 Eizerold，吴福辉《梁遇春散文全编》注为"未详"，学者马海甸认为是Fitzgerald（菲茨杰拉德）的误植。——编者注

学者。他大学毕业后和大学里的后辈常常来往，他一位熟识的大学生对于波斯文学有很深的研究，他们一同读波斯古诗人 Omar Khayyam 的诗，这个诗人那时在波斯已成大家赞美，大家都读的诗人了。Eizerold 的譒译是很自由的意译，但是懂得波斯文的学者都说很能达原文风韵，远胜过一切直译。

丁尼生（Tennyson，1809—1892）——他是一个生性害羞恬静，不喜和人们交接的诗人。他的一生完全被诗的冲动支配着，他在做桂冠诗人之前，过着清贫而自得的生活，这和华兹华斯很相似。他的最大长处有两点：一是能够好似毫不费力地用简单的字句烘染出夺目的画图，这一方面是由于他会观察自然细微的地方，所以淡淡地描摹一两笔都非常逼真。一方面是由于他具有艺术家精益求精的态度，字字都要使成为无瑕的白璧。第二个长处是他在诗的音乐有极大的成就。无论那个人只要他不是个聋子，一念起他的诗，都会很纳罕，文字能够产生这么美的音调。据说从前有一位不懂英文的人家读他的诗，就知道是一定是大诗人的作品。凡是诗里的艺术奥妙，他无有不精通，不臻上乘的。他靠他的想像力，将颜色和音乐应用到种种不同的题材上，结果总是那么可喜。他尤长于小诗，在十几行里音调和情境千变万化，说到艺术方面的确是鬼斧神工。他的思想近乎平凡，没有什么深刻的地方，但是他的诗材真当得起一代宗师的名称。他最有名的长篇诗是"In Memoriam"，那是哭他朋友的挽歌，里面信仰和怀疑相冲突着，最终是信仰战胜了一切，所以有人说他是个肯定的诗人。

白朗宁（Browning，1812—1889）——他也是一位肯定的诗人，然而他和丁尼生却大不相同。丁尼生多少带些悲观主义者的色彩和定命论的精神，所以他的肯定是出于个体服从全部的演进。白朗宁却是极看重个人意志，他的福音是个性绝不可被压下，个人可以打倒世上一切的障碍。白朗宁顶喜欢歌颂爱情和预言人生胜利的乐天人生观。丁尼生是句斫字琢的，白朗宁却乘一时盛气，信笔写去，有时生出至妙的音乐，有时变为噪音。丁尼生是艺术先于人生哲学，白朗宁却全注目于他那挺拔的意思，几乎不大管音调的和谐与否。然而有时白朗宁情诗的悦耳反胜过斤斤于字句间的人们。白朗宁的情调永远是热烈豪放，喘不过气的样子。他的诗的勇敢，有力和具有独立的精神完全是他个人人格的表现。他是最足感发人们的意志，带有兴奋剂的诗人。他的诗可说是人类灵魂的研究录，他不记人们外面的生活，却一开头就钻到人们的心里去，用解剖刀将个个人灵魂的构造一一呈现出来。白朗宁的诗晦涩难读，这一半是因为他草率从事，一半是因为他的情绪太紧张，他的意思挤得太紧，他的联想太快，所以才使念他诗的人好像完全莫名其妙，但是他的佳处是值得我们用苦心细读的。有人说，有一回有一个人拿他的一句诗请他解释，他自己也弄不清，说不知道当时指的是什么了。他一生除开和他妻子那段浪漫事情外，没有什么大事，他常侨居于意大利。《尾声》是他去世那年做的，那时已七十多岁了。他对于人生有极深切的了解，他相信宇宙是具有一个最后的好目的。

安诺德（Arnold，1822—1888）——这位十九世纪批评大家也是一位诗人。他的诗在形式方面简洁拘谨，深得希腊文学三味。他诗的内容表现出一个对于宇宙人生均感疑惑的人的态度。他的理智太强，不能相信宗教，但是同时亦不能屈服于科学的唯物论，所以心里有不断的纷扰，常带了失望的口吻。他对于宇宙悲哀地穷究着；同时又拿坚忍的态度接受人世不可免的苦痛和忧愁。他真可以代表近代的一种心情。

罗赛谛（D. G. Rossetti，1828—1882）——他是一位画家，娶有一个美丽的太太，过了两年，这位太太死了，他就把他所有尚未出版的诗全放在棺材里，伴他的妻子长眠。后来经许多朋友的劝告，他才让他们将他的诗掘出，拿去出版。他是逃开现实，从想像里找一块乐土的人。他的诗意象鲜明，声调轻柔，兼有图画和音乐的好处，此外还含有神秘的意思，那种看穿事物外膜的能力是不下于勃莱克的。

罗赛谛妹妹（Christine Rossetti，1830—1894）——爱和死是她唯一的题目。她和她的哥哥不同，她的宗教色彩极浓，她甚至于因为宗教的信仰的缘故，和她的爱人离异，这也许是她生平诗歌里悲声的由来罢！她最长于描写悲哀和虔信混在一起的情感。她简洁的文字明白地露出她的真挚，她那绝妙的音乐增加她悲哀的诗情。她和安诺德刚刚相反，可称做信仰的诗人。

Morris（1834—1896）——他的一心都向往于中古时代，他的诗和罗赛谛一样地带着虹霓般的轻盈，是神仙国里歌音的回响。他的著作极多，最爱叙述中古的浪漫故事，那都现有一种梦也似的美丽光辉。他是乌托邦式的社会主义者，最反对近代的商业文明，努力于美化家庭屋内的装饰。他又是一位画家，他真可说是完全住在美的境界里。

史文朋（Swinburne，1837—1909）——他受法国诗人嚣俄（Hugo），高谛蔼（Gautier）和波特来耳（Baudelaire）的影响甚深。他的诗完全是一片谐音，一种情调。我们如果执着他的字句来仔细推究，常觉得他的意思模糊。若使只去领略里面的音乐和意境，我们却能明白了解他。他是英国诗人里最能应用韵的好处的大师，又是一反英国向来习俗道德，染有法国人放荡不羁的精神的人。他诗里奇怪的美感任何人都赶不上。他是维多利亚时代最后一位大诗人，可算做一幅极好的夕照图。

近代诗歌

Dolson[1]（1840—1921）——他十六岁就到英国政府商业部当书记，过了四十五年的部员生活。和兰姆（Charles Lamb）一样，单调的生活却反使他到文学去找安慰，他的诗始终保着形式的新鲜，精神的甜蜜和字句的恰当这几个好处。他的心盘绕于有风趣的小巧事情上面，用可爱的辞句轻轻地呈出可爱的思想。他介绍许多法国诗的形式到英国来，他自己的诗也很有法国文学里柔美和欢欣的色彩。

---

1 Dolson，吴福辉《梁遇春散文全编》注为"未详"，学者马海甸认为是Dobson之误植，今译为多布森。——编者注

Bridges（1844—1930）——这位在今年四月里才去世的桂冠诗人和济慈一样，本来是一位医生，喜欢音乐同旅行。他的诗恬退静默，又严肃，又细腻。思想紧张，独立不倚，却又有一种温文的甜蜜。他早年漫游大陆和东方，三十八岁后住在边僻的所在，过读书做诗的生活，同华兹华斯很有些相似。他是个精明的古典学者，所以他的诗有希腊文豪简洁明了的作风。

汉烈（Henley，1849—1903）——他从小就患了肺病，过了一年的病室生活。他许多描写医院的诗是建设于这时的经验。他后来做了好几个报纸的编辑。他的身体虽弱，却具有大无畏的精神，他的诗也常歌颂这种不屈不挠的态度。他不单题目新鲜，他的诗式也很特别的，是无韵的，全凭自然的节奏的，这却很合于表现他那种冲口而出的豪爽雄句。

史梯文生（Stevenson，1850—1894）——他家里三代都是建筑灯塔，他却弃了世业，起先学法律，后来极用心去练习写文章。他是汉烈的好朋友，也是患痨病的。他为着增加自己健康的缘故旅行许多地方，最后在南海一个野蛮岛上做酋长。他的浪漫小说《金银岛》和他的散文集《贻少年少女》都是不朽的杰作。他的诗呈现出天真烂缦的童心教我们对于日常事物里，取个好玩的观察点。

Meynell（1850—1923）——她的短诗的好处是简易同恳挚，此外微带些含有诗情的愁绪。这几乎是许多女诗人的共有色彩。白朗宁夫人和罗赛谛妹妹以及 Sara Teasdale 等都是如此。这几种特色实在根原于她感觉的敏锐。她的心灵是易感过人的，她年轻时候在日记里记下有两句动情的话：If I look inward, I find tears. If outward, rain.这真可译做"心中泪共阶前雨"了。她诗里最显明的是宗教的情调，但是却表现得极可喜。她后来皈依天主教也是由于她感到天主教仪式的壮美，并不是出于干燥的教义的辩证，所以她入教后，没有去一心修道，却仍然过她那诗人的生涯。她一生里对于朋友的情是非常认真的，她和Patmore，Meredith都缔有极纯洁，极透澈的交情。Patmore死了，她独自闭在暗室里哭了一整天。

Thompson（1857—1907）——他年青时在大学读过书，后来试过各条混饭的路子，鞋店的助手，替书铺收买旧书的伙计，甚至于做街头上卖火柴的人。他当了多年的流浪汉，Alice Meynell的丈夫发现他的天才时候，他正穷得不堪。他又有鸦片瘾，后来虽然戒了，可是他的身体永没有复原。他的生活和高尔斯密士，辜勒律己都有些仿佛，不过比他们更坎坷些罢！他诗中处处现出他是一位不知有外面世界，只看见自己心里世界的神秘的人。

Watson（1858—　）[1]——他是一个信心坚强，感情热烈的人。他带着我们去领略人生的光荣和价值。他那伟大的心灵从他的精悍的文字同富有想像力的意境里给我们以安慰。

霍斯曼（Housman，1858—　）[2]——他的作品极少，他的

---

[1] Watson，英国诗人，卒于1935年。——编者注
[2] 霍斯曼（Housman），英国诗人，卒于1936年。——编者注

诗是用微酸的诙谐来说人世的凄凉苦辛。他的文学简明无疵，却含有很深的意思，淡淡的几笔隐括了人生里微妙的情感。他现在是牛津大学的拉丁文教授。

Symons（1865—　）[1]——这位英国象征派的领袖，同时是个大批评家。他深受法国诗人的影响，他的诗常充满了浓芳的浪漫情绪，很具有史文朋的作风。

夏芝（Yeats，1865—　）[2]——他是爱尔兰文艺复兴的领袖，想建立一种浸在爱尔兰情调里的国民文学。他的父亲是个名画家，他在儿时听了许多爱尔兰农民的神话和故事，这做了他的诗歌戏曲的背境。神秘的色彩和抒情的飘忽生姿是他的特点。他的诗很多，此外还有散文和剧曲。

道生（Dowson，1867—1900）——这位唯美派的诗人过的生活是最颓唐不过的。他身体本来孱弱，再加上自己的摧折，打吗啡针，吃鸦片以及种种放荡的事情。人们都说他是喝酒喝死的。总之，他这微脆的心灵受不了粗暴冷酷的环境，他于是渐渐自杀死了。

A. E.（George William Russell）（1867—　）[3]——他是个热烈的爱国者，享有盛誉的社会学者同经济学者，演说家，有名

---

1 Symons，英国诗人，卒于1945年。——编者注
2 夏芝（Yeats），现译叶芝，爱尔兰诗人、作家，卒于1939年。——编者注
3 A. E.，乔治·威廉·罗素的笔名，爱尔兰作家及画家，卒于1935年。——编者注

的画家，同时他又是一个神秘的诗人。夏芝对于他的诗批评道："他从一切东西里找出在深处燃烧着的一种芬芳的火焰"。

Phillips（1868—1915）——他才入大学一学期就跑去当一个戏班里的小脚色，一连过了六年优伶的生活。他的诗意象显明，最能说出人间世的悲情。他是爱"悲情"的人，他觉得人世的悲哀比着无聊赖的神仙生活还高明得多。他的诗的确是内心的呼声，所以能打到我们的心坎。

Davies（1870— ）[1]——他本来是个乡下牧牛的人，当了许久的流浪汉，他在坎拿大沿着火车轨道赶路时，他的右脚被车轮碾断了。他的天才是萧伯纳发现的。他的诗清新可喜，真可算做躺在自然怀中的娇儿，很天真地赞美自然，丝毫没有人间烟火气。萧伯纳说"我还没有念过三行，就看出这个作家是个真诗人"，大概谁念他的诗都会有同样的感觉。

De la Mare（1873— ）[2]——他常将极普通，极细小的东西说得非常微妙，非常有魔力，这是因为他始终是个具有小孩子心情的诗人。他还能传出人们意识里近乎神秘的心境，呈现一种不即不离的美，好像都是我们自己本来怀有未曾十分明了的思想。他还低诉人类幽怨的情绪和凄然的心境，将人们共有的悲哀，用简朴的词令，诚恳地表现出来。

Gibson（1878— ）[3]——欧战牺牲了无数人的生命，可是

---

[1] Davies，英国诗人、作家，卒于1940年。——编者注
[2] De la Mare，英国诗人、小说家，卒于1956年。——编者注
[3] Gibson，英国"乔治亚诗人"，卒于1962年。——编者注

同时也产生不少关于战争的绝妙诗歌。Drinkwater，Gibson，Rupert Brooke都十分感动地歌咏着战争的各种色相。Gibson的诗兼有精悍的语气和怅惘的诗情，很能描写战争的浪费。

Masefield（1874— ）[1]——他还是一个小孩时候就从家里跑出，到商船里当一个茶房，做了好几年的水手，步行过许多国土；在纽约酒店里做伙计，又到织地毡工厂做工人。一天买了一本英国十四世纪大诗人孝素（Chaucer）的诗集，读到天亮，他终身的志向就决定了。他是歌颂人生的诗人，他始终保留着老舟子的口吻，雄奇英猛地高歌着，他的气魄真是冠绝一时，人生在他的诗里放出罕见的异彩。他对于一切穷苦潦倒的生活，施以化腐朽为神奇的本领，于是我们得到无限的安慰，敢肯定地来睐着人生了。

史蒂芬斯（Stephens，1882— ）[2]——他也是爱尔兰新兴文学的健将，他那不规则的音节是和当代一般无韵的新诗很相似的。他那种热烈的讥讽和清冷的诙谐多半是劝人努力实现自己的梦，来完成自己的性格。

十九年五〈月〉九〈日〉于北平报房胡同

---

1 Masefield，英国诗人、小说家、剧作家，生卒年又作1878—1967年。——编者注
2 史蒂芬斯（Stephens），爱尔兰诗人、小说家，卒于1950年。——编者注

Old English Ballads

The Call

My blood so red,
For thee was shed,
Come home again, come home again,
My own sweet heart, come home again!

You've gone astray
Out of your way,
Come home again, come home again! [1]

Barbara Allen's Cruelty

All in the merry month of May,
When green buds they[2] were swelling,
Young Jemmy Grove on his death-bed lay
For love o' Barbara Allen.

呼 唤

我这么鲜红的血是为着你流了,请你回到家里来罢,回到家里来罢,我亲亲的爱人,回到家里来罢!

你已经走错了路头,走进歧途了,回到家里来罢,回到家里来罢!

Barbara Allen 的残忍

在快乐的五月里,当绿蕾涨大的时候,年青的Jemmy Grove总是将死地躺在床上,因为他爱上了Barbara Allen。

---

1 这是一首失恋人的哀歌,在短短七行里,把 come home again 这句话重复了五遍,因此念起来格外觉得沉痛。这种重复是民歌所最喜欢用的,可说是民歌的一个特色。

2 在民歌里 Subject 常常重说一遍, they 所代的就是 green buds。

He sent his man unto her then,
To the town where she was dwelling;
"O haste and come to my master dear,
If your name be Barbara Allen."

Slowly, slowly rase¹ she up,
And she cam² where he was lying;
And when she drew the curtain by,
Says "Young man, I think you're dying."

"O it's I³ am sick and very, very sick,
And it's a'⁴ for Barbara Allen."
"O the better for⁵ me ye'se⁶ never be,
Tho' your heart's blude⁷ were a-spilling!"

"O dinna⁸ ye min⁹, young man," she says,
"When the red wine ye were filling,
That ye made the healths gae¹⁰ round and round,
And ye slighted Barbara Allen?"

---

1 rose
2 came
3 少了一个 who 字，民歌里的文法总是很随便的，因为民歌的作者并不是读过文法的文学士先生们。
4 all

他就派个仆人到她那里，到她所住的那个市镇。这个仆人对她说道："若使你的名字是 Barbara Allen，请你赶快来到我亲爱的主人家里。"

她慢慢地起来，她来到他躺着的地方；当她拉开帐幔时候，她说，"年青的人，我想你快死了。"

"我病了，病得狠利害，全是为着 Barbara Allen。"

"你绝不能够得我把你医好，虽然你的心血是在溢流！你还记得吗，年青的人，"她说道，"当你们盛起满杯红酒，你们一连举杯祝别个女郎的健康，却忽略了 Barbara Allen？"

---

5 to be the better for：to be in a better condition because of 因……而变为较佳。比如 I am the better for his medicine，就是说"吃了他的药，我病好了许多"。Allen 表示她是绝不来安慰他的，所以说你绝不能够因为我而能病好。

6 you shall

7 blood

8 did not

9 remember

10 go

He turn'd his face unto the wa',
And death was wi' him dealing:
"Adieu, adieu my dear friends a';
Be kind to Barbara Allen!"

As she was walking o'er the fields;
She heard the dead-bell[1] knelling
And every jow[2] the dead-bell gave,
It cried "woe to Barbara Allen!"

"O mother, mother, mak' my bed,
To lay me down in sorrow.
My love has dide[3] for me to-day;
I'll die for him to-morrow."

O Gin My Love Were You Red Rose

O Gin[4] my love were you red rose,

---

1 death-bell
2 stroke
3 died

他转过脸来向着墙壁，死神正在处置他，他叹道"别了，别了，我所有的亲爱朋友；你们好好地看待 Barbara Allen 罢！"

当她走过田里的时候，她听到报丧的钟声，一声叫道，"Barbara Allen 真不幸！"

"母亲，母亲，"她回家时喊道，"给我铺床罢，悲哀地把我放在床上。我的爱人今天为着我死了，我明天也得为着他死去。"

若使我的爱人是那朵红蔷薇

若使我的爱人，是那朵长在堡墙上面的红蔷薇，我自己又

Barbara Allen 衔恨 Jemmy Grove 过去的失礼，硬着心肠，说出刺心的冷话，让她的情人死去，宁愿自己后来再去殉情；而 Jemmy Grove 到死还是毫无怨意，仍然叫他的朋友们好好地待她——这二种的性格的确是刚相反的，所以演出这出悲剧。世上真正的悲剧都是起于性格的冲突，这篇民歌伟大的地方就在这点。难怪 Goldsmith 说他年青时一听人们唱到这首，就会流下泪来。

这首同下面那首都是苏格兰的民歌，用的是苏格兰土话。所以古怪的字特别多一点。

4 if

That grows upon castle wa' [1].
And I myself a drap[2] of dew,
Down on that red rose I would fa'[3].
O my love's bonny, bonny, bonny,
My love's bonny, and fair to see,
Whene'er I look on her weel-fared[4] face,
She looks and smiles again to me.

O gin my love were a pickle[5] of wheat,
And growing upon yon lily[6] lee[7],
And I mysel' a bonny wee bird,
Awa'[8] wi'[9] that pickle o' wheat I wad[10] flee,
O my love's bonny, bonny, bonny,
My love's bonny and fair to see;
Whene'er I look on her weel-fared face,
She looks and smiles again to me.

O gin my love were a coffer[11] o' gowd[12],
And I the keeper o'[13] the key,
I wad open the kist[14] whene'er I list[15]
And in that coffer I wad be.

---

1 wall
2 drop

是一滴露水,那么我一定坠到那蔷薇花上。我的爱人是轻盈好看,每回我瞧她那美丽的庞儿时节,她总是回看着我,向我轻轻一笑。

若使我的爱人是长在那可爱的田地上的一颗小麦,我自己又是个轻盈的小鸟,那么我一定要带那麦粒远飞。我的爱人是轻盈好看,每回我瞧她那美丽的庞儿时节,她总是回看着我,向我轻轻一笑。

若使我的爱人是一箱黄金,我又是管着钥匙,我高兴时我

---

3 fall
4 well-favored, handsome
5 grain
6 lovely
7 field
8 away
9 with
10 would
11 box
12 gold
13 of
14 chest
15 wish

O my love's bonny, bonny, bonny,
My love's bonny and fair to see;
Whene'er I look on her weel-fared face,
She looks and smiles again to me.

The Twa[1] Corbies[2]

As I was walking all alane[3],
I heard twa corbies making a maen[4]:
The tane[5] unto the t'ither[6] did say,
"Whaur[7] shall we gang[8] and dine the day?"

"O doun[9] beside you auld[10] fail[11] dyke[12],
I wot[13] there lies a new-slain knight;
And naebody[14] kens[15] that he lies there
But his hawk, his hound, and his lady fair.

---

1 two
2 ravens
3 alone
4 moan
5 one

就要打开箱子，把自己存在里头。我的爱人是轻盈好看，每回我瞧她那美丽的庞儿时节，她总是回看着我，向我轻轻一笑。

两 个 乌 鸦

我正在踽踽地独行，听到了两个乌鸦呻吟：一个对着那一个说道，"今天我们要去那里觅食？"

那个答道："在那方古老的土沟旁边，我知道躺有一个新被人杀死的骑士；谁也不晓得他躺在那里，除开了他的鹰鸟，他的猎狗同他美丽的夫人。

---

6 the other
7 where
8 go
9 down
10 old
11 turf
12 ditch
13 knew
14 nobody
15 knows

"His hound is to the hunting gane[1],
His hawk to fetch the wild-fowl hame[2],
His lady's ta'en[3] another mate,
Sae we may mak'[4] our dinner sweet.

"O we'll sit on his white hause bane[5],
And I'll pyke[6] out his bonny blue e'en[7];
Wi'ae lock o'[8] his gowden[9] hair
We'll theek[10] our nest when it blaws[11] bare.

"Mony a ane[12] for him makes maen,
But nane shall ken whaur he is gane.
Over his banes when they are bare,
The wind shall blaw for evermair[13]."

---

1 gone
2 home
3 has taken
4 make
5 neck bone
6 pick
7 eyes
8 with a lock of

"他的猎狗跑去打猎了，他的鹰鸟跑去捕野兽了，他的夫人跟着另外一个丈夫去了。所以我们可以吃到甜蜜的大餐。

"我们要坐在他的白颈骨上，我要啄出他那秀美的蓝眼睛；拿着一束他的金黄头发，我们来补密我们的巢窝，当它被风吹得一无遮蔽的时候。

"许多人为着他发出哀啼，但是没有人晓得他到那里去了。当他的骨头白花花的露着时候，风儿将老在上面狂吹。"

9　golden
10　thatch
11　is blown
12　many a one
13　evermore

这首诗借荒野里两只乌鸦的问答，客观地将武士死后的凄凉描写得非常动人；全诗里却没有一句牵情的话。因此更能深切的打动读者的心灵。这种天衣无缝的绝技也是民歌独到之处。

The Douglas Tragedy

"Rise up, rise, now, Lord Douglas, " she says,
"And put on your armor so bright;
Let it never be said that a daughter of thine
Was married to a lord under night.

"Rise up, rise up, my seven bold sons,
And put on your armor so bright,
And take better care of your youngest sister,
For your eldest's awa'[1] the last night."

He's[2] mounted her on a milk-white steed,
And himself on a dapple grey,
With a bugelet horn[3] hung down by his side,
And lightly they rode away.

Lord William lookit[4] o'er[5] his left shoulder,

---

1 was away
2 he has
3 small bugle horn

Douglas 家的悲剧

"起来,现在就起来 Douglas 爵士,"她(Douglas 夫人)说,"穿上你那么光亮的盔甲罢;千万别让人家说道,你的一个女孩在夜里偷嫁给一个爵士。"

"起来,起来,我七个勇敢的儿子,穿上你们那么光亮的盔甲罢,要好好地当心你们顶小妹妹了,因为你们的大妹妹前晚上跟了人家偷跑。"

他(William 爵士,Douglas 女孩的情人),把她(Douglas 的女孩)放在一匹乳白的马上,自己骑着一匹杂灰色的马儿,小喇叭挂在身旁,他们就轻轻地偷跑了。

William 爵士回过头来,从左肩上看去,瞧一瞧他能够看见

---

4 looked
5 over

To see what he could see,
And there he spied her seven brethren bold,
Come riding over the lee[1].

"Light down, light down, Lady marg'ret," he said,
"And hold my steed in your hand,
Until that against your seven brethren bold,
And your father, I mak' a stand[2]."

She held his steed in her milk-white hand,
And never shed one tear.
Until that she saw her seven brethren fa[3]
And her father hard fighting, who loved her so dear.

"O hold your hand, Lord William!" she said,
"For your strokes they are wond'rous[4] sair[5];
True lovers I can get many a ane[6],
But a father I can never get mair[7]."

---

1 lea
2 to stand and fight 站起来打仗
3 fall

什么,他望见她七个勇敢的兄弟,骑着马从草地那里奔来。

"下马来,下马来,Margaret 小姐(Douglas 女孩的名字),"他说,"拿着我的马儿罢,等我站住来同你的父亲和七个勇敢的兄弟一斗。"

她用她乳白的手牵着马儿,一点的眼泪也没有流下。一直等到她看见她的七个兄弟一一伤倒,她的父亲正在拼命地接战,她的父亲一向是那么爱她。

"停住你的手,William 爵士!"她喊道,"你的打击使他们非常苦痛;真心的爱人我能够找到许多,但是我再也不能得到一个父亲。"

---

4 wonderous
5 sore
6 one
7 more

O she's ta'en out[1] her handkerchief,
It was o' the holland sae[2] fine,
And aye[3] she dighted[4] her father's bloody wounds,
That ware[5] redder than the wine.

"O chuse[6], O chuse, Lady Marg'ret, "he said,
"O whether will ye gang[7] or bide?"
"I'll gang, I'll gang, Lord William, "she said,
"For ye have left me no other guide."

He's lifted her on a milk-white steed.
And himself on a dapple grey,
With a bugelet horn hung down by his side,
And slowly they baith[8] rade[9] away.

O they rade on, and on they rade,
And a'[10] by the light of the moon,
Until they came to yon wan[11] water,

---

1 taken out
2 so
3 continually
4 prepared
5 were

她抽出她的手帕,那是这么好的荷兰布做的,她裹好她父亲血肉糢糊的伤口,流的血是比酒还红。

"你拣罢,Margaret 小姐,"他说,"你是跟我去呢,还是滞在这儿?"

"我要去,我要去,William 爵士,"她说,"因为你杀得没有人剩下带我走路。"

他把她放在一匹乳白的马上,自己骑着一匹杂灰色的马儿,小喇叭挂在身旁,他们俩慢慢地走去。

前行又前行,月色照路旁,他们走到透明无色的水边,他

---

6 choose
7 go
8 both
9 rode
10 all
11 colorless

And there they lighted down.

They lighted down to tak' a drink
Of the spring that ran sae clear;
And down the stream ran his gude[1] heart's blood,
And sair she 'gan[2] to fear.

"Hold up, hold up[3], Lord William," she says,
"For I fear that you are slain!"
"'Tis naething[4] but the shadow of my scarlet cloak,
That shines in the water sae plain."

O they rade on, and on they rade,
And a' by the light of the moon,
Until they cam' to his mother's ha'[5] door.
And there they lighted down.

"Get up, get up, lady mother," he says,
"Get up, and let me in!
Get up, get up, lady mother!" he says,
"For this night my fair lady I've win[6].

---

1 good

们就在那里下马。

他们下马来饮水,喝些这么清澈的泉水;他可贵的心血滴到水里,她立刻心慌,害怕起来。

"别倒下去,别倒下去,William 爵士,"她说道,"我恐怕你是受了致命的重伤!""没有事,这不过是我红色大衣的影子,鲜明地照耀在水里。"

前行又前行,月色照路旁,他们来到他母亲的家。他们就在那里下马。

"起来,起来,母亲,"他说道,"起来,让我进去罢!起来,起来,母亲!今晚上我得到我的美丽爱人。"

---

2 began
3 to keep from falling 支撑着
4 nothing
5 hall
6 won

"O mak' my bed, lady mother, " he says,
"O mak' it braid¹ and deep!
And lay Lady Marg'ret close at my back,
And the sounder I will sleep."

Lord William was dead lang ere midnight,
Lady Marg'ret lang ere day—
And all true lovers that go thegether²,
May they have mair³ luck than they!

Lord William was buried in St. Mary's kirk⁴,
Lady Margaret in Mary's quire⁵;
Out o' the lady's grave grew a bonny red rose,
And out o' the knight's a brier.

And they twa met, and they twa plat,
And fain they wad be near;
And a'⁶ the warld might ken⁷ right weel⁸,
They were twa lovers dear.

---

1 brood
2 together
3 more

"铺我的床,母亲,"他说道,"铺得宽点,铺得厚点!把 Margaret 小姐紧紧地靠在我的背后,我就可以更沉酣地睡去。"

不到中夜 William 爵士就早已死去,不到天亮,Margaret 小姐也早已死去——普天下携手同行的真心爱人们,愿他们不像他俩这样无福!

William 爵士埋在圣玛利教堂里面,Margaret 小姐埋在圣玛利教堂圣台的傍〔旁〕边;从小姐的坟里长出一株可爱的红玫瑰,从武士坟里长出一株荆棘。

两株树织成连理,它们爱这么偎偎依依;全世界里的人们都会明白,他们是一双挚爱的情侣。

4　church
5　choir
6　all
7　know
8　well

But by and rade[1] the Black Douglas,
And wow[2] but he was rough!
For he pulled up the bonny brier,
And flanged[3] in St. Mary's Loch[4].

---

1 by and rode: rode by.
2 表示怜惜的感叹词。
3 flung
4 lake

但是黑Douglas骑马走过,唉,他是多么粗暴!他拔起美丽的荆棘,把它掷在圣玛利的湖里。

The Sixteen Century
(The Elizabethan Age)

Sir Walter Raleigh
(1552—1618)

The Silent Lover

I

Passions are liken'd best to floods and streams;
The shallow murmur, but the deep[1] are dumb;
So, when affection yields discourse, it seems
The bottom is but shallow whence they come.
They that are rich in words, in words discover
That they are poor in that which makes a lover.[2]

II

Wrong not, sweet empress of my heart,
The merit of true passion,

---

1 the shallow, the deep: adjective 加上 article the，可以当 noun 用，所以这两字作"浅水"同"深水"解。

静默的爱人

I

热情好比是河流；浅水会潺潺，深水反无声；所以爱情若使产生出情话，这些话仿佛不是从心的深处流来。言辞富丽的人们，单是他们的言辞就现出他们缺乏了爱人所以为爱人的要素。

II

管理我的心的甜蜜皇后，别弄错了真诚爱情的价值，别以

---

2 第一个 that 是 relative pronoun，代 they 字；第二个 that 是 conjunction；第三个 that 是 demonstrative pronoun。

With thinking that he feels no smart,
That sues for no compassion.

Silence in love bewrays[1] more woe
Than words though ne'er so witty[2]:
A beggar that is dumb, you know,
May challenge double pity.

Then wrong not, dearest to my heart,
My true, though secret passion;
He smarteth most that hides his smart
And sues for no compassion.

Edmund Spenser
(1552—1599)

Like as a ship, that through the ocean wide,
By conduct of some star doth make her way[3],
Whenas[4] a storm hath d'mmed her trusty guide;
Out of her course doth wander far astray.[5]

---

[1] involuntarily reveals the presence of

为未曾大声乞怜的人就没有觉到苦痛。

爱河里面的静默比千言万语显出更大的悲哀,不管那话儿是多么巧妙迷人:一声不则的叫花子,你晓得,是会加倍地动人矜怜。

那么,最亲爱的,别误会了我这真诚的而静默的热情;最觉到苦痛的是那个把苦痛藏起,不去求怜的人儿。

☆ ☆ ☆

像一只靠着星的指示,渡过大海的船儿,当一阵狂风蒙蔽住了她这可靠的引导(指星儿),她就离开了航路,远入迷途。

---

2 though ne'er so witty:though they(words)are never so witty.
3 to make one's way:to advance 前进。
4 when 的古写。
5 开头四行里面 subject 同 verb 的关系如下:Like ship,that...doth make...doth wander...;再下四行里面 subject 同 verb 的关系如下:So I,whose star,that wont...is overcast,do wander...。

So I, whose star, that wont with her bright ray
Me to direct[1], with clouds is overcast,
Do wander now, in darkness and dismay,
Through hidden perils round about me placed[2].

Yet hope I well that, when this storm is past,
My Helice[3], the lodestar of my life,
Will shine again, and look on me at last,
With lovely light to clear my cloudy grief.

Till then I wander care-full, comfortless,
In secret sorrow, and sad pensiveness.

Sir Philip Sidney
(1554—1586)

To the Moon

With how sad steps, O Moon, thou climb'st the skies!
How silently, and with how wan a face!
What! may it be that even in heavenly place
That busy archer[4] his sharp arrows tries?

同样地，素来用着她的光辉带我行路的星儿一被黑云遮住，我现在就彷徨于黑暗恐惧之中，穿着围在四面的暗险前行。

　　但是我很希望风灭时节，我的 Helice，——我生命的引导星——会重现光明，还肯用她可爱的清辉照我，洗净了我心里云雾般的忧愁。

　　在那时以前，我总是满心烦恼地，不安地，暗里伤情地，黯然多虑地彷徨。

呈　月　亮

　　你是多么愁步慢移地走近中天，月亮吓！多么沉默的，又是多么脸容惨淡！怎么！难道那个好事的弓手也到天堂去试他的利箭吗？

　1　that wont to direct me with her bright ray.
　2　round about me placed：placed round about me 形容 perils。
　3　他爱人的名字
　4　指爱神 Cupid，他是一个小孩，拿着了箭，到处射人，谁的心被他射中了，谁就是钟起情来。

Sure, if that long-with-love-acquainted eyes
Can judge of love, thou feel'st a lover's case:
I read it in thy looks; thy languish'd grace
To me, that feel thy like, thy state descries[1].

Then, even of fellowship, O Moon, tell me,
Is constant love deem'd there but want of wit?
Are beauties there as proud as here they be?
Do they above love to be loved, and yet
Those lovers scorn whom that love doth possess?
Do they call "virtue" there — ungratefulness?[2]

William Shakespeare
(1564—1616)

Sonnets

XXIX

When, in disgrace with fortune and men's eyes,
I all alone beweep my outcast state,

若使我这个久谙爱情的眼睛能够鉴别爱情，我敢说你必定是害了相思：我从你的形容看出了此中消息；你那憔悴风姿对于患了同病的我告诉出你的心情。

那么，为着同病相怜，月亮吓，告诉我罢，在你那里历久不变的钟情也被看做失丢了智慧吗？那里的美人也像我们这里这么骄傲吗？天上的人们也是爱人见爱，然而这班多情的人们又看不起了情迷的人们吗？他们难道也把忘恩看做美德吗？

十 四 行 诗

第二九首

当我失爱于运命，遭着人们的白眼，我独自哭我这流落的

---

1 show
2 Do they call ungratefulness a virtue there?
近代大批评家Saintsbury在他的《伊利沙伯文学史》*Elizabethan Literature*〔*A History of Elizabethan Literature*〕里说这首是"the first perfectly charming sonnet in English language."

And trouble deaf Heaven with my bootless cries,
And look upon myself, and curse my fate.

Wishing me like to one more rich in hope,
Featur'd[1] like him, like him with friends possess'd,
Desiring this man's art, and that man's scope,
With what I most enjoy contented least.[2]

Yet in these thoughts myself almost despising,

---

1 featur'd（featured）：shaped，这处是指生活的方式，不是指人们的相貌。

2 with what I most enjoy contented least: contented least with what I most enjoy.

这是莎翁十四行诗集里的第二十九首。莎翁的十四行诗共有一百五十二首（通行说法是一百五十四首。——编者注）。关于莎翁写这些诗的动机和这些诗所赞美的对象，几百年来，聚讼不已。大概说起来这一百多首诗可分两系，第一系（从一至一百二十六）是对于一位年青貌美，尚未结婚的朋友而发的。莎翁赞美他的朋友的美貌，劝他结婚，把这可喜的容姿留传人世（一至二十六首）。当莎翁和这位朋友分离了，他倾吐出凄恻的怀念（二十七至三十二）。后来他的朋友偷去他的情人，他只好伤心，还是恋着这位翩翩公子（三十三至四十二）。四十三首至五十五首又是离别的怨辞。他的朋友和他好像有些隔膜，莎翁迫切地向他一再声明自己的悃挚，这时莎翁是满腹的忧愁（五十六至六十五）。他的朋友同坏人来往，他又丢到悲哀的深渊里去了（六十六至七十四）。七十五至七十七首申辩他的诗为什么好似是很单调的，因为他觉得只有这位朋友是值得歌颂的。莎翁和其他诗翁竞争，想独占这位青年的友谊（七十八首至八十七首），他的朋友仿佛跟他生疏了（八十八至九十六首），莎翁就想法去夺回他朋友的爱情（九十苦境，用我那无用的悲啼，去向聋子般的青天麻烦，看看自己，咒诅我的运命。

只想我能够像那个更有希望的人儿，像他那么一种的生涯，像他那样有了好友，想有这个人的本领，想有那个人的淹博，平常最使我满意的东西，现在倒觉得索然。

可是当我想到这些，几乎嫌恶了自己，偶然我记起"你"

七首至九十九首），分离好久之后，他们又和好如初了（一百首至一百二十九〔六〕首）。莎翁对于一位男朋友发生出这段湾湾〔弯弯〕曲曲的爱情，做了这许多一往情深的十四行诗，后世有些批评家就非〔飞〕长流短，说出不妙的话来。近代诗人 John Masefield 在他的 William Shakespeare 书里，挥他那如椽之笔替莎翁辩护，他说"Men with imagination enjoy sweeter and closer friendships than the many know. The many, mulish as ever, therefore imagine evil"，这话的确是真的，不看人们在 Gray 写给他朋友的信，有许多简直好像人们在初恋时所写的情书。第二系（从一百二十七首至一百五十二首止）是关于一位黑头发黑眼睛（在中国这是不足为奇的，从夷人的眼看去，这样人的确是罕见，所以被人们称做"the dark lady"了）的女人。莎翁自己疯狂的爱了这个杨花水性的女人，经过了海中的一切惊涛骇浪，这些风波全反照在这一系的诗里。莎翁一身〔生〕的事实，我们不大晓得，他在戏曲里又是使各种的人们都有说话的余地，不露出自己的性情，批评家因此说他的戏曲是 impersonal，所以这一百多首的十四〈行〉诗几乎是莎翁唯一的自白语，几百年来批评家们要那样杀得血肉模糊，来争着解释这一百多首诗的背境，也就是这个缘故了。但是这些十四行诗本身的好处是无疑的。

Haply I think on thee, — and then my state,
Like to the lark at break of day arising
From sullen earth, sings hymns at heaven's gate.

For thy sweet love remember'd such wealth brings,
That then I scorn to change my state with kings.

LVII

Being your slave, what should I do but tend[1]
Upon the hours and times of your desire?
I have no precious time at all to spend,
Nor services to do, till you require.

Nor dare I chide the world-without-end[2] hour
Whilst I, my sovereign, watch the clock for you,
Nor think the bitterness of absence sour
When you have bid your servant once adieu.

Nor dare I question with my jealous thought
Where you may be, or your affairs suppose[3],
But, like a sad slave, stay and think of nought

---

1 attend
2 never-ending

来——顿然间我的心情,像破晓时节从昏暗的地上飞起的天鹨,在天门上唱出赞美的歌来。

因为你那甜蜜的爱情在回忆里带来了这么多的财富,那时我真是不屑将我的境地来和帝王对调。

第五七首

既是你的奴才,我除开随你的高兴,伺候着你外,还有别的什么可做?我的时间简直算不得宝贵,我也没有什么事情要干,当你想用我之前。

我也不敢骂那悠悠似岁的时日,当我,我的君王呀,为着你等候;我也不敢说离别的苦痛叫人心酸,当你对你的仆人(指自己)说过了一声再会。

我也不敢怀着妒忌的念头,问你是到那里去了,或者去猜你有了什么事情,却是像个愁闷的奴才,静静地等候着,什么

---

3 to conjecture

Save, where you are how happy you make those.

So true a fool is love, that in your will,
Though you do any thing, he thinks no ill.[1]

LXXI

No longer mourn for me when I am dead
Than you shall hear[2] the surly sullen bell
Give warning to the world that I am fled
From this vile world, with vilest worms to dwell.

Nay, if you read this line, remember not
The hand that writ it; for I love you so,
That I in your sweet thoughts would be forgot,
If thinking on me then should make you woe[3].

O, if, I say, you look upon this verse,
When I perhaps compounded[4] am with clay,
Do not so much as my poor name rehearse,
But let your love even with my life decay.

---

1 He believes that your intentions are always good.
2 only so long as you hear

也不想，除非是想现在同你在一起的人们是多么快乐。

爱情是这么一个真真的傻子，不管你做了什么，他总以为你的存心不会是坏的。

第七一首

当我死后，抑郁惨憺的丧钟向世间宣告我逃出了这丑恶的世界，去和最丑恶的蠕虫同住，钟声歇后，你也不要再为我悲哀。

不，当你念起这行诗时，请你不要记着这个作诗的人；因为我是这么爱你，我情愿被你的甜蜜的思想忘却，若使那时一想到我，会使你生愁。

我说，若使当我或者已经同尘土混在一起的时候，你看到了我这首小诗，请你连我的名字都不要念着罢，最好的却是你的爱情简直随着我的生命一同凋零。

---

3 sorrowful
4 unitd

Lest the wise world¹ should look into your moan,
And mock you with² me after I am gone.

LXXIII

That time of year thou may'st in me behold
When yellow leaves, or none, or few, do hang
Upon those boughs which shake against the cold —
Bare ruin'd choirs where late the sweet birds sang.

In me thou see'st the twilight of such day
As after sunset fadeth in the west,
Which by and by black night doth take away,
Death's second self, that seals up all in rest.

In me thou see'st the glowing of such fire
That on the ashes of his³ youth doth lie,
As the death-bed whereon it must expire,
Consumed with⁴ that which it was nourish'd by.

---

1 这句含有讥笑的意思，因为世上许多人们的确是太乖巧了，爱人一死，他们就揩干眼睛，觅新欢去了。

2 with: because of.

怕的是伶俐乖巧的世界，会看出你这呻吟的意味，拿着我来讥笑你，当我已经不在人间。

第七三首

你在我身上可以看到那个时令，当黄叶，全已凋零，或者遗留一点，挂在那冷风里摇曳的枝上——这群荒废的圣台（指残枝）不久以前还是甜蜜的鸟儿的歌唱之所。

你在我身上看到这样一个薄暮，当太阳下去了，朦胧的微光也渐渐西沉，这微光渐渐地被黑夜吞没，那真是死的化身，把世上的一切全封在休息里去。

你在我身上看到这样火的燃烧，它躺在它盛时的余烬上面，好像那是它与世永诀的死床，它是随着燃料而俱尽。

---

3 his: its.
4 together with; fire and fuel disappear together.

This thou perceiv'st which makes thy love more strong
To love that well which thou must leave¹ ere long.

LXXXVII²

Like as the waves make towards the pebbled shore,
So do our minutes hasten to their end;
Each changing place with that which goes before,
In sequent toil all forwards do contend.

Nativity, once in the main of light,
Crawls to maturity, wherewith being crown'd,
Crooked eclipses, 'gainst his glory fight,
And time that give doth now his gift confound.

Time doth transfix the flourish³ set on you'h,
And delves the parallels in beauty's brow;
Feeds on the rarities of nature's truth⁴,
And nothing stands but for his scythe to mow⁵.

---

1 leave: give up.
2 这首诗在1609年首次出版的版本中为第六十首，而非第八十七首。——编者注
3 pierce through the glass

你看了这些,会更热烈地爱我,好好地爱着你所快将失丢的东西罢。

第八七首

好像波浪奔向沙砾的海岸,我们的光阴是同样地急趋于消亡;个个时刻都是取过去而代之,这样子接连着齐向前面竞驰。

我们的命星诞生后,走向光海里去,渐渐地走到成熟时期,既然达了绝顶,不利的遮蚀就来和它的光荣相争,给我们这许多东西的"时间之神"现在把它从前的礼物一一收回。

"时间之神"将青春的光辉穿破,在美人的眉梢掘出并行的皱痕,吃去了难得的,真真天生的美丽;那里会有屹然不动的东西,什么也逃不了他那镰刀的刈割。

---

4 世间上许多的美丽都是妆饰出来的,天生的佳质的确是很稀少。因为是天然本色,所以叫做 nature's truth,因为很难得,所以说做 the rarities of nature's truth。

5 时间之神拿了一把镰刀,凡事过去,变成了无痕的陈迹,就说是给他镰刀割去。

And yet, to times in hope¹ my verse shall stand,
Praising thy worth, despite his cruel hand.

CIX

O, never say that I was false of heart,
Though absence seem'd my flame to qualify².
As easy might I from myself depart
As from my soul, which in thy breast doth lie:

That is my home of love: if I have rang'd,
Like him that travels, I return again;
Just³ to the time, not with the time exchang'd⁴,
So that myself bring water for my stain.

Never believe, though in my nature reign'd
All frailties that besiege all kinds of blood⁵,
That it could so preposterously be stain'd,
To leave⁶ for nothing all thy sum of good.

---

1 times in hope: ages yet to come 未来的时代。
2 qualify: diminish.

然而，不管他是多么毒手，在将来时候，我的诗会屹然不动，赞美着你的好处。

第一〇九首

千万别说我是负心，虽然不见好像灭了我的情焰。我是不能离开了自己，同样地我不能同躺在你胸里的我的灵魂相离。

你的胸里是我爱情的归宿：若使我曾出去漫游，那么像旅行的人们一样，我仍然还家；是准时地回来，并没有时久情迁，真好似自己带水来洗净我的污痕。

虽然，我的心情含有包围着种种人们的一切弱点，千万别相信我的心情会那样悖性地染污，会为着追求虚无，离开了你的一切好处。

---

3 punctually
4 altered
5 people of different temperaments
6 as to leave

For nothing this wide universe I call,
Save thou, my rose; in it thou art my all.

Man's Ingratitude

Blow, blow, thou winter wind,
Thou art not so unkind[1]
As man's ingratitude;
Thy tooth is not so keen,
Because thou art not seen,[2]
Although thy breath be rude.
Heigh ho![3] sing, heigh ho! unto the green holly[4]:
Most friendship is feigning, most loving mere folly:
Then heigh ho, the holly!
This life is most jolly.

Freeze freeze, thou bitter sky,
Thou dost not bite so nigh[5]
As benefits forgot:
Though thou the waters warp[6],
Thy sting is not so sharp

---

1 unnatural

这个宽大的世界我是当做个虚无，除开了你，我的蔷薇；你是我的一切。

人 的 忘 恩

刮着罢，刮着罢，你这冬天的凄风，你还没有人们的忘恩那么不情；你的牙齿也没有那么锋利，因为你是无形，虽然你的气息是那么粗暴。哈哈！唱，哈哈！还是对着冬青高歌罢：友谊多半是假的，爱情多半都是傻的：那么，哈哈，冬青！此生真快乐。

冻住罢，冻住罢，你这苦冷的天气，你还没有忘恩的人那样刺人心肠；虽然你会使水织成细纹，你的刺没有像忘了友谊的人

---

2 因为风是看不见的，所以我们不认得它，也不晓得它从前受过我们的恩惠没有，因此不管它是多么凄凉，我们总觉得不及人情的冷淡那么刺心。
3 快乐时候的欢呼声音。
4 快乐的象征。
5 so deeply
6 weave

As friend remember'd not.[1]
Heigh ho! sing, heigh ho! unto the green holly:
Most friendship is feigning, most loving mere folly:
Then heigh ho, the holly!
This life is most jolly.

O Mistress mine, where are you roaming?
O, stay and hear, your true love's coming,
That can sing both high and low:
Trip no further, pretty sweeting[2],
Journeys end in lovers' meeting,
Every wise man's son doth know.

What is love? 'tis not hereafter;
Present mirth hath present laughter;
What's to come is still unsure:
In delay there lies no plenty[3],—
Then come kiss me, sweet-and-twenty,[4]

---

1 the forgetting of one friend by another
这首诗是在莎翁喜剧 *As You Like It* 里。

那么尖利。哈哈，唱，哈哈，还是对着冬青高歌罢！友谊多半都是假的，爱情多半都是傻的：那么，哈哈，冬青，此生真快乐。

☆　☆　☆

我的情人，你走到那里去呢？停住来听罢，你真真的爱人正在前来，他能唱出高高低低的调子：别再望〔往〕前走了，可爱的乖乖，爱人的相会是行路的终点，这道理个个聪明人都会知道。

什么是爱情？并不是属于将来；眼前的快乐发出眼前的笑声；将来是如何，谁能说准：迟延一下，就要减少了许多，——那么，来吻我罢，甜蜜的二十年华，青春不是长留不

---

2 甜蜜的苹果，移作亲爱的称呼。
3 In delay there lies no plenty: delay leads to no good.
4 这句的意思有许多的说法，数百年来，聚讼不决，但是多半的人们都以为twenty是指年纪，sweet是讲这个女子的可爱，我们也只好这么解释了。其他的说法是"sweet and twenty times sweet," "sweet and gives me twenty kisses," 等等。一句微妙的好诗，这班发白齿摇的注解家却争得你生我死，这是何必呢！

Youth's a stuff¹ will not endure.

A Sea Dirge

Full fathom five² thy father lies,
Of his bones are coral made,
Those are pearls that were his eyes:
Nothing of him that doth fade,
But doth³ suffer a sea-change
Into something rich and strange.
Sea-nymphs hourly ring his knell:
Ding-dong,
Hark! now I hear them, — ding — dong bell.

Ariel's Song

Where the bee sucks, there suck I,
In a cowslip's bell I lie,
There I couch when owls do cry;
On the bat's back I do fly
After summer merrily.⁴

1　stuff之后略去一个which。

变的东西。

海葬的挽歌

　　五㖊下躺着你的父亲，他的骨化作珊瑚，从前的眼睛现在变为明珠：他那消失的躯体没有一处不受了海里的变化，变成了富丽奇巧的东西。海里的女神常常摇起他的丧钟：叮当，听吓！现在我听到了，叮当。

Ariel 的小歌

　　蜂儿吮啜的地方，我也在那里吮啜，我躺在一朵莲香花的萼里，我偃卧在里面，当鸮鸟悲啼的时候；我快乐地坐在蝙蝠肩上随着夏天飞翔。我现在要快乐地，快乐地在垂枝的

　　上面第一首是莎翁 *Twelfth Night* 里小丑唱的小调。
　2 Full fathom five 当人们把两手向左右伸开，从手指末端到那边手指末端的距离叫做 fathom，这大概是六呎，所以五个 fathom 可以译做三十呎。
　3 which does not
这是莎翁 *Tempest* 里小神仙 Ariel 的短歌。
　4 像燕子那样随着夏天南北漫游。

Merrily, merrily shall I live now
Under the blossom that hangs on the bough.

Thomas Campion
(1567—1619)

Silly boy, 'tis full moon yet, thy night as day shines clearly;
Had thy youth but wit to fear, thou couldst not love so dearly.
Shortly wilt thou mourn when all thy pleasures are bereaved[1];
Little knows he how to love that never was deceived.

This is thy first maiden flame, that triumphs yet unstained;
All is artless[2] now you speak, not one word, yet, is feigned;
All is heaven that you behold, and all your thoughts are blessed;
But no spring can want his fall, each Troilus hath his Cressid[3].

花儿底下过活。

☆ ☆ ☆

傻孩子，这还是月圆时节，你的午夜是同白天一样的光明。假使你虽年青，也晓得害怕，你绝不会这样地一往情深。不久你就要感到悲哀，当你一切的快乐全被斩除；从来未曾受人骗过的人们是不大知道应当怎样去钟情。

这是你初次的新鲜的情焰，不沾俗虑地飞扬；你现在所说的全是天然流露出真话，还没有一句假语夹在里头；你所看见的全是天堂，你的思想都极洁净；但是没有一个春天会没有秋天，个个的 Troilus 都有他的 Cressid。

Ariel 是莎翁 Tempest 这出喜剧里一个最可喜的小神仙。这是他唱的调子，里面充满着轻盈的幻想，真是有不吃人间烟火的风韵，唱起来又是甜蜜可口，所以几百年来，歌咏神仙生活的小诗，没有一首能够赶得过它。

1　are destroyed
2　artless: without guile.
3　希腊预言家 Calchas 的漂亮女儿，负了她的情人 Troilus。

Thy well-ordered locks ere long shall rudely hang neglected;
And thy lively pleasant cheer read grief on earth dejected,
Much then wilt thou flame thy saint, that made thy heart so holy,
And with sighs confess, in love that too much faith is folly.

Yet be just and constant still! Love may beget a wonder,
Not unlike a summer's frost, or winter's fatal thunder.
He that holds his sweetheart true, unto his day of dying,
Lives, of all that ever breathed, most worthy the envying.

Come, cheerful day, part of my life to me;
For while thou view'st me with thy fading light,
Part of my life doth still[1] depart with thee,
And I still onward haste to my last night:
Time's fatal wings do ever forward fly,
So every day we live a day we die.

But, O ye nights, ordained for barren rest,

你这整齐不紊的鬈发不久会粗野地不加梳理地垂着四旁；你现在这活泼高兴的情怀全归消沉，看见的只是世上的悲哀；那时你会大大地怨你的圣神，为什么起先使你的心这么高超，你会长叹一声说道太相信爱情了只是愚蠢。

然而还是诚实有恒罢！爱情或者可以生出奇迹，好似夏天的严霜同冬天的恶雷。到死还是爱着他的情人，这是众生里最值得羡慕的人儿。

☆ ☆ ☆

来罢，快乐的日子，这也是我生命的一部分；因为当你的余晖照我时候，我生命的一部分总是随你俱亡，我也总是急趋于我的末夜："时间之神"的凶翼老是向前飞去，因此活了一天，我们是死了一天。

但是，你们这黑夜呀，注定了花在无聊的睡眠里去，我的

---

1 always

How are my days deprived of life in you
When heavy sleep my soul hath dispossest,
By feigned death life sweetly to renew!
Part of my life in that, you life deny;
So every day we live a day we die.[1]

Ben Jonson
(1573—1637)

To Celia

Drink to me only with thine eyes,
And I will pledge with mine;
Or leave a kiss but in the cup
And I'll not look for wine.
The thirst that from the soul doth rise
Doth ask a drink divine;
But might I of Jove's nectar sup,
I would not change[2] for thine.

I sent thee late[3] a rosy wreath,
Not so much honouring thee

日子给你减丢了不少的生气，当沉酣的睡眠逐出了灵魂，甜蜜地用假死来把生命更新！这也是我生命的一部分，你却使它失了生气；因此活了一天，我们是死了一天。

呈 Celia

只用你的眼波来醉我罢，我也用我的双盼酬你的深情；或者你留一吻在杯里，我再也不去饮别的美酒。从心之深处来的干渴要一杯神圣的饮水；但是我若使能够畅饮天帝的甘露，我也不愿拿你吻过的杯水来相换。

我近来送你一环蔷薇，并不是这样地看重你，会希望它在

---

1 Night is a part of life, because, although spent in sleep which is feigned death and the negation of activity (in that you life deny), its purpose is life sweetly to renew.
2 take it in exchange
3 lately

As giving it a hope that there
It could not wither'd be;
But thou thereon didst only breathe,
And sent'st it back to me;
Since when it grows, and smells I swear,
Not of itself but thee!

John Donne
(1573—1631)

Stay, O sweet, and do not rise!
The light that shines comes from thine eyes;
The day breaks not, it is my heart,
Because that you and I must part.
Stay! or else my joys will die
And perish in their infancy.

Death, be not proud, though some have called thee
Mighty and dreadful, for thou art not so;
For those whom thou think'st thou dost overthrow
Died not, poor Death; nor yet canst thou kill me.

你那里能常春不萎；但是你只需轻轻一吹，再将这花环还我；我敢说从此后它不是自己长大，带着自己的气息，却是被你培养大了，染了你的芬芳！

☆　☆　☆

滞下去罢，甜蜜的人儿，别耍起来！这些亮光是来自你的双眸；天还没有破晓，破的是我的心儿，因为你我现在是不得不别离。滞下去罢！不然我的欣欢会死去，在他的稚年时就告灭亡。

☆　☆　☆

死神，别耍骄傲，虽然有人说你是伟大可怕，其实你并不是这样；因为你所认做被你打倒了的人们是没有死去，可怜的死神；你也不能够把我杀死。

From rest and sleep, which but thy picture be,
Much pleasure, then from thee much more must flow;
And soonest our best men with thee do go,
Rest of their bones, and souls' delivery.¹

Thou art slave to Fate, chance, kings and desperate men.
And dost with poison, war, and sickness dwell,
And poppy or charms can make us sleep as well,
And better than thy stroke; why swell'st thou, ² then?

One short sleep past, we wake eternally,
And Death shall be no more; Death, thou shalt die.

---

1 这句同前行的 thee 是同位的。
2 why swellest thou with pride?

休息同睡眠，那只是你的影子，给了我们不少的快乐，那么从你我们一定会得到更大的欣欢；我们里最好的人们最快地跟你走去，你是他们躯体的休息，他们灵魂的得救。

你是命运，机会，帝王同拼命的人们的奴隶，你和毒药，战争，疾病同居在一起；鸦片同催眠能使我们同样地安眠，而且比你的手段还要高明。那么你为甚这样地骄傲？

短短的一睡过后，我们是永生地醒着，"死"是无能为力了；死神，你自己却是会死。

The Seventeenth Century

Robert Herrick
(1591—1674)

To the Virgins, to Make Much of[1] Time

Gather ye rosebuds while ye may,
Old time is still a-flying;
And this same flower that smiles to-day,
To-morrow will be dying.

The glorious lamp of heaven, the sun,
The higher he's a-getting,
The sooner will his race[2] be run,
And nearer he's to setting.

That age is best which is the first,
When youth and blood are warmer;
But being spent, the worse, and worst
Times still succeed the former.

呈少女们,劝她们看重青春

有花堪折直须折,时间老人总是在飞驰,你不看眼前的好花,今天微笑明朝萎。

天上的明灯,那个太阳,愈走到高处,他的路程就愈快走完,他也愈近于西沉。

小小年华是最佳,青春热血共沸腾;青春既已过去了,时间总是每况愈下地接连。

---

1 to make much of:看重。
2 race:日月的行程。

Then be not coy, but use your time,
And while ye may, go marry:
For having lost but once your prime,
You may for ever tarry.

To Anthea, Who May Command Him Anything

Bid me to live, and I will live
Thy protestant[1] to be;
Or bid me love, and I will give
A loving heart to thee.

A heart as soft, a heart as kind,
A heart as sound and free
As in the whole world thou canst find,
That heart I'll give to thee.

Bid that heart stay, and it will stay
To honour thy decree;
Or bid it languish quite away,

别害羞罢,好好用你的时间,趁时嫁人罢:

为的是浓艳良时一错过,你会永久空迟延。

呈 Anthea,她能叫他干任何事情

叫我活,我就活着,向你诉出我的衷情;

或者叫我爱,我就要给你一个深情的心儿。

全世界里你所能找到的最柔软,最温和,最纯洁无瑕的,未曾给过别人的心儿,这样的心我要献给你。

叫那心停住,它就要停住来恪遵你的命令;或者叫它憔悴死去,为着你它也要

---

1 protestant: one who makes a protestation (a solemn declaration) of his devotion (一个虔诚地宣言他自己的恳挚的人)。

And 't shall do so for thee.

Bid me to weep, and I will weep
While I have eyes to see;
And, having none, yet will I keep
A heart to weep for thee.

Bid me despair, and I'll despair
Under that cypress-tree;
Or bid me die, and I will dare
E'en death to die for thee.

Thou art my life, my love, my heart,
The very eyes of me;
And hast command of every part
To live and die for thee.

To Daffodils

Fair Daffodils, we weep to see
You haste away so soon;

这么做去。

叫我哭，我就要哭，当我有眼睛的时候；没有了眼睛，我也要为着你暗自心酸，来代啼痕。

叫我失望，我要在柏树下失望；或者叫我死，我也敢冒死，为着你死去。

你是我的生命，我的爱情，我的赤心，简直是我的眼睛；你能够命令我的任何部分，叫它为着你生着或者死去。

呈　水　仙

水仙，我们哭着看你这么匆匆地过去

As yet the early rising sun

Has not attained his noon.

Stay, stay,

Until the hasting day

Has run

But to the even-song[1];

And, having prayed together, we

Will go with you along.

We have short time to stay, as you,

We have as short a spring;

As quick a growth to meet decay,

As you, or anything.

We die

As your hours do, and dry

Away,

Like to the summer's rain,

Or as the pearls of morning's dew,

Ne'er to be found again.

---

1 even-song: 晚祷的时候，就是黄昏。

（萎谢的意思）；清早起来的太阳还没有走到它的中天。请你停住罢，停住罢，再等这匆匆的日子到了黄昏；既是一块祈祷过，我们将和你一同辞世。

我们停留的时间同你一样地短促，我们的春天也是一样地难留；我们的从长成到衰老是同你和一切有生一样地倏忽。我们生下不久也就死去，同你的朝生暮死一样，我们是像夏雨那么易干，或者似早上的露珠，一现后再难追寻。

Edmund Waller
(1606—1687)

Go, lovely Rose!
Tell her that wastes her time and me.
That now she knows,
When I resemble her to thee,
How sweet and fair she seems to be.

Tell her that's young,
And shuns to have her graces spied,
That hadst thou sprung
In deserts, where not men abide,
Thou must have uncommended died.

Small is the worth
Of beauty from the light retired[1];
Bid her come forth,
Suffer herself to be desired,
And not blush so to be admired.

---

1 retired: withdrawn.

☆　☆　☆

去罢，可爱的蔷薇！告诉她，那个浪费了自己的同我的光阴的她。她现在要知道当我将你比她，她是多么甜蜜美丽呀。

告诉她，那个年青而怕人瞧着她的美丽的她，若使你是长在无人烟的沙漠中间，你就会未曾受过赞美地死去。

躲着光线的美丽是不大值钱；叫她出来，让人们来欣慕罢，别要听到颂辞就这样子酡颜。

Then die! that she
The common fate of all things rare
May read in thee;
How small a part of time they share
That are so wondrous sweet and fair!

John Milton
(1608—1674)

To Mr. Lawrence

Lawrence, of virtuous father virtuous son,
Now that the fields are dank and ways are mire,
Where shall we sometimes meet, and by the fire
Help waste a sullen day, what may be won
From the hard season gaining?[1] Time will run
On smoother, till Favonius[2] re-inspire
The frozen earth, and clothe in fresh attire
The lily and rose, that neither sow'd nor spun.[3]
What neat repast shall feast us, light and choice,

然后，你再死去！使她从你可以看出一切希奇东西的共同命运；知道了这么怪甜美丽的东西是多么难得久留！

呈 Lawrence 先生

　　Lawrence，你这贤父的贤子，现在是地湿途泥的时候，我们要去何处相会，依着火做些这种天气能做的娱乐，消磨去一个沉闷的长日呢？那么光阴就会过得快些，等到西风吹醒了冰冻的大地，替天然生出的百合蔷薇换上新衣。那时我们要用什么微妙精美的佳餐同来尽欢，饮着好酒，然后再起来细听

1　taking such enjoyments as the weather permits（gaining what may be won from the hard season）
2　the west wind
3　见《圣经》里马太福音第六章第二十八节："Consider the lilies of the field, how they grow; they toil not, neither do they spin."

Of Attic taste[1], with wine, whence we may rise
To hear the lute well touch'd, or artful[2] voice
Warble immortal notes and Tuscan[3] air?
He who of those delights can judge, and spare
To interpose them oft[4], is not unwise.

On His Blindness

When I consider how my light is spent,
Ere half my days, in this dark world and wide,
And that one talent which is death to hide
Lodged with me useless, though my soul more bent
To serve therewith my Maker, and present
My true account, lest He returning chide, —
Doth God exact day-labour, light denied?
I fondly[5] ask. But Patience, to prevent

---

1 雅典人是非常秀雅温文的，所以 Attic taste 是等于"refined elegance"。
2 skilful
3 Italian
4 avoid indulging in them too often
5 foolishly

琵琶的逸响,或者练熟的声音唱出不死的奇韵同意大利的名歌?晓得这些快乐而不常去放恣地享受,这可说是真真的智者。

他自己的失明

当我想起还不到半生,我的眼睛就在这黑暗广大的世界里失去了他的光明,当我想起书写的能力(隐存起那能力不用就是等于死亡)放在我的身上无用,虽然我的心更愿意用它(指这能力)来服事我的创造主,说出我的真情,怕的是回头来他会责备,——我痴痴地问道,"上帝不给人以眼力,还会要人做事吗?"但是"耐心"

开头八行是一个introductory sentence,第七行,第八行是principal sentence。Doth God...denied? 是一个noun clause,做I ask的object。

That murmur, soon replies, "God doth not need
Either man's work, or His own gifts: who best
Bear His mild yoke, they serve Him best. His state
Is kingly; thousands[1] at His bidding speed
And post o'er land and ocean without rest, —
They also serve who only stand and wait."

Richard Lovelace
(1618—1658)

To Lucasta, Going to the Wars

Tell me not, Sweet, I am unkind,
That from the nunnery
Of thy chaste breast and quiet mind
To war and arms I fly.

True, a new mistress now I chase,
The first foe in the field;

---

1 thousands of angels

为要阻着这个怨言，立刻回答道，"上帝用不着人们的工作同他所给与人们的才能：谁最能忍受他的温和的束缚，谁就是服事得最好的人。他的地位是帝王的地位；他一开口，有千万天使立刻飞跑，不停地越山过海赶到他的面前，——只是站住耐心地等着，也可说是服事他的人们。"

出征前呈 Lucasta

别说我，甜蜜的人儿，我是忍心，因为从你贞洁的胸同安详的心这个尼庵里，我飞跑到战争同武器中去。

不错，现在我追着一个新的爱人，那是战场里站在最前的敌人；我还用更强烈

And with a stronger faith[1] embrace
A sword, a horse, a shield.

Yet this inconstancy is such
As thou too shalt adore;
I could not love thee, Dear, so much,
Loved I not Honour more.

John Dryden
(1631—1700)

No, no, poor suffering heart, no change endeavor;
Choose to sustain the smart, rather than leave her.
My ravished eyes behold such charms about her,
I can die with her, but not live without her;
One tender sigh of hers to see me languish,
Will more than pay the price of my past anguish.
Beware, O cruel fair, how you smile on me,
'Twas a kind look of yours that has undone me.

---

1 stronger faith: a faith stronger than he had in pursuit of love.

的诚恳去拥抱一把剑，一匹马和一只盾。

但是这个无恒，就是你也会钦重；我不会这样爱你，亲爱的，若使我不是更爱我的令名。

☆　☆　☆

不，不，可怜的受苦的心儿并不去企图移情；我甘心忍受着刺痛，却不肯离开她的身旁。我那被迷醉的眼睛看出她有万般美丽，我情愿死在她的旁边，却不能够活着同她隔离；她的一声柔情的微喟，当她看我憔悴，是偿了我过去的一切哀伤，尚且有余。小心点，忍心的美人，你怎样向我微笑，这全因为曾送过一次怜惜的眼波，才使我愁损如今。

Love has in store for me one happy minute,
And she will end my pain who did begin it;
Then no day void of bliss or pleasure leaving,
Ages shall slide away without perceiving.
Cupid shall guard the door, the more to please us,
And keep out Time and Death, when they would seize us:
Time and Death shall depart, and say, in flying,
Love has found out a way to live by dying.

　　有人以为古典文学是冷冰冰的，可是这首诗的内容是多么浪漫，里面的情感多么真挚，而它的作者却是十八世纪里古典文学大师的 Dryden。

爱神替我留有一分愉快的光阴，起先给我苦痛的她会来结束我的悲怀；从此后我再不会有不宁不乐的日子，几世纪也只是不知不觉地消磨。爱神会守起门来，更加我们的欣欢，挡住了时间老人同死神，当他们意存擒缚地来临：时间老人同死神会走开了，飞行时说道爱情是用死来求生。

The Eighteenth Century

Alexander Pope
(1688—1744)

The Quiet Life

Happy the man[1], whose wish and care
A few paternal acres bound,
Content to breathe his native air,
In his own ground.

Whose herds with milk, whose fields with bread,
Whose flocks supply him with attire,
Whose trees in summer yield him shade,
In winter fire.

Blest, who can unconcern'dly find
Hours, days, and years slide soft away,
In health of body peace of mind,
Quiet by day,

---

1 Happy the man 即是 Happy is the man。

恬静的生涯

　　这样的人真快乐，他的希望同烦恼出不了他祖传的几亩薄田，自愿在他自己的地上吸着家乡的空气。他的牛群给他以牛奶，他的田园给他以面包，他的绵羊给他以衣服，他的树林夏天有浓荫，冬天好生火。

　　这样的人真有福，他能够无忧无虑地任刻刻朝朝年年轻轻地过去，体健心宁，

Sound sleep by night; study and ease
Together mix'd; sweet recreation;
And innocence, which most does please
With meditation.

Thus let me live, unseen, unknown;
Thus unlamented let me die;
Steal from the world, and not a stone
Tell where I lie.

Henry Carey

(1693—1743)[1]

Sally in Our Alley

Of all the girls that are so smart,
There's none like pretty Sally;

第三、四段若把全句写出是如下：
Blest (is the man), who...night; (in) study and ease...; (in) sweet recreation, and innocence...meditation.
这首诗整齐不放〔?〕，可以做十八世纪里古典文学的代表。

白天里安详度日，黑夜到纳头酣睡，读书同游息混在一起，还有甜蜜的娱乐同耽心冥想的天真。

这样子让我不被世人看见同晓得地活着；这样子让我不受人们的哀悼死去；偷偷地走出世界，连一块石头都没有说出：我是在那里长眠。

我们巷里的 Sally

世上许多那么漂亮的女孩，却都没有一个赶得上 Sally；她是我心中的爱人，她

---

1 另一说法是他出生于1689年之前，可能早在1687年。——编者注

She is the darling of my heart,
And she lives in our alley.
There is no lady in the land
Is half so sweet as Sally;
She is the darling of my heart,
And she lives in our alley.

Her father he makes cabbage-nets,
And through the streets does cry 'em;
Her mother she sells laces long
To such as please to buy 'em:
But sure such folks could ne'er beget
So sweet a girl as Sally!
She is the darling of my heart,
And she lives in our alley.

When she is by I leave my work,
I love her so sincerely;
My master comes like any Turk,
And bangs me most severely —
But let him bang his bellyful,
I'll bear it all for Sally;

住在我们的巷里。全国没有一位姑娘,有Sally一半的可爱;她是我心中的爱人,她住在我们的巷里。

她父亲编织煮菜用的网子,做好了他就去沿街叫卖;她母亲出卖长长的花边,给那爱买的人们:但是这样的人家绝不会生出女孩,像Sally这么可爱!她是我心中的爱人,她是住在我们的巷里。

当她来我身旁,我丢开了我的事情,我爱她是爱得这么诚恳;我的师父像一个顶凶恶的土耳其人走近前来,结结实实地打我一番——但是让他打得一个饱罢,为着Sally我能够忍受这些;她是我心中的爱

She is the darling of my heart,
And she lives in our alley.

Of all the days that's in the week
I dearly love but one day,
And that's the day that comes betwixt
A Saturday and Monday;
For then I'm drest all in my best,
To walk abroad with Sally;
She is the darling of my heart,
And she live in our alley.

My master carries me to Church,
And often I am blamed
Because I leave him in the lurch
As soon as text is named;
I leave the Church in sermon-time,
And slink away to Sally;
She is the darling of my heart,
And she lives in our alley.

人,她住在我们的巷里。

全星期里的日子,我深深地只爱一天,那是在星期六同星期一的中间;因为那天我全身穿着顶好的衣服,跟Sally同到外面去闲行;她是我心中的爱人,她住在我们的巷里。

我师父带我到教堂里去,我常常挨他的怒骂,因为牧师才说出当天演讲的圣经章节,我就把他丢在那里,独自偷跑;当说教时候,我离开教堂偷偷地去找我的Sally;她是我心中的爱人,她住在我们的巷里。

When Christmas comes about again,
O then I shall have money;
I'll hoard it up, and box it all,
I'll give it to my honey:
I would it were ten thousand pounds,
I'd give it all to Sally;
She is the darling of my heart,
And she lives in our alley.

My master and the neighbours all
Make game of me and Sally.
And, but for her, I'd better be
A slave and row a galley;
But when my seven long years[1] are out,
O then I'll marry Sally, —
O then we'll wed, and then we'll bed...
But not in our alley!

---

1 他当徒弟的时间。

当圣诞节又到了的时候,那时我就会有钱;我把它积下,全放在匣里,我要将它给我那甜蜜蜜的爱人:我真希望里面能有千磅〔镑〕,我要全把它给我的Sally;她是我心中的爱人,她住在我们的巷里。

我的师父同所有的邻居全拿我同Sally来开玩笑。若使不是有她,我还愿意当个奴隶,罚去摇橹;但是当我的七年长期一旦结束,那时我要娶来我的Sally——那时我们结婚了,一床同梦……但是不是在我们的巷里!

Thomas Gray

(1716—1771)

On a Favorite Cat, Drowned in a Tub of Goldfishes

'Twas on a lofty vase's side,
Where China's gayest art had dyed
The azure flowers that blow,
Demurest of the tabby kind,
The pensive Selima, reclined,
Gazed on the lake below.

Her conscious tail her joy declared:
The fair round face, the snowy beard,
The velvet of her paws,
Her coat that with the tortoise vies,
Her ears of jet, and emerald eyes,
She saw;[1] and purr'd applause.

---

1 第八行至第十一行都是 saw 的 object, i.e. she saw them reflected in the water。

一个人们钟爱的猫儿泅死金鱼缸里

　　这是一个巍然的花瓶,中国最艳的艺术在上画了怒放的碧色花儿;一个最端壮〔庄〕不过的猫儿,深思默想的 Selima(猫儿的名字),躺在一旁,瞧着她眼下的明湖。

　　她那自觉的尾巴说出她的欣欢:她看到了自己团团的庞儿,雪白的胡子,丝绒般的脚爪,堪同玳瑁比美的外皮,黑玉似的耳朵同翡翠色的眼睛;她呜呜地喝出采来。

Still had she gazed, but 'midst the tide
Two angel forms were seen to gilde,
The Genii of the stream:
Their scaly armour's Tyrian[1] hue
Through richest purple to the view
Betray'd a golden gleam.

The hapless Nymph with wonder saw:
A whisker first, and then a claw
With many an ardent wish
She stretch'd, in vain, to reach the prize —[2]
What female heart can gold despise?
What Cat's averse to Fish?

Presumptuous maid! with looks intent
Again she stretch'd, again she bent,
Nor knew the gulf between —
Malignant Fate sat by and smiled —
The slippery verge her feet beguiled;

---

1 古时 Tyre 人善做紫色的颜料，那是用骨螺做的。
2 因为隔了一层玻璃。

她正在注目,但是那水里有一对仙人儿漫漫地游泳,那是水里的神灵:他们鳞甲的紫色是紫得现出一线金黄。

这个不幸的仙女(指猫儿)暗自纳罕地看着:先用胡须试一试,再伸出一只脚爪,她满心热望地伸出去抓这宝物,可是终归枉然——那个女人的心能够看轻金子?那个猫儿不喜小鱼?

放肆的姑娘!带着专心的脸孔,她又伸出爪来,她又湾〔弯〕下身去,她不懂得中间的一道鸿沟——恶意的命运之神坐在一旁微笑——光滑的边缘欺骗了她的四脚;她

She tumbled headlong in!

Eight times[1] emerging from the flood,
She mew'd to every watery God,
Some speedy aid to send: —
No Dolphin came, no Nereid stirr'd,
Nor cruel Tom nor Susan[2] heard —
A favourite has no friend!

From hence, ye Beauties, undeceived
Know one false step is ne'er retrieved,
And be with caution bold;
Not all that tempts your wandering eyes
And heedless hearts, is lawful prize,
Nor all that glisters[3], gold!

---

1 西谚谓一个猫儿有九条命，要等到九条命全死亡了，她才算完全死去。

2 外国很多男孩子叫做Tom（Thomas），很多女孩叫做Susan，所以用了这两个专有名词来代表男女小孩。

3 glister: glitter.

Gray是个禀性忧愁的人，忧愁的人有时说出笑话，总会比别人更见清新，所以这首诗的滑稽情绪会这么可喜。Cowper也是天生愁种，他的倒装地摔到里头！

有八次从这洪水中露出了头，她呜呜地向一切的水神哀鸣，求他们迅速地送出救援：——河豚也不来，海女也不移驾，残忍的 Tom 和软心的 Susan 也没听到——一个人们钟爱的猫儿却得不到朋友！

美人们，你们从此可以清醒，要晓得一失足成了千古恨，凡事该在大大地一再思维；引动了你们那浏览一切的眼睛同经浮粗忽的心灵的并不一定全是合法的东西，闪闪发光的并不一定全是真金！

John Gilpin（《痴汉骑马歌》，辜汤生有译本，商务出版）是绝妙的长篇滑稽诗。中国的诗被"六义"弄得正经得有如泥菩萨，最缺乏这种轻松的微笑情调。其实诗人并非阎罗王，何妨开开笑口。

Oliver Goldsmith

(1728—1774)

When lovely woman stoops to folly
And finds too late that men betray, —
What charm can soothe her melancholy?
What art can wash her guilt away?

The only art her guilt to cover,
To hide her shame from every eye,
To give repentance to her lover
And wring his bosom is—to die.

William Blake

(1757—1827)

Introduction to "Songs of Innocence"

Piping down the valleys wild,

这首诗见他的长篇小说 *The Vicar of Wakefield* 中。

☆　☆　☆

当可爱的女人屈身去做出愚蠢的事情，晓得太迟了男人是会负心，——什么魔力能够慰藉她的愁怨？什么法术能够洗清她的罪恶？

惟一的法子盖住她的罪恶，遮起她的凌辱，避着人们的眼睛，使她的爱人深深追悔，心痛如割——就是自裁。

《天真的歌》的序诗

吹着笛子，走下荒野的山谷，吹出快

Piping songs of pleasant glee,
On a cloud I saw a child,
And he laughing said to me.

"Pipe a song about a Lamb!"
So I piped with merry cheer.
"Piper, pipe that song again;"
So I piped; he wept to hear.

"Drop thy pipe, thy happy pipe;
Sing thy songs of happy cheer!"
So I sung the same again,
While he wept with joy to hear.

"Piper, sit thee down and write
In a book, that all may read."
So he vanished from my sight;
And I plucked a hollow reed.

And I made a rural pen,
And I stained the water clear,
And I wrote my happy songs,
Every child may joy to hear.

乐的调儿,我看见一个小孩站在云端。他大笑地向我说道:"吹一曲来赞美小羊罢!"我就高兴地吹着。"吹,吹,再吹一遍罢";我又吹着;他听得泪流。"放下笛子,你那可喜的笛子,唱出你快乐的小歌罢!"我又唱一遍,他听着喜得泪流。"吹笛人坐下来,写在书里,使大家都能念到罢。"我不见他了;我拔起一根空心的芦苇。我做成一管粗野的笔,沾着清水,就写了个个小孩所爱听的短歌出来。

　　Blake 的诗集有一部叫做《天真的歌》里面是天真地歌咏自然同人生;有一部叫做《经验的歌》,狰狞的世态,阴险的想头,一切人世辛酸的经验全反映在里面,一个人既看出人间世的种种乌烟瘴气,仍然不失其天真的童心,这真是天才。

Love's Secret

Never seek to tell thy love,
Love that never told can be;
For the gentle wind doth move
Silently, invisibly.

I told my love, I told my love,
I told her all my heart,
Trembling, cold, in ghastly fears.
Ah! she did depart!

Soon after she was gone from me,
A traveller came by,
Silenlty invisibly:
He took her with a sigh.

　　Blake 以为爱情是不可言说的，真是"一落言诠，便非真谛"了，所以他用了那不可捕捉的风来打比。Blake 的诗辞句是极简单的，所含的意思却非常奥妙，这是他的难懂处，也就是他的妙处。

爱情的秘密

别说出你的爱情,爱情那能说出;因为和风也只是静静地,隐隐地吹着。

我说出我的爱情,我说出我的爱情,我告诉她我的真心,战栗着,出着冷汗,惊恐得难言。唉!她却离我而去!

去后不久,来了一个旅人,静静地,隐隐地:他微微一叹,就得到她的深情。

Auguries of Innocence

To see a world in a grain of sand,
And a heaven in a wild flower;
Hold infinity in the palm of your hand,
And eternity in an hour.

Robert Burns

(1759—1796)

To a Mouse

On Turning Her Up in Her Nest with the Plough, November 1785

Wee[1], sleepit[2], cow'rin'[3], tim'rous[4] beastie[5],

　　Blake 觉得天下里极细微的东西都含有神秘的意味，你如果能够懂了一件极细微的东西，你就也能够了解宇宙的大谜。他以为宇宙是整个的，是一元的，宇宙中只有一个神秘，这是一切事物都分有的，所以一事通，百事通，由芥子可以测知苍溟了。这是神秘主义者的共同色彩，这首哲理

"天真"的推测

从一粒沙砾里看到宇宙，从一朵野花里看到天堂；把无限拿在你的掌里，把永劫存在一个瞬间。

呈 耗 子

（犁一下去，把她从窝里赶出）
一七八五年十一月

小小的，光滑的，畏缩的，胆怯的，

诗可说是神秘主义者的共同信条。宇宙的神秘只有天真的人们才能猜到，所以他这诗的题目是"天真"的推测。

1 little
2 sleep
3 cowering
4 timorous
5 diminutive of beast

O what a panie's in thy breastie¹!
Thou need na² start awa³ sae⁴ hasty⁵,
Wi' bickering brattle⁶!
I wad⁷ be laith⁸ to rin⁹ an' chase thee
Wi murdering pattle¹⁰!

I'm truly sorry man's dominion
Has broken Nature's social union,
An justifies that ill opinion
Which makes thee startle
At me, thy poor, earth-born companion,
An' fellow-mortal!

I doubt na, whyles¹¹, but thou may thieve;
What then? poor beastie, thou maun live!

---

1 diminutive of breast
2 not
3 away
4 so
5 hurrying
6 scamper
7 would
8 loath

小畜生，呵，你的小胸膛有多么大的惊惶呀！你用不着这么迅速地吓走了，这么急急地飞跑！我绝不愿跟着赶你，带了那当凶手的小锹！

我真伤心人们的威权破坏了自然的一体，使你会有理由，见我就害怕地飞逃，其实我也不过是你的同生在世上的可怜伴侣，而且是一样地同会死亡！

我相信有时你会偷窃，这有什么要紧？可怜的畜生，你也是为着要生存！一束麦

---

9 run
10 paddle
11 sometimes

A daimen[1] icker[2] in a thrave[3]
'S[4] a sma'[5] request;
I'll get a blessin' wi' the lave[6],
An' never miss 't[7]!

Thy wee bit housie[8], too, in ruin!
Its silly[9] wa's[10] the win's[11] are strewin!
An' naething[12] now to big[13] a new ane[14],
O' foggage[15] green!
An' bleak December's win's ensuin,
Baith[16] snell[17] an' keen!

Thou saw the fields laids bare an' waste,
An' weary winter comin fast,
An' cozie here beneath the blast,

---

1 occassional
2 ear of grain
3 twenty-four sheaves
4 is
5 small
6 rest
7 it
8 diminutive of house
9 poor

里的一二小穗是个很细微的要求,剩下的我得着尚要谢谢上帝,绝不会觉得到〔倒〕少了些收成!

你那小屋,也已毁灭!他那可怜的四墙风儿正在吹散!现在也没有青草去盖个新房!接着来的凄冷的冬风是有刺有锋!

你看田野里空无一物,讨厌的冬天又快到头,你当初想在这里安逸地住下,避

---

10 walls
11 winds
12 nothing
13 now
14 build
15 rank grass
16 both
17 piercing

Thou thought to dwell—
Till, Crash! the cruel coulter[1] passed
Out thro' thy cell!

That wee bit heap o' leaves an' stibble[2]
Has cost thee monie a weary nibble!
Now thou's turned cut for a'[3] thy trouble,
But[4] house or hald[5],
To thole[6] the winter's sleety dribble,
An' cranreuch[7] cauld[8]!

But mousie, thou art no thy lane[9]
In proving foresight may be vain:
The best-laid schemes o' mice an' men
Gang aft agley[10],
An' lea'e[11] us naught but grief an' pain
For promised joy!

---

1 blade in front of the ploughshare
2 stubble
3 in spite of
4 without
5 holding
6 endure
7 hour-frost

着那狂风，等到猛的一声，残忍的犁铲的铁口穿过你的小房！

那一些树叶同刹〔槎〕蘖费了你不少的辛苦细咬！现在你却被赶出来了，虽然从前费过多少辛苦，仍然无家无屋，可以避冬天的雨雪霏霏和苦冷的严霜！

但是，小耗子，不单是你一个证明出未雨绸缪也许会变成无用：耗子同人们的打算得最好的计划也常常走到错途，只剩下悲哀同苦痛来换那预期的快乐！

---

8 cold
9 not alone
10 amiss
11 leave

Still thou art blest compared wi' me!
The present only toucheth thee,
But och! I backward cast my e'e[1],
On prospects drear!
An' forward, tho' I canna see,
I guess an' fear!

John Anderson

John Anderson, my jo[2], John,
When we were first acquent[3],
Your locks were like the raven,
Your bonie brow was brent[4];
But now your brow is beld[5], John,
Your locks are like the snaw[6],
But blessings on your frosty pow[7],
John Anderson, my jo!

---

1 eye
2 sweetheart
3 acquainted
4 clear, without lines

你还是有福,同我一比!你只是感觉到现在,但是唉!我回头来看的是过去的惨淡光景!向前瞻,虽然不见,我暗自猜着,正在担心!

John Anderson

John Anderson,我的爱人,John,我们当初认得时候,你的头发是黑得像乌鸦,你的额也是丰润无痕,但是现在你的额已经秃了,John,你的头发宛如白雪,愿上帝赐福给你这斑白的头颅,John Anderson,我的爱人!

---

5 bald
6 snow
7 head

John Auderson, my jo, John,
We clamb¹ the hill thegither²;
And monie³ a cantie⁴ day, John,
We've had wi' ane anither⁵:
Now we maun⁶ totter down John,
And hand in hand we'll go,
And sleep thegither at the foot,⁷
John Anderson, my jo!

A Red, Red Rose

O, my luv⁸ is like a red, red rose,
That's newly sprung in June;
O, my luv is like the melodie⁹,
That's sweetly played in tune.

As fair art thou, my bonie lass,

---

1 climbed
2 together
3 many
4 merry
5 we have had with one another
6 must

John Anderson，我的爱人 John，我们曾齐爬上那小山，有许多快乐日子，John，我俩同在一处；现在我们要蹒跚走下，John，但是我们也要携手同行，到那山脚下同眠，John Anderson，我的爱人！

一朵红红的玫瑰花

我的爱人像一朵红红的玫瑰花，六月里刚刚吐萼；我的爱人像一曲妙乐，甜蜜地演奏和谐。

你是多么美丽，我的标致姑娘，我的

---

7 这是拿来代表人生的道路，老年人精力日衰，好似走下山一样，最后到了平地，那又是恢复本来无生的境界，去长眠了。

8 love

9 melody

So deep in luve am I;
And I will luve thee still, my dear,
Till a' the seas gang¹ dry.

Till a'² the seas gang dry, my dear,
And the rocks melt wi' the sun;
And I will luve thee still, my dear,
While the sands O' life shall run.

And fare thee weel³, my only luve!
And fare thee weel awhile!
And I will come again, my luve,
Tho' it were ten thousand mile!

---

1 go
2 all
3 well

爱情也是多么样深;我还是要爱着你,亲爱的,虽然普天下的大海全已枯干。

海也枯了,山也给太阳晒到溶了;过了这么久,我还是爱你,我总是爱你,我亲爱的,当我的生命尚有一点的残留。

再会罢,我惟一的爱人!暂时别离一下罢!我是必定回来的,我的爱人,虽然有万里的路程!

The Nineteenth Century

William Wordsworth
(1770—1850)

Lucy

I

Strange fits of passion have I known:
And I will dare to tell,
But in the lover's ear alone,
What once to me befell.

When she I loved look'd every day
Fresh as a rose in June,
I to her cottage bent my way,
Beneath an evening moon.

Upon the moon I fix'd my eye,
All over the wide lea;

Lucy

I

我经历过热情的奇怪激发:我只敢向爱人们的耳朵里说出我的一段奇情。

当我的爱人天天都同六月里的蔷薇一样新鲜,我向她的茅屋走去,月儿高挂在中天。

我的眼睛老钉〔盯〕着月儿,穿过广阔的草场;

With quickening pace my horse drew nigh
Those paths so dear to me.

And now we reach'd the orchard-plot;
And, as we climb'd the hill,
The sinking moon to Lucy's cot
Came near and nearer still.

In one of those sweet dreams I slept,
Kind Nature's gentlest boon!
And all the while my eyes I kept
On the descending moon.

My horse moved on, hoof after hoof.
He raised, and never stopp'd.
When down behind the cottage roof,
At once, the bright moon dropp'd.

What fond and wayward thoughts will slide
Into a lover's head!
"O mercy!" to myself I cried,
"If Lucy should be dead!"

我的马儿一步快一步地走近我所爱的小途。

现在我们到了果园；当我们爬上小山，渐沉的月儿渐渐地行近Lucy的茅屋。

我迷醉在我生平所做的一个好梦里面，这些梦真是自然最温柔的恩赉！我的眼总是不断地瞧着那下沉的月儿。

我的马儿前进，他的蹄子接连地举起，老没有一会儿的停歇。当那明亮的月儿向着茅屋的屋顶后面顿然地下沉。

什么可笑古怪的想头，都会偷跑到爱人的心里！"唉，天呀！"我对自己叫道，"若使Lucy是死了！"

II

She dwelt among the untrodden ways
Beside the springs of Dove,
A maid whom there were none to praise,
And very few to love.

A violet by a mossy stone
Half hidden from the eye!
Fair as a star, when only one
Is shining in the sky.

She lived unknown, and few could know
When Lucy ceased to be;
But she is in her grave, and oh,
The difference to me!

III

I travell'd among unknown, men,
In lands beyond the sea;
Nor, England! did I know till then
What love I bore to thee.

Ⅱ

她住在人迹不到的地方,Dove 的流边,她是无人称赞,很少人钟爱的一位姑娘。

像铺着苍苔的石头旁边的紫罗兰,一半遮着不被人眼看见!像星儿那么美丽,当只有一个明耀在天中。

她活着不被人们知道,仅仅几个人晓得 Lucy 是已辞世;但是她已在她的坟里了,呵,对着我这是个多么大的不同!

Ⅲ

我在海外他乡的生人里旅行;英国,不到那时,我真不晓得我是多么爱你。

'Tis past, that melancholy dream!
Nor will I quit thy shore
A second time; for still I seem
To love thee more and more.

Among thy mountains did I feel
The joy of my desire;
And she I cherish'd turn'd her wheel
Beside an English fire.

Thy mornings show'd thy nights conceal'd
The bowers where Lucy play'd;
And thine too is the last green field
That Lucy's eyes survey'd.

IV

Three years she grew in sun and shower;
Then Nature said, "a lovelier flower
On earth was never sown;
This child I to myself will take;
She shall be mine, and I will make
A lady of my own.

这是过去了,这一场的愁梦!我再也不会离开你的海岸;我真像一天一天地更爱着你。

在你的群山里,我觉到我所想得的欣欢;我心里所爱恋的她也是在个英国的火旁转着她的纺纶。

你的清早照着,你的昏黑蒙着 Lucy 游玩所在的小亭;那也是你的 Lucy 弥留时最末一次所看到的绿田。

IV

三年里她在阳光同雨中长大;"自然"于是说道,"地上从来没有种过个更可爱的花儿;这孩子我要拿来给我自己;她将算是我的,我要把她做成个我中意的姑娘。

"Myself will to my darling be
Both law and impulse; and with me
The girl, in rock and plain,
In earth and heaven, in glade and bower,
Shall feel an overseeing power
To kindle or restrain.

"She shall be sportive as the fawn
That wild with glee across the lawn
Or up the mountain springs;
And hers shall be the breathing balm,
And hers the silence and the calm
Of mute insensate things.

"The floating clouds their state shall lend
To her; for her the willow bend;
Nor shall she fail to see
Even in the motions of the storm
Grace that shall mould the maiden's form
By silent sympathy.

"我自己对着我这个乖乖既去束缚又去鼓舞；这女孩跟着我在岩石同平原里，大地同青天里，在林中空地同园中小亭里要感到一个监临的势力，来点起心灵之火或者来范围住种种的任性胡为。

"她要像那狂欢着飞跑过草地，或者飞奔上山坡的小鹿那么喜欢玩耍；她具有气味薰人的芬芳，又具有默然不语的静物的那种静默同安详。

"舒卷自如的白云借她以他们的风韵；杨柳也是为着她而湾〔弯〕腰（她从杨柳学到她的袅娜态度）；甚至于从风浪的暴动里，她也看出轻柔的秀美，她暗地里同情着，因此她那年轻的身体也渐化轻柔。

"The stars of midnight shall be dear
To her; and she shall lean her ear
In many a secret place
Where rivulets dance their wayward round
And beauty born of murmuring sound
Shall pass into her face.

"And vital feelings of delight
Shall rear her form to stately height,
Her virgin bosom swell;
Such thoughts to Lucy I will give
While she and I together live
Here in this happy dell."

Thus Nature spake — The work was done —
How soon my Lucy's race was run!
She died, and left to me
This heath, this calm and quiet scene;
The memory of what has been,
And never more will be.

V

A slumber did my spirit seal;

"午夜的星儿将受她的见爱；她将倾耳于许多秘密的地方，那里小河自恣地跳跃，潺潺妙音的清美将现在她的脸上。

"快乐的生气勃勃使她长得玉立堂堂，使她的小女之胸也膨胀起来；我要使Lucy有这些精神，当她同我一起住在这快乐的山谷里头。"

"自然"这么说——这场工作也就做成了——但是Lucy的一生是多么快就结束呀！她死去，留下给我的是这个草原，这个静寂同这悄悄的风景；还有的是那不可复得的前尘影事的追忆。

V

一场甜睡紧封住我的灵魂；那时我没有人间的

I had no human fears;

She seem'd a thing that could not feel

The touch of earthly years.

No motion has she now, no force;

She neither hears nor sees;

Roll'd round in earth's diurnal course,

With rocks, and stones, and trees.

Lines Written in Early Spring

I heard a thousand blended notes,

While in a grove I sate reclined,

In that sweet mood when pleasant thoughts

Bring sad thoughts to the mind.

To her fair works did Nature link

The human soul that through me ran;

  Wordsworth诗的命题几乎全是"自然",这几首可说是他所仅有的情诗。他主张我们写诗时,不应当让情感任意奔放,却该有个恬静的胸怀做背境,把情感反映出来;他一写情诗,难免有些情不自禁,所表现的情绪

忧虑;她好像是个不受人世岁月影响的不老人儿。

现在她不动了,也没有丝毫的力气;她已是无视无闻;却只跟着岩石树林一起,天天照着地球自转的轨道而滚旋。

早春偶成

我听到融在一气的成千妙音,当我斜倚地坐在林中,我是怀着那个甜蜜的心境,当快乐的思想勾上愁来。

"自然"将我身里的这种人的灵魂同她美丽的作品(指大地的风光)连在一起;我真是伤心,一想

因此也甚紧张,这是违了他的主张。因为要言行一致,他宁可焚琴煮鹤,少写情诗,后世的读者因此少读了许多的绝妙情诗。

And much it grieved my heart to think
What man has made of man.

Through primrose tufts, in that green bower,
The periwinkle trailed its wreaths;
And 'tis my faith that every flower
Enjoys the air it breathes.

The birds around me hopped and played,
Their thoughts I cannot measure: —
But the least motion which they made,
It seemed a thrill of pleasure.

The budding twigs spread out their fan
To catch the breezy air;
And I must think, do all I can,
That there was pleasure there.

If this belief from heaven be sent,
If such be Nature's holy plan,
Have I not reason to lament
What man has made of man?

到人们是怎地去糟塌〔蹋〕自己。

穿过莲馨花的团簇,在绿色的圆亭里面,雁来红拖曳他的须叶;我是相信个个花儿都喜悦他所呼吸的空气。

四旁的小鸟跳动游戏,他们的想头我那能度量:——但是他们极细微的一动好像都是快乐的震动。

含苞的小枝张开他们的叶子,去捉和风;无论如何我总以为这里是蕴有欣欢。

若使这个信仰是从天降下,若使这是"自然"的神圣计划,我是不是有理去哀悼,人们是怎样地去糟塌〔蹋〕自己?

My heart leaps up when I behold
A rainbow in the sky;
So was it when my life began;
So is it now I am a man;
So be it when I shall grow old,
Or let me die!
The Child is father of the Man;
And I could wish my days to be
Bound each to each by natural piety[1].

The Solitary Reaper

Behold her, single in the field.
You solitary Highland Lass!
Reaping and singing by herself;
Stop here, or gently pass!
Alone she cuts and binds the grain,
And sings a melancholy strain;

☆ ☆ ☆

我的心跳起来,当我看到天上的一曲虹儿;我生命开始时,我就是这样;现在成人了,我仍然如此;将来老大,就也这样罢,否则还是让我死去!"小孩"是"大人"的根芽;我希望,我的一生天天都是虔敬地瞧着"自然"。

寂寞的刈禾人

看她罢,独自在田中。那个寂寞的山地里姑娘!独自刈禾,独自歌唱;有时停着,有时轻轻地慢行!她孤单单地割下禾来,成束扎起,唱出一曲凄迷的

---

1 natural piety: the feeling of reverent exaltation with which I have always witnessed the beauty and grandeur of nature.

O listen! for the Vale profound
Is overflowing with the sound.

No Nightingale did ever chaunt
More welcome notes to weary bands
Of travellers in some shady haunt,
Among Arabian sands:
A voice so thrilling ne'er was heard
In spring-time from the Cuckoo-bird,
Breaking the silence of the seas
Among the farthest Hebrides[1].

Will no one tell me what she sings?
Perhaps the plaintive numbers[2] flow
For old, unhappy, far-off things,
And battles long ago:
Or is it some more humble lay,
Familiar matter of to-day?
Some natural sorrow, loss, or pain,
That has been, and may be again?

---

1 苏格兰西方的小群岛，以风景幽雅著名。有一位批评家说Hebrides这字念起来有袅袅不绝之音，使人生辽远之感，以为这是Wordsworth用专有名词用得神化的地方。

调儿；呵，听着罢！深谷是满溢着歌声。

夜莺对着亚拉伯沙漠里阴凉处的疲倦旅人们未曾唱出比这个更欢然的歌声：像这么动人的歌声从来没有从杜鹃嘴里听到，当春天时候，他在辽远的 Hebrides 里冲破了大海的静寂。

谁也不能告诉我，她唱的是什么吗？也许这悲伤的词句缕述着古昔不幸的事情，同久已过去的战争；或者是些更低微的小调，说出当今的日常故事吗？一些天然会有的悲哀，损失同苦痛，古而有过，现在也还会发生？

---

2 numbers: verse，作此解时常居复数。

Whate'er the theme, the Maiden sang
As if her song could have no ending;
I saw her singing at her work,
And o'er the sickle bending;
I listened motionless and still;
And, as I mounted up the hill
The music in my heart I bore,
Long after it was heard no more.

I wandered lonely as a cloud
That floats on high o'er vales and hills,
When all at once I saw a crowd,
A host, of golden daffodils;
Beside the lake, beneath the trees,
Fluttering and dancing in the breeze.

Continuous as the stars that shine
And twinkle on the milky way,
They stretched in never-ending line
Along the margin of a bay;
Ten thousand saw I at a glance,

不管是什么题材,这姑娘唱着好似她的歌儿是不会完的;我看她工作时唱着,湾〔弯〕下腰拿着镰刀;我不动地宁静地聆着;当我走上山去,我心里还存着那歌声,虽然我早已不会听见。

☆ ☆ ☆

我独自遨游,像高居在上,越谷过山的一片白云,忽然间我看到一群,一大队的金黄色水仙;在湖旁,在树下,在和风里摇着舞着。

像在银河里照耀闪烁的众星那么接连着,他们(指水仙)舒展成无起无终的一线,沿着堰堤的边旁;我一眼看去有十万[1]朵活泼跳舞着摇荡他

---

[1] 此处"十万"据英文原文应为"一万"。——编者注

Tossing their heads in sprightly dance.

The waves beside them danced; but they
Out — did the sparkling waves in glee:
A poet could not but be gay,
In such a jocund company:
I gazed — and gazed — but little thought
What wealth the show to me had brought.

For oft, when on my couch I lie
In vacant or in pensive mood,
They flash upon that inward eye
Which is the bliss of solitude;[1]
And then my heart with pleasure fills.
And dances with the daffodils.

The Inner Vision

Most sweet it is with unuplifted eyes
To pace the ground, if path be there or none,

---

1 这两行是 Wordsworth 夫人当枪手的，他自己以为这两行是全篇里的精华，这也许是出自他的谦让美德罢。

们的花冠。

他们旁边的波浪也在跳舞,但是他们的欣欢胜过灿烂的浪花:一个诗人对着这样喜悦的伴侣,安得不喜逐颜开!我瞧着——恣意地瞧着——却不大想到这壮观会给我多少的幸福。

常常当我躺在床上,心中是悠然或者愁然,这班花朵会顿现在心眼上,那真是寂寞的无上至福;那时我的心满着快乐,会同水仙花一同跳舞。

心中的幻影

这是最甜蜜的,垂着眼睛慢步,脚下有路或是

While a fair region round the traveller lies
Which he forbears again to look upon.

Pleased rather with some soft ideal scene,
The work of Fancy, or some happy tone
Of meditation, slipping in between
The beauty coming and the beauty gone.

If Thought and Love desert us, from that day
Let us break off all commerce with the Muse:
With thought and Love companions of our way —

Whate'er the senses take or may refuse, —
The Mind's internal heaven shall shed her dews
Of inspiration on the humblest lay.

To Sleep

A flock of sheep that leisurely pass by,
One after one; the sound of rain, and bees
Murmuring; the fall of rivers, winds and seas,
Smooth fields, white sheets of water, and pure sky; [1]

无路,旅人的四围是美丽的风光,他却不再去流连。他只高兴一些缥渺的意想境界,那是"幻想"的作品或者一些恬然自适的冥想的,暗暗地插在快来的美景同已过的美景中间。

若使"思想"同"爱"弃着我们而去,从那天起让我们不再和诸神往来;若使有"思想"同"爱"做我们途中的伴侣——不管感官所受的同所拒的是什么——心灵的方寸天堂会洒下她那灵感的甘露于最低微的调儿。

呈 睡 神

一群徐徐地接连着走过的小羊,雨的声音同蜜蜂的细吟;河的奔流,狂风,大海,平野,一片白

---

1 这些东西全是非常单调的,具有催眠的能力,所以他故意去想这些东西来下眠,同我们睡不着时,把数目拿来一一数过,是有同样的作用的。

I have thought of all by turns, and yet do lie
Sleepless; and soon the small birds' melodies
Must hear, first uttered from my orchard trees,
And the first cuckoo's melancholy cry.

Even thus last night, and two nights more, I lay,
And could not win thee, Sleep! by any stealth:
So do not let me wear to-night away:
Without thee what is all the morning's wealth?
Come, blessed barrier between day and day,
Dear mother of fresh thoughts and joyous health!

Samuel Taylor Coleridge
(1772—1834)

Love

All thoughts, all passions all delights,
Whatever stirs this mortal frame
All are but ministers of Love,
And feed his sacred flame.

茫茫的大水，洁净无尘的青天；这些东西我一一都拿来想过，但是我还是躺着不能入眠！不久我一定要听到小鸟的歌声，先从我果园里的树林吐露出来，还有最先起来的杜鹃的哀啼。

昨晚如是，前两晚也如是，我躺着，却不能得你的欢心，睡神！连偷偷地一息也是不能；今晚别让我再这样消磨去罢：没有你，清晨的一切幸福算得什么？来罢，朝朝中间的可谢的间隔，你是新鲜的思想同快乐的健康的母亲！

爱

一切思想，一切情感，一切欣欢，凡是可以撩乱这血肉之躯的，全不过是"爱情"的部下培养起他那神圣的火焰。

Oft in my waking dreams do I
Live o'er again that happy hour,
When midway on the mount I lay,
Beside the ruined tower.

The moonshine, stealing o'er the scene,
Had blended with the lights of eve;
And she was there, my hope, my joy,
My own dear Genevieve!

She leaned against the armed man,
The statue of the armed Knight;
She stood and listened to my lay,
Amid the lingering light.

Few sorrows hath she of her own,
My hope! my joy! my Genevieve!
She loves me best whene'er I sing
The songs that make her grieve.

I played a soft and doleful air;
I sang an old and moving story—

在白天的梦里，我常常重温起那个快乐的时光，当我躺在半山里，颓废的古塔站在一旁。

偷偷地照地的月色同暮色杂在一起；她也是在那里，我的希望，我的喜悦，我亲亲可爱的Genevieve姑娘！

她倚着那披甲的人，那是披甲武士的石像；她站住听我的歌声，在那淹留未去的微光里。

她自己没有多少悲哀，我的希望！我的喜悦！我亲亲可爱的Genevieve！她最爱我，每当我唱出那使她心酸的歌曲。

我奏出一曲轻柔凄然的调子；我唱出一个动人

An old rude song, that suited well
That ruin wild and hoary.

She listened with a flitting blush,
With downcast eyes, and modest grace;
For well she knew I could not choose
But gaze upon her face.

I told her of the Knight that wore
Upon his shield a burning brand;
And that for ten long years he wooed
The Lady of the Land.

I told her how he pined: and ah!
The deep, the low, the pleading tone
With which I sang another's love,
Interpreted my own.

She listened with a flitting blush,
With downcast eyes, and modest grace;
And she forgave me, that I gazed
Too fondly on her face!

的故事——一个朴实的故事,刚合这荒芜古老的废墟。

她聆时脸上常有红霞流走,低着眼睛含羞得可人;她实在晓得我是免不了钉〔盯〕着她的庞儿。

我告诉她在盾上画有正在燃烧的火把的武士;同他一连十年向着"国内的绝色佳人"求婚。

我告诉她他怎样地憔悴:呀!我歌唱别人的情史时所用的深沉的,低微的,恳求的声音说出我自己的衷情。

她聆时脸上常有红霞流走,低着眼睛含羞得可人;她赦宥我那样痴痴地钉〔盯〕着她的庞儿!

But when I told the cruel scorn¹
That crazed that bold and lovely Knight,
And that he crossed the mountain-woods,
Nor rested day nor night;

That sometimes from the savage den,
And sometimes from the darksome shade,
And sometimes starting up at once
In green and sunny glade, —

There came and looked him in the face
An angel beautiful and bright;
And that he knew it was a Fiend,
This miserable Knight!

And that, unknowing what he did,
He leaped amid a murderous band,
And saved from outrage worse than death
The Lady of the Land; —

And how she wept and clasped his knees;
And how she tended him in vain —
And ever strove to expiate

我说出佳人那种残忍的藐视弄疯了这勇敢的可爱武士,他望〔往〕深山的森林里走去,朝夜不停;

有时从野蛮人的洞里,有时从黑暗暗的阴处,有时忽然从青青朝阳的空地上,——

来了一个美丽光明的天使,对着他脸上尽瞧;可怜的武士,他知道这是一个恶魔!

不懂得自己干的是什么,他跳进一群凶手里去,救出"本国的绝色佳人"免她受了那尤甚于死的耻辱;——

我又说她怎样哭泣,抱着他的双膝;她怎样枉然地看护着他——她老是竭力想去补偿那使他疯狂

---

1 the cruel scorn: i.e. of the Lady.

The scorn that crazed his brain; —

And that she nursed him in a cave;
And how his madness went away,
When on the yellow forest-leaves
A dying man he lay; —

His dying words — but when I reached
That tenderest strain of all the ditty,
My faltering voice and pausing harp
Disturbed her soul with pity!

All impulses of soul and sense
Had thrilled my guileless Genevieve;
The music and the doleful tale,
The rich and balmy eve;

And hopes, and fears that kindle hope,
An undistinguishable throng,
And gentle wishes long subdued,
Subdued and cherished long!

的藐视；——

她在穴里看护他；他的疯疾是怎样好了，当他是躺着黄叶上的死人；——

他临终时所说的话是——但是当我唱到这小歌里最动人的一节，我那吞吐的声音同停住了的琴韵使他的心灵深感到哀怜！

心灵同感官的一切刺激震动了我这天真的Genevieve；那种音乐同那凄然的故事，再加上华美芬芳的黄昏；

希望同点燃着希望的恐惧，化成分不开的一团，久已压下的些微想愿，虽已压下却久已涵蓄在心头！

She wept with pity and delight,
She blushed with love and virgin-shame;
And like the murmur of a dream,
I heard her breathe my name.

Her bosom heaved — she stepped aside,
As conscious of my look she stepped —
Then suddenly, with timorous eye
She fled to me and wept.

She half enclosed me with her arms,
She pressed me with a meek embrace;
And bending back her head, looked up
And gazed upon my face.

'Twas partly love, and partly fear,
And partly 'twas a bashful art,
That I might rather feel, than see,
The swelling of her heart.

I calmed her fears, and she was calm,
And told her love with virgin pride;
And so I won my Genevieve,

她为着怜悯同喜悦而泪流,她为着爱情同处女的害羞而脸红;像梦中的喃喃,我听她吐出我的小名。

她的胸部起伏——她走到旁边,觉得我的注视,她走到旁边——然后突然地,带着怯懦的眼神,她跑到我跟前,呜咽泪下。

她用双臂一半围着我的全身,她迫近我以柔和的拥抱;向背湾〔弯〕着头,她仰视我的脸孔。

这有几分是爱情,有几分是恐惧,还有几分是怕羞的狡计,她要我觉到,不是看到,她心儿的膨胀。

我安下她的恐惧,她跟着就安心了,她带着小女的骄羞诉出她的爱情;这样子我得到了我的

My bright and beauteous Bride.

Walter Savage Landor
(1775—1864)

Ianthe

From you, Ianthe, little troubles pass
Like little ripples down a sunny river;
Your pleasures spring like daisies in the grass,
Cut down and up again as blithe as ever.

Why

Why do our joys depart
For cares to seize the heart?
I know not. Nature says,
Obey; and man obeys.
I see, and know not why,
Thorns live and roses die.

Genevieve，我这光明美丽的新娘。

Ianthe

Ianthe，小小的苦恼离你而去，有如小波流下一条晒着太阳的小河；你的快乐像草里的雏菊一样地产生，割下去，和先前同样快乐地又长出来。

此 何 故 耶

为什么我们的欣欢走去，让烦恼来抓着心儿？我不知道。"自然"说"服从"；人们就服从了。我眼见荆棘生着蔷薇死，我却不晓得是为什么。

The Maid's Lament

I loved him not; and yet now he is gone,
I feel I am alone.
I check'd him while he spoke; yet, could he speak,
Alas! I would not check.
For reasons not to love him once I sought,
And wearied all my thought
To vex myself and him; I now would give
My love, could he but live
Who lately lived for me, and when he found
'Twas vain, in holy ground
He hid his face amid the shades of death.
I waste for him my breath
Who wasted his for me; but mine returns.
And this lorn[1] bosom burns
With stifling heat, heaving it up in sleep,
And waking me to weep
Tears that had melted his soft heart: for years
Wept he as bitter tears.
"Merciful God!" such was his latest prayer,

小女的哀语

我从前并不爱他;但是现在他死了,我感到我的孤单。从前他一说话,我就拦住;可是现在他若能说,唉!我绝不会再拦。我曾故意找出理去不爱他,竭思尽虑来麻烦自己同他;我现在要献出我的爱情,若使他还是活着,他不久以前是为我而活,当他看出这是枉然,他在神圣的地里掩藏起他的脸孔,在死的阴影中间。他从前为我叹息,我现在也为他唏嘘;但是我的叹息回返身来,这个无依的胸膛燃着闷热,睡眠中起伏无定,使我醒来流下从前溶化了他的软心的那种热泪。他有好多年都是流着这同样辛酸的眼泪。"仁慈的上帝!"这是他最后的

---

1 lorn: deserted.

"These may she never share!"
Quieter is his breath, his breast more cold
Than daisies in the mould,
Where children spell, athwart[1] the churchyard gate,
His name and life's brief date.
Pray for him, gentle souls, whoe'er you be,
And, O, pray too for me!

Finis

I strove with none, for none was worth my strife.
Nature I loved and, next to nature, Art:
I warm'd both hands before the fire of life;
It sinks, and I am ready to depart.

Death

Death stands above me, whispering low
I know not what into my ear;
Of his strange language all I know

---

1 athwart: across, 从门的上头看去。

祷告，"这些苦痛愿她永不尝到！"同墓上的雏菊相比，他的气息是更恬静，他的胸部是更冰冷，小孩们隔着教堂坟园的门，一字字念出他的名字同他那短促一生的日期。为他祈祷罢，温和的灵魂（指小孩），不管你是谁呵，也替我祈祷罢！

尾　　声

我不同谁去争胜，因为谁也不值得我的竞争。"自然"是我所爱的，其次就是"艺术"：我伸出双手烘着生命的火；它消沉了，我也愿意走开。

死

死神站在上面，低低地向我的耳朵说了些我不懂的话儿；他那奇怪的言语，我所知道的只是里面

Is, there is not, a word of fear.

Thomas Moore

(1779—1852)

'Tis the last rose of summer,
Left blooming alone;
All her lovely companions
Are faded and gone;
No flower of her kindred,
No rosebud is nigh
To reflect back her blushes,
Or give sigh for sigh!

I'll not leave thee, thou lone one,
To pine on the stem;
Since the lovely are sleeping,
Go, sleep thou with them;
Thus kindly I scatter
Thy leaves o'er the bed
Where thy mates of the garden
Lie scentless and dead.

没有一句使人害怕的话儿。

☆ ☆ ☆

这是夏天最后的一朵蔷薇,剩下来孤单地吐华;她所有可爱的伴侣全已凋谢;没有她的姊妹花,没有一粒的蔷薇蕊在近傍〔旁〕来反射出她的羞颊或者跟着叹息,声声相和!

我将不让你,你这孤寂的蔷薇,在枝头憔悴;可爱的同伴既全入睡,去,你也和她们同眠罢;所以我慈爱地散你的花瓣在花床之上,在那里你园中的好友全是无香地死死地稳眠。

So soon may I follow,
When friendships decay,
And from love's shining circle
The gems drop away!
When true hearts lie withered,
And fond one are flown,
O, who would inhabit
This bleak world alone!

George Noel Gordon, Lord Byron
(1788—1824)

When we two parted
In silence and tears,
Half broken-hearted,
To sever for years,
Pale grew thy cheek and cold,
Colder thy kiss;
Truly that hour foretold
Sorrow to this!

The dew of the morning
Sunk chill on my brow;

当朋友尽凋零了，爱的光圈上的宝石也一颗颗地掉下，我也能这么快地随他们而去罢！当真心的人儿已经萎谢，可爱的人儿早已不存，啊，谁愿意独自住在这荒凉的世界！

☆ ☆ ☆

当我俩静静地含着满泡眼泪分手，心儿半破，因为一别要几年，你的颊灰白变冷，你的吻更是如冰；真的，那时就预言到这刻的悲哀！

那天早上的清露冷冷地滴到我眉上；我的眉梢

It felt like the warning
Of what I feel now.
Thy vows are all broken,
And light is thy fame;
I hear thy name spoken
And share in its shame.

They name thee before me,
A knell to mine ear;
A shudder comes o'er me —
Why wert thou so dear?
They know not I knew thee
Who¹ knew thee too well:
Long, long shall I rue thee
To deeply to tell.

In secret we met,
In silence I grieve
That thy heart could forget,
Thy spirit deceive.
If I should meet thee
After long years,

好像感到个警告,警告了此刻的痛心。你的誓言全背了,你的名誉也就不受人看重;我听到人们提起你的名字,我也分有你的可羞。

他们当我面前提到你的名字,对于我的耳朵这是个殡葬的哀音;我浑身战栗起来——为什么你从前是那么可人?他们不晓得我认得你,我却是认得太深:我将久久地为你悲伤,感伤得太深了那能说出。

从前我们偷偷地相会,现在我暗暗地哀悼你的心是会忘却旧情,你的灵魂是肯骗人。若使年久月长后,我再会到你,我要怎样地向你招呼?也只好

---

1 who 的 antecedent 是 I。

How should I greet thee?
With silence and tears.

All for Love

O talk not to me of a name great in story;
The days of our youth are the days of our glory;
And the myrtle and ivy of sweet two-and-twenty
Are worth all your laurels, though ever so plenty.

What are garlands and crowns to the brow that is wrinkled?
'Tis but as a dead flower with May-dew besprinkled:
Then away with all such from the head that is hoary —
What care I for the wreaths that can only give glory?

O Fame! — if I e'er took delight in thy praises,
'Twas less for the sake of thy high-sounding phrases,
Than to see the bright eyes of the dear one discover
She thought that I was not unworthy to love her.

静静地含着满泡的眼泪。

一切全是为爱情

别同我说历史上什么伟大的名字，青春的日子就是我们光荣的日子；甜蜜的廿二年华欢宴时戴在头上的番石榴花同常春藤是值得你们一切纪功的桂花冠，虽然这花冠是那么多。

花冠和皇冕配着已皱的眉头，这算得什么？这不过像残花上洒着五月的清露：那么，发已斑白的头还是不要这些罢——只能给我以光荣的花冠，我做甚还去关心？

呵名誉呀！——若使我有时高兴你的赞美，那不是为着你那说来动听的颂辞，却是因为看到可爱人儿的眼睛表示出她以为我是配得上爱她。

There chiefly I sought thee, there only I found thee;
Her glance was the best of the rays that surround thee;
When it sparkled o'er aught that was bright in my story,
I knew it was love, and I felt it was glory.

She walks in beauty, like the night
Of cloudless climes and starry skies,
And all that's best of dark and bright
Meet in her aspect and her eyes,
Thus mellow'd to that tender light
Which heaven to gaudy day denies.

One shade the more, one ray the less,
Had half impair'd the nameless grace
Which waves in every raven tress,
Or softly lightens o'er her face,
Where thoughts serenely sweet express
How pure, how dear their dwelling-place.

我只从那里（指爱人的眼睛）去求你（指名誉），我在那里才能找到你；她的青盼是你旁边最好的光辉；当他的双眸对着我生平里光荣的事情现出光辉，我晓得这是爱情，我觉到这才是光荣。

☆　☆　☆

她在美丽中走着，像无云天气，满天繁星的静夜，凡是明暗的至美都聚在她的颜色的同双眸，因此做成了恬柔的光彩，那好处浓艳的白昼焉能得到。

浓了一些，暗了一些，就去了一半那说不出的风韵，这是随着她每束乌鸦般的黑发飘动，或者轻轻地照着她的庞儿，恬〔甜〕蜜的思想在她脸上现出她的心地是多么洁白可爱。

And on that cheek and o'er that brow
So soft, so calm, yet eloquent,
The smiles that win, the tints that glow
But tell of days in goodness spent,
A mind at peace with all below,
A heart whose love is innocent.

To Thomas Moore

I

My boat is on the shore,
And my bark is on the sea:
But, before I go, Tom Moore,
Here's double health to thee!

II

Here's sigh to those who love me,
And a smile to those who hate;
And, whatever sky's above me,

在她这么柔软的，安详的，又是那么解语的颊边同眉梢，有那可人的微笑同灿烂的神采告诉出她的日子是用在仁慈事上，她的思想是与万物无忤，她的心是怀着天真的爱。

呈 Thomas Moore

我的小艇是在岸旁，我的帆船是在海里：但是在我动身之前，Tom Moore，我饮了双杯一再祝你的康健！

爱我的人们，我现在给他们以一声浩叹，恨我的人们，我现在给他们以微微一笑；不管我的遭遇

Here's a heart for every fate.

III

Though the ocean roar around me,
Yet it still shall bear me on;
Though a desert should surround me,
It hath springs that may be won.

IV

Were't the last drop in the well,
As I gasped upon the brink,
Ere my fainting spirit fell,
'Tis to thee that I would drink.

V

With that water, as this wine,
The libation I would pour
Should be — peace with thine and mine,
And a health to thee, Tom Moore.

会是如何,我这里有个敢历一切遭遇的心儿。

虽然海水在四围狂啸,可是他会带我向前;虽然四围会是个沙漠,它也有那可以找到的清泉。

若使这是井里的最后一滴,当我口干得喘在一旁,在我快消失的精神凋谢之前,那是为着你我要饮祝健康。

用了那水,好像用这酒一样,我饮酒时的颂词是——愿你的一切同我的一切都能平安,还祝你的康健,Tom Moore。

Percy Bysshe Shelley

(1792—1822)

Stanzas Written in Dejection near Naples

The sun is warm, the sky is clear;
The waves are dancing fast and bright,
Blue isles and snowy mountains wear
The purple noon's transparent might;
The breath of the moist earth is light
Around its unexpanded buds;
Like many a voice of one delight[1]—
The winds, the birds, the ocean-floods—
The City's voice itself is soft like solitude's.

I see the Deep's[2] untrampled floor
With green and purple seaweeds strown;
I see the waves upon the shore,[3]
Like light dissolved in star-showers thrown;
I sit upon the sands alone;
The lightning of the noontide ocean

Naples 湾畔愁中书怀

太阳是温暖的,天空是清彻的;波浪跳得清快又光明,蓝色的小岛同雪盖的高山都戴上了艳丽中天的明晖;湿壤的气息轻轻地围着尚未吐华的花蕾;风声,鸟语同涛声合起来像整个快乐的种种呼声,城市的声音也清柔得有似荒凉的幽处。

我看见漫布着青紫海草,人迹未经的海底;我看见浪儿打到岸上,像光明化作一阵的星雨;我独自坐在沙上;中午的海里波光在我旁边四射,从大

---

1 声音虽然不同,所表现的乐绪则一。
2 the Deep:海。诗中常常这样用。
3 I see the waves upon the shore: I see the waves thrown upon the shore.

Is flashing round me, and a tone
Arises from its measured motion —
How sweet! did any heart now share in my emotion.

Alas! I have nor hope nor health,
Nor peace within, nor calm around,
Nor that content, surpassing wealth,
The sage in meditation found,
And walked with inward glory crowned —
Nor fame, nor power, nor love, nor leisure;
Others I see whom these surround —
Smiling they live, and call life pleasure;
To me that cup[1] has been dealt in another measure.

Yet now despair itself is mild
Even as the winds and waters are;
I could lie down like a tired child,
And weep away the life of care
Which I have borne, and yet must bear

---

1 that cup: 此处 cup 意指 something alloted to one as a portion to be received or endured，即上帝派定的运命，典出《圣经·约翰福音》中"The cup which the Father hath given, shall I not drink it?"（天父赐我之杯，我岂有不饮之理）。

海的合于韵律的起伏来了一阵清音——多么甜蜜呀！有谁现在和我怀着同样的幽情。

唉！我没有希望，没有健康，心里不安，四围不宁，也没有那可说是胜过巨富的知足，这是贤人在冥想里找到的，所以走动时带着有内心的光荣——没有名誉，没有权力，没有爱情，没有余暇；我看到别人是享这许多的幸福——他们微笑地活着，口说生活是快乐；对着我生命的杯却没有这样斟满杯缘。

可是现在失望也就同和风静浪一样的温驯；我能够躺下像个疲倦了的小孩，把我已经忍受过，而一定还要忍受的恼烦付之一哭，等到死神像睡一样

Till death like sleep might steal on me,
And I might feel in the warm air
My cheek grow cold, and hear the sea
Breathe o'er my dying brain its last monotony.

Ode to the West Wind

I

O Wild West Wind, thou breath of Autumn's being[1];
Thou from whose unseen presence the leaves dead
Are driven like ghosts from an enchanter fleeing,
Yellow, and black, and pale, and hectic red,
Pestilence-stricken multitudes! O thou
Who chariotest to their dark wintry bed
The winged seeds, where they lie cold and low,
Each like a corpse within its grave, until
Thine azure sister of the spring shall blow
Her clarion o'er the dreaming earth, and fill
(Driving sweet buds like flocks to feed in air)
With living hues and odours plain and hill;

会偷偷地来临，我会在温暖的空气里觉得颊儿生凉，听到大海向我这快死的脑海吹出他最后的单调呼声。

西　风　歌

啊，狂恣的西风，你是秋神的气息；你虽然无形，死叶却给你追逐四散，像群鬼那样逃避着巫人，黄色，黑色，惨澹色，痨病人发烧时脸上的红色，种种的枯叶，真是像患瘟的大众；呵，你将有翅的种子运到它们黑暗的冬床，它们就冷冷地平躺在那里，只只像个坟里的死尸，等到春天里你那青妹（指春天的东风，它一来到，天也变青澄了，所以叫做青妹）拿起她的喇叭吹向梦着的大地，满山满野，都生满了活色生香，（他吹开甜蕾去吸新鲜的空气，

---

1 Autumn's being：凡有生命的东西都可以叫作 being，所以这两字可作"秋神"解。

Wild Spirit, which art moving everywhere;
Destroyer and preserver: hear, O hear!

II

Thou on whose stream, 'mid the steep sky's commotion
Loose clouds like earth's decaying leaves are shed,
Shook[1] from the tangled boughs of heaven and ocean,
Angels of rain and lightning! there are spread
On the blue surface of thine airy surge,
Like the bright hair uplifted from the head
Of some fierce Maenad[2], even from the dim verge
Of the horizon to the zenith's height,
The locks of the approaching storm. Thou dirge
Of the dying year, to which this closing[3] night
Will be the dome of a vast sepulchre,
Vaulted with all thy congregated might
Of vapours, from whose solid atmosphere
Black rain, and fire, and hail will burst: O hear!

III

Thou who didst waken from his summer dreams

---

1 shook: shaken.

如赶就草的绵羊);狂恣的精灵,到处飘忽;你是破坏者又是保护者:听呀,啊,听呀!

你的奔流是在峻峭天空的骚乱之中,贯穿海天的缠结巨枝散下了,有如地下衰叶的漫云,这云儿也流落在你的周流里面,那是送雷雨的专差!此外四布在你的气浪的蓝色表面,像一二疯女头上怒飘着的鲜明散发,甚至从模糊的极边直到中天,那是前来的风浪的鬓丝。你是将逝之年的哀音,这个残宵将做一个大顶,上铺着你全军的氤氲水汽,从这结实的大气里会破裂出黑雨,电火和冰雹:呵,听呀!

你把鲜蓝的地中海从夏梦里唤醒,他本是躺在

---

2 古代的酒神祭日,加入行礼的妇女都是披发,手执火炬,所以被人叫作疯女——Maenad。
3 closing: closing in, 夜的黑暗是四面八方围拢来的。

The blue Mediterranean, where he lay,
Lull'd by the coil of his crystalline streams,
Beside a pumice isle in Baiae's bay[1]
And saw in sleep old palaces and towers
Quivering within the wave's intenser day,
All overgrown with azure moss and flowers
So sweet, sense faints picturing them! Thou
For whose path the Atlantic's level powers
Cleave themselves into chasms, while far below
The sea-blooms and the oozy woods which wear
The sapless foliage of the ocean, know
Thy voice, and suddenly grow gray with fear.
And tremble and despoil themselves[2]: O hear!

IV

If I were a dead leaf[3] thou mightest bear;
If I were a swift cloud to fly with thee;
A wave to pant beneath thy power, and share
The impulse of the strength, only less free
Than thou, O uncontrollable! If even
I were as in my boyhood, and could be

那里，被他晶明流水的回圈所催眠，在Baiae海湾里一个浮石岛的旁边，他在睡眠里看到故宫同古塔在水中的更明净的中天里颤摇，他们全长有天青的苔同芳花，那么甜蜜呀，描状时我的感官也会醉晕！大西洋水面的平均威力也为你而裂开深穴，当深渊下，海花同带着海里无汁枝叶的湿树听到你的声音，忽然怕得色变苍灰。战抖着，落叶纷纷：呵，听呀！

若使我是个你能吹动的残叶；若使我是片与你同飞的流云；若使我是在你的威力下喘息着，分有你大力的浩然之气的波浪，只赶不上你那样的自由，呵，不可拘束的大力呀！甚至于若使我还在稚年，

---

1 在Naples湾的西北。
2 雪莱说这是科学家都知道的一种现象，海里，河里，湖里底下的植物是同陆地上面的一样地受季候的影响，所以西风也影响到它们。
3 leaf之后省掉了一个relative pronoun。

The comrade of thy wanderings over heaven,[1]
As then, when to outstrip thy skiey speed
Scarce seen'd a vision — I would ne'er have striven[2]
As thus with thee in prayer in my sore need.
O! lift me as a wave, a leaf, a cloud!
I fall upon the thorns of life! I bleed!
A heavy weight of hours has chain'd and bow'd
One too like thee — tameless, and swift, and proud.

V

Make me thy lyre[3], even as the forest is:
What if my leaves are falling like its own?
The tumult of thy mighty harmonies
Will take from both a deep, antumnal tone,
Sweet though in sadness. Be thou, Spirit fierce,
My spirit! Be thou me[4], impetuous one!
Drive my dead thoughts over the universe,
Like wither'd leaves, to quicken a new birth!

---

1 风云在天上狂奔，小孩在地下乱跑，好像是一双游侣。

2 从第四十三行 If I were a dead leaf 起到第五十一行的 Scarce seemed a vision 止全是副句，正句是 I would ne'er have striven...。

3 make me thy lyre：拿我做你的乐器，发出人生同高超思想的新调，传布到全世界去。

能做你在天上漫游的伴侣,那时我以为跑得比你在天上的遨游还快是属可能,我也不会这样深感到需要,努力来向你祷告。呵!吹我起来,像一波浪花,一片白云,一叶枯叶罢!我坠在人生的荆棘上!我流血着!时光的重担锁住同压着一个太像你的人儿和你一样的难驯,迅速同自骄。

把我来当做你的琴罢,正像那树林一般:若使我生命的叶子也似树林一样地凋零那也无妨。你那伟大音乐的起伏会从他俩得到一个深沉的秋声,虽然凄迷,却又轻柔勇悍的精灵,你的精神来做我的精神!你我合一罢,直前不顾的精灵!将我这死般的思想吹散四方,像枯叶一样去做成一个新生!应

---

4 Be thou me:照文法说,此处应作 I,但是用起 me 来,却悦耳得多了,习惯上亦常有这种用法,如"It is I"通常说总是"It is me"。

And, by the incantation of this verse,
Scatter, as from an unextinguish'd hearth
Ashes and sparks, my words among mankind!
Be through my lips to unawaken'd earth.
The trumpet of a prophecy! O Wind,
If Winter comes, can Spring be far behind?

The Indian Serenade

I arise from dreams of thee
In first sweet sleep of night,
When the winds are breathing low
And the stars are shining bright:
I arise from dreams of thee,
And a spirit in my feet
Has led me — who knows how?
To thy chamber-window, sweet!

The wandering airs they¹ faint
On the dark, the silent stream —

我这诗的咒召罢,将我的话传遍人间,好似从不灭的火炉里吹出灰烬同火花!用我的嘴唇,你对这未醒的大地吹出一声预言的号角罢!呵,风呀,若使冬天到了,春天那能久迟?

印度的良夜之歌

我起来,当我刚梦着你,在夜里初入睡的甜蜜时候,那时风儿轻轻地吹着,星儿灿烂地发亮:我起来,当我刚梦着你,脚里的一个精灵带着我走——谁晓得是怎样带着?带到你卧室的窗下,甜蜜的人儿!

飘游的风儿晕倒在黑暗静寂的河流上——黄金

---

1 The wandering airs they:they 即指 the wandering airs,为同位词(appositive),下面第十四行的"it"也是如此,与"The nightingale's complaint"同位也。

The champak[1] odours fail
Like sweet thoughts in a dream;
The nightingale's complaint
It dies upon her heart,
As I must die on thine,
O beloved as thou art!

O lift me from the grass!
I die, I faint, I fail!
Let thy love in kisses rain
On my lips and eyelids pale.
My cheek is cold and white, alas!
My heart beats loud and fast;
O! press it ⟨to thine own again,
where⟩ it will break at last.

Love's Philosophy

The fountains mingle with the river
And the rivers with the ocean,
The winds of heaven mix for ever
With a sweet emotion;

花的香味,消失去像梦里的乐事;夜莺的哀啼,声音沉灭在她的心头,同样地我也一定是死在你的心头,呵,你是多么可爱!

呵,从草上把我拖起罢!我死去了,我晕倒了,我无力了!让你的爱情像霖雨般降下热吻在灰白的唇上眼皮,我的颊儿是冰冷无血,唉!我的心跳动得响而且快;呵!再拿你的心来紧压着我的心罢,它最终也是碎在那里。

爱 的 哲 学

泉水和河水相合,河水同海水不分,天上的和风永久是跟甜蜜的情调互应;世界里没有孤单的东

---

1 印度的一种树,常植在神庙旁边,开的花是金黄色的,香味极浓。

Nothing in the world is single,
All things by a law divine
In one another's being mingle —
Why not I with thine?

See the mountains kiss high heaven,
And the waves clasp one another;
No sister-flower would be forgiven
If it disdain'd its brother;
And the sunlight clasps the earth,
And the moonbeams kiss the sea —
What are all these kissings worth,
If thou kiss not me?

To a Skylark

Hail to thee, blithe spirit!
Bird thou never wert, —
That from heaven, or near it,
Pourest the full heart
In profuse strains of unpremeditated art.

西，神圣的律例定好了万物都是精神一致地相遇相混——为什么，你我偏不连理一气？

请看高山吻着青天，波浪互相拥抱；没有个连枝的花儿会得到原宥，若使它看轻了它的姊妹花；阳光拥着大地，月色吻着深渊——这许多接吻值得什么，若使你偏不肯吻我？

云　雀　歌

你这快乐的精灵呀！你绝不是一只鸟儿，从天上或者近天倾泻下你的满怀欣欢，巧技天生，浪唱出畅快的歌声。

Higher still and higher
From the earth thou springest
Like a cloud of fire;
The blue deep thou wingest,
And singing still dost soar, and soaring ever singest.

In the golden lightning
Of the sunken sun,
O'er which clouds are brightening,
Thou dost float and run,
Like an unbodied joy whose race is just begun.

The pale purple even
Melts around thy flight;
Like a star of heaven,
In the broad daylight
Thou art unseen, but yet I hear thy shrill delight —

Keen as are the arrows
Of that silver sphere,
Whose intense lamp narrows
In the white dawn clear,
Until we hardly see, we feel that it is there.

你从地上像一朵火云那样一再上升；你在苍穹里飞翔，唱着同时上飞，飞着不停地歌唱。

在落照的金黄闪光里，上面映着云儿，你浮游飞动着，像初生而尚未成体的快乐。

淡紫的暮色随着你的飞翔而消失；像光天化日里的一粒星儿，你是不可见的，可是我听到你那溜亮的欢唱——

你的歌声是像日轮的光箭那么锋利，这一盏极亮的明灯到了清彻皎白的中天反形缩小，等到我们几乎不能看见了，却只感到它高挂在那儿。

All the earth and air
With thy voice is loud,
As, when night is bare,
From one lonely cloud
The moon rains out her beams, and heaven is overflow'd.

What thou art we know not;
What is most like thee?
From rainbow clouds there flow not
Drops so bright to see,
As from thy presence showers a rain of melody.

Like a poet hidden
In the light of thought,
Singing hymns unbidden,
Till the world is wrought,
To sympathy with hopes and fears it heeded not.

Like a high-born maiden
In a palace tower,
Soothing her love-laden
Soul in secret hour
With music sweet as love, which everflows her bower.

地上同空中响彻了你的歌喉,好似清夜里从一朵孤单的云儿,月亮洒下他的万线银光,满天溢着清辉。

你是怎样,我们不知,什么是最像你呢?从虹霓落下的雨花没有你所洒的倾注歌声那么光明。

像隐在思想之光里面的诗人,任情唱出他的颂歌,等到俗世对于本不关心的希望同恐惧动起了同情。

像宫中高塔里的贵胄姑娘,深夜地用音乐慰她那不胜春思的心灵,那妙音是甜蜜得有似爱情,洋溢着她的小亭。

Like a glow-worm golden
In a dell of dew,
Scattering unbeholden[1]
Its aerial hue
Among the flowers and grass which screen it from the view.

Like a rose embower'd
In its own green leaves,
By warm winds deflower'd[2],
Till the scent it gives
Makes faint with too much sweet these heavy-winged thieves.

Sound of vernal showers
On the twinkling grass,
Rain-awaken'd flowers —
All that ever was
Joyous and clear and fresh — thy music doth surpass.

Teach us, sprite or bird,
What sweet thoughts are thine:

像夕露润滋的山谷里的金黄流萤,谁也没有看见地它散出它的浮光在花草的中间,它也借着花草才能隐身。

像一朵蔷薇,存在它自己的绿叶丛中,被和风偷去它的香气!等到它所发的芬香使翅儿载得沉重的狂风被香醉得晕眩。

滴在萤萤〔荧荧〕的青草同雨后苏醒的花儿上的春雨潺潺——一切欣欢,清彻,新鲜的妙乐,全比不上你的歌声。

教我罢,精灵也好,飞鸟也好,你到底蕴有什

---

1 unseen
2 robbed of its scent

I have never heard
Praise of love or wine
That panted forth a flood of rapture so divine.

Chorus hymeneal,
Or triumphal chant
Match'd with thine would be all
But an empty vaunt —
A thing wherein we feel there is some hidden want.

What objects are the fountains
Of thy happy strain?
What fields, or waves, or mountains?
What shapes of sky or plain?
What love of thine own kind? What ignorance of pain?

With thy clear keen joyance
Languor cannot be;
Shadow of annoyance
Never came near thee:
Thou lovest, but ne'er knew love's sad satiety.

么甜蜜的想头：我从没有听过对于爱情同醇酒的赞美，吐出过这么神圣可喜的歌泉。

婚乐同凯旋的歌唱和你一比，全变做无内容的空响，——我们觉得那里面有了说不出的不足。

什么是你这快乐歌唱的源泉？泉的四面有什么田野，波浪同高山？泉上面的青天，泉地下的平原是何形态？是爱你同类里的那个？是那样子的未尝苦恼？

你有了这么清利的欣欢，绝不会感到疲倦；烦恼的影子绝不至走近你的身旁：你爱着，却不晓得爱的可悲的厌烦。

Waking or asleep,

Thou of death must deem

Things more true and deep

Than we mortals dream,

Or how could thy notes flow in such a crystal stream?

We look before and after,

And pine for what is not:

Our sincerest laughter

With some pain is fraught;

Our sweetest songs are those that tell of saddest thought.

Yet, if we could scorn

Hate and pride and fear,

If we were things born

Not to shed a tear,

I know not how thy joy we ever should come near.

Better than all measures[1]

Of delightful sound,

---

1 music measures

这首诗开头六段迷醉地赞美云雀的歌声,其次六段是用别种的美来同他的歌声相比,其次六段将云雀快乐无穷的歌声和人们杂有悲愁,未臻尽醒着或者睡着，你必是把死看做是真实而有深意的东西，不是我们世上的人们所尝梦到——否则你的音调怎能如斯流利晶清？

我们前瞻后顾，常感不足而心酸：我们最真挚的大笑声杂有苦辛；我们最甜蜜的歌曲是诉出最哀伤的忧愁。

可是若使我们能够看轻怨恨骄傲同恐惧，若使我们是生下不要流一滴清泪的人们，我不晓得我们怎样能赶得到你的欣欢。

对于诗人，你的绝技是胜过一切欢乐的调子，

美尽善的音乐相比，最后三段，他说出自己对于云雀歌喉的希冀，有人以为这是 Shelley 最妙的抒情诗。

Better than all treasures
That in books are found,
Thy skill to poet were, thou scorner of the ground!

Teach me half the gladness
That thy brain must know;
Such harmonious madness
From my lips would flow,
The world should listen then, as I am listening now.

The World's Wanderers

Tell me, thou Star, whose wings of light
Speed thee in thy fiery flight,
In what cavern of the night
Will thy pinions close now?

Tell me, Moon, thou pale and gray
Pilgrim of Heaven's homeless way,
In what depth of night or day
Seekest thou repose now?

一切书中的妙理,你这地的藐视者!

教我们以你心中所知的一半乐绪罢;那么我的唇也会唱出和谐的狂歌,世人将听着我——有如我现在的静聆。

世界的漂泊者

告诉我,你这星儿,你的光带着你这样地猛烈飞奔,你现在要在夜里的那个窟里去安下你的双翼?

告诉我,月亮,你这天上渺茫路里的惨白漂泊者,在夜或日的那个深渊里你现在去求安息?

Weary Wind, who wanderest
Like the world's rejected guest,
Hast thou still some secret nest
On the tree or billow?

A Lament

I

O world! O life! O time!
On whose last steps[1] I climb,
Trembling at that where I had stood before;
When will return the glory of your prime?
No more — Oh, never more!

II

Out of the day and night
A joy has taken flight;
Fresh spring, and summer, and winter hoar,
Move my faint heart with grief, but with delight
No more — Oh, never more!

疲倦的风,你流荡着世界里的逐客,你在树上或者在浪上,还有一些秘密的栖所吗?

哀 歌

呵世界!呵人生!呵光阴!我踏着我的残年上登,看到我从前站足的地方,我浑身发颤;青春的光荣那时回来?再也不——呵,绝不再来!

朝朝夜夜欣欢渐渐地远走高飞;阳春,夏天同皓冬使我微弱的心儿感到悲哀,但快乐之感是再也不——呵,绝不再来!

---

1 雪莱想到自己的将死,所以说 last steps,他果然在翌年死去,也可说是一句诗谶。

John Keats

(1795—1821)

Ode to a Nightingale

My heart aches, and a drowsy numbness pains
My sense, as though of hemlock I had drunk,
Or emptied some dull opiate to the drains[1]
One minute past, and Lethe-wards[2] had sunk:
'Tis not through envy of thy happy lot,
But being too happy in thine happiness[3] —
That[4] thou, light-winged Dryad[5] of the trees.
In some melodious plot
Of beechen green, and shadows numberless,
Singest of summer in full-throated ease.

O, for a draught of vintage! That hath been
Cool'd a long age in the deep-delved earth,

---

1 to the dregs

夜 莺 歌

　　我的心痛着,一种昏睡的麻痹使我难受,好似前一分钟我饮了鸩酒或者干了满杯的雅片,我渐渐地走近忘却一切的境地:这不是因为妒忌你的幸运,却是看到你的幸福自己也太感到欣欢,——当我想到你是森林里一位轻翅的女神,在绿荫如织树影无穷的妙处,畅快地放开歌喉,唱出盛夏的光荣。

　　啊,来一杯葡萄酒呀!那是久冻在深窟里,喝起

---

　　2 在希腊神话中,地狱里的忘川叫做Lethe,我们在出世以前,喝了这水,就把前生事迹全忘了。

　　3 too happy...：诗人的心痛是由于他对于夜莺生出灵敏精妙的同情;他由同情而生的快乐太强烈了,反变为痛苦,有如太甜的东西尝到舌上反觉的难过一样。

　　4 in the thought that

　　5 森林的女神

Tasting of Flora¹ and the country green,
Dance, and Provençal² song, and sunburnt mirth!
O, for a beaker full of the warm South,
Full of the true, the blushful Hippocrene³,
With beaded bubbles winking at the brim,
And purple-stained mouth⁴;
That I might drink, and leave the world unseen,
And with thee fade away into the forest dim.

Fade far away, dissolve, and quite forget
What thou among the leaves hast never known,
The weariness, the fever, and the fret
Here, where men sit and hear each other groan;
Where palsy shakes a few, sad, last grey hairs,
Where youth grows pale, and spectre-thin, and dies;
Where but to think is to be full of sorrow
And leaden-eyed despairs;
Where Beauty cannot keep her lustrous eyes,

---

 1 春天同司花的女神
 2 Provence：居法国南部，出产佳酿，住民常在户外作种种的游戏，古时常有沿途唱歌的诗人（troubadour）。
 3 文艺女神的泉
 4 mouth 指杯嘴。

来使人记到阳春，芳花，同绿野，跳舞，Provence 的小调同太阳底下的乐事！来一杯满载着暖和南方的风味的美酒呀，这酒好像 Hippocrene 诗泉的泉水在日光里娇羞地发红，一粒粒的酒泡在杯缘霎眼，杯口也染得鲜紫；那么我可以一口呷下偷偷地离了尘世，与你同消失在暗澹的丛林。

悠悠地消失了，化解了，全忘却了绿叶里从不晓得的那些苦恼，那是这里的厌倦，狂热同麻烦，在这里人们坐着互听彼此的呻吟；在这里瘫痪的老人摇着凄凉的，最后几根的白发，年青的人们脸容日见惨淡，鬼一样的瘦削，而死去；在这里一想起来就是满腹牢愁，同两眼无光的失望；在这里美貌不能永留着她那明媚的双眸，再过一两天新的爱人

Or new Love pine at them beyond tomorrow.

Away! away! for I will fly to thee,
Not charioted by Bacchus[1] and his pards,
But on the viewless[2] wings of Poesy,
Though the dull brain perplexes and retards:
Already with thee! Tender is the night,
And haply the Queen-Moon is on her throne
Cluster'd around by all her starry Fays;
But here there is no light,
Save what from heaven is with the breezes blown
Through verdurous glooms and winding mossy ways.

I cannot see what flowers are at my feet,
Nor what soft incense hangs upon the boughs,
But in embalmed darkness[3], guess each sweet
Wherewith the seasonable month endows
The grass, the thicket, and the fruit-tree wild;
White hawthorn, and the pastoral eglantine;
Fast fading violets cover'd up in leaves;

---

1 希腊神话中的酒神。
2 viewless: invisible.
3 embalmed darkness 言黑暗浸在那季的花的芳香之中也。

会哀悼着它们的消失。

去罢！去罢！我要飞到你的身旁，不须酒神同他的豹子来运送，却坐在看不见的诗情翅膀，虽然傻人们是莫名其妙而迟步不前：已经同你一块了！夜是柔软的，也许月后高坐宝座，四围拥有他那许多的星神；但是这里却是黑沉沉的，除了一些微光给和风从天上吹下，经过了这青翠的浓荫同羊肠的苔径。

我看不见我足下有什么花草，也不知道枝上挂的是什么馨香，却只好在这芬芳的黑暗里，按着当前的时令去猜猜草地上，矮树上，野果树上长的是何花；是乳白色的山楂花，有刺的野蔷薇，隐在密叶里快将凋谢的紫罗兰；还有初夏最先开的，将来

And mid-May's eldest child,
The coming musk-rose, full of dewy wine,
The murmurous haunt of flies on summer eves.

Darkling[1] I listen; and for many a time
I have been half in love with easeful Death,
Call'd him soft names in many a mused rhyme[2],
To take into the air my quiet breath;
Now more than ever seems it rich to die,
To cease upon the midnight with no pain,
While thou art pouring forth thy soul abroad
In such an ecstasy!
Still wouldst thou sing, and I have ears in vain —
To thy high requiem become a sod.

Thou wast not born for death, immortal bird!
No hungry generations tread thee down;
The voice I hear this passing night was heard
In ancient days by emperor and clown[3]:
Perhaps the self-same song that found a path

---

1 Darkling: in the darkness.
2 mused rhyme: long thought-on verse.
3 clown: rustic.

临的麝香玫瑰,溢着露酒,夏天傍晚时那是蚁〔蝇〕子嗡嗡的聚处。

在黑暗里我细听;有许多回我几乎钟情于安逸的死亡,用了许多再三咏味的诗句,叫出他(指死神)许多亲爱的小名,请他将我这恬静的气息收到太空;我现在比从前更深深地觉得死去是很快乐的,半夜里一些不疼地停了生机,当你在外面这样狂欢地倾吐出你的心灵!你还唱着,当我听不见了——化成坏土,你正唱着这高超的安灵歌调。

你生下是不会死的,不死的鸟儿!没有饥饱的人们能残害你们;这个残宵里我所听到的声音古时的帝王农夫也曾听过:或者就是穿过Ruth忧愁的心灵的那

Through the sad heart of Ruth[1], when, sick for home,
She stood in tears amid the alien corn;
The same that oft-times hath
Charm'd magic casements, opening on the foam
Of perilous seas, in faery lands forlorn.

Forlorn! The very word is like a bell
To toll me back from thee to my sole self!
Adieu! The fancy cannot cheat so well
As she is fam'd to do, deceiving elf.
Adieu! Adieu! thy plaintive anthem fades
Past the near meadows, over the still stream,
Up the hill-side; and now 'tis buried deep
In the next valley-glades:
Was it a vision, or a waking dream?
Fled is that music: — Do I wake or sleep?

Ode on a Grecian Urn

Thou still unravish'd[2] bride of quietness,

---

1 见《圣经》中 Ruth II.3, 23。

Keats 写这诗时，他的兄弟肺病死去不多久，他大概已看出他自己肺病的征候，死的影子已横在他面前，所以这首诗格外沉痛。

个调儿,当她怀着家乡,泪人儿似地站在异国的谷里;古时魔术家在波涛上起盖的楼阁,内中被囚的姑娘所听到的也许也是这个调儿,在那被人弃的仙乡。

被弃!这个字好像个叫我从你那里回到寂寞的我的钟声!再会!幻想,你这骗人的小鬼,并不像人们所传的会编得那么美妙。再会!再会!悲歌消失了,过了近处的草场,过了静寂的小河,上了山边现在是深深在邻谷的旷地之中:这是幻想或者是张开着眼睛甜梦?歌声去了——我现在醒耶梦耶?

希腊古瓶歌

你是"宁静"的贞洁新娘,你是"寂默"同

---

2 因为保存它的美丽同洁白,所以说是贞洁的。

Thou foster-child of silence and slow time,
Sylvan historian, who canst thus express
A flowery tale more sweetly than our rhyme:
What leaf-fring'd legend haunts about thy shape
Of deities or mortals, or of both,
  In Tempe or the dales of Arcady[1]?
  What men or gods are these? What maidens loth?
  What mad pursuit? What struggle to escape?
  What pipes and timbrels? What wild ecstasy?

Heard melodies are sweet, but those unheard
Are sweeter; therefore, ye soft pipes, play on;
Not to the sensual[2] ear, but, more endear'd,
Pipe to the spirit ditties of no tone:
Fair youth, beneath the trees, thou canst not leave
Thy song, nor ever can those trees be bare;
Bold Lover, never, never canst thou kiss,
Though winning near[3] the goal — yet do not grieve;
She cannot fade, though thou hast not thy bliss,
For ever wilt thou love, and she be fair!

---

1 都是希腊的名胜之区。
2 sensual: physical or bodily.
3 winning near: approaching.

"日长似岁的时光"的养子,你是林谷的历史家,能将一假花簇锦绣的故事比我们的诗歌说得如此更见甜蜜:你的外皮永留有关于 Tempe 或者 Arcady 山谷里的神或人或者两者的绿叶围住的一个什么传说?这些画在上面的是何人或何神?这个害羞躲避的是那个姑娘?这是什么疯狂的追逐?这是什么逃避的努力?这是什么箫鼓?这是什么狂欢?

听得到的曲调是美妙的,但是这些听不到的曲调却更见悦耳;所以,你们这曼声的笛子,吹下去罢;不是对着肉体的耳朵,却是,更可爱的,吹出无音的心调。树下久立的美少年,你不能停奏,这些树也不能见凋;勇敢的爱人,你绝不能吻到你的情人,虽然是已近身边——然而也用不着悲伤;她永不能消失,虽然你得不到你的幸福,但是你会永爱不忘,她也是美貌长留!

Ah, happy, happy boughs! That cannot shed
Your leaves, nor ever bid the Spring adieu;
And, happy melodist, unwearied,
For ever piping songs for ever new;
More happy love! more happy, happy love!
For ever warm and still to be enjoy'd,
For ever panting, and for ever young;
All breathing human passion far above, [1]
That leaves a heart high-sorrowful and cloy'd,
A burning forehead, and a parching tongue.

Who are these coming to the sacrifice?
To what green altar, O mysterious priest,
Lead'st thou that heifer lowing at the skies,
And all her silken flanks with garlands drest?
What little town by river or sea shore,
Or mountain-built with peaceful citadel,
Is emptied of this folk, this pious morn?
And, little town, thy streets for evermore
Will silent be; and not a soul to tell
Why thou art desolate, can e'er return.

呀，快乐，快乐的绿枝！你们不会落叶，也从不和春天告别；还有快乐的音乐家，不倦地永久吹出永久是新鲜的调子；更快乐的爱情！更快乐的爱情！永久是热烈的，始终是可乐的，永久恋慕着，永久是青春远胜过人间世一切的热情，那只留下个悲伤厌倦的心境，发烧的额头同一个干燥的苦舌。

这班到神庙去献上牺牢的是谁？到那个绿色的祭坛去，呀，神秘的神甫，你带着这向天叫叫的牝牛同他那饰着花环的柔软如丝的胁腹？是河旁海滨或盖着和平的堡垒的高山上的那个小镇里的居民今早上倾城出来？这小镇呀，你的街道将永归于寂寞；再也没有人回来说你是为甚这么荒凉。

---

1 All breathing human passion far above: far above all breathing human passion.

O Attic shape! Fair attitude! With brede
Of marble men and maidens overwrought,
With forest branches and the trodden weed;
Thou, silent form, dost tease us out of thought
As doth eternity: cold pastoral!
When old age shall this generation waste,
Thou shalt remain, in midst of other woe
Than ours, a friend to man, to whom thou say'st,
"Beauty is truth, truth beauty,"[1] —That is all
Ye know on earth, and all ye need to know.

La Belle Dame sans Merci

"O what can ail thee, knight-at-arms,
Alone and palely loitering[2]?
The sedge has wither'd from the lake,
And no birds sing.

---

1 从第十一行至三十行,表现出人生的短促同艺术品的美的永留人间,造这个瓷器的人创造出这些人物,他们就永久生动地留在世间,他们的真实几乎超我们这班具有骨肉的活人。所以 Keats 慨然说道美即是真,真即是美,这句话也就做了后来唯美派文学的中心思想同主要信条。

呀，雅典的作风！美丽的姿态！满载着一束的雕刻的男女，树枝同足下践踏的青草；你，静默的模型同永劫一样使我们失掉思想的能力：冷冷的田舍风光！当老年销磨了这代的人们，你将在与我们不同的别种悲哀中仍然做人们的一个朋友，你对他们说道"美即是真，真即是美，"——这是你在地上所知道的一切，你也只需知道了这些。

没有慈心的美丽姑娘

"呀，什么使你难过，可怜的骑士，独自憔悴地徜徉？现在芦苇枯死在湖里，鸟儿也早已不歌唱。

按：这个古瓶上面画了两个不同的景致，一边是画男女的嬉戏（诗中第八行至第十行），一边是画到神庙的人众（诗中第三十一行至三十七行）。

2 palely loitering: loitering with pale looks.

"O what can ail thee, knight-at-arms,
So haggard and so woe-begone?
The squirrel's granary is full,
And the harvest's done.

"I see a lily on thy brow
With anguish moist¹ and fever dew,
And on thy cheeks a fading rose
Fast withereth too?

"I met a lady in the meads,
Full beautiful — a fairy's child,
Her hair was long, her foot was light,
And her eyes were wild.

"I made a garland for her head,
And bracelets too, and fragrant zone;
She look'd at me as² she did love,
And made sweet moan.

---

1 moist: 形容 brow。
2 as: as if.

"呀,什么使你难过,可怜的骑士,瘦削悲伤得如斯?松鼠的小谷仓是已经满了,秋收也已割完。

"我看你的眉梢好似一朵湿着悲哀热露的白莲,你的颊儿真是一朵也快就枯萎的将谢蔷薇。

"我在牧场上遇到一位姑娘,满美丽的,可说是仙人的女儿;她的发悠长,她的步轻盈,她的双眼却是浪狂。

"我替她的头编顶花冠,还有花镯同芬香的腰带;她睇着我,好似钟情,唤出甜蜜的呻吟。

"I set her on my pacing steed
And nothing else saw all day long,
For sidelong would she bend, and sing
A fairy's song.

"She found me roots of relish sweet,
And honey wild and manna dew,
And sure in language strange she said,
'I love thee true.'

"She took me to her elfin grot,
And there she wept, and sigh'd full sore,
And there I shut her wild, wild eyes
With kisses four.

"And there she lulled me asleep,
And there I dream'd — Ah! Woe betide!
The latest dream I ever dreamt
On the cold hill side.

"I saw pale kings and princes too,
Pale warriors, death-pale were they all;
They cried — 'La Belle Dame sans Merci

"我放她在我那溜蹄的马上,整天里没有看到别的东西,因为她是倒身斜倚着,唱出神仙的歌儿。

"她为我找出美味的草根,还有野蜜和甘露,的确用奇怪的言词,她说道,'我爱你一往情深'。

"她带我到她仙洞,在那里她流泪而叹息深深,在那里我再四吻闭着她那浪狂的双眼。

"在那里她抚我入眠,在那里我就做梦,——唉!大祸临头!那是我一生里最后的一梦,在那凄冷的山旁。

"我看见颜色惨白的帝皇同皇子,脸色惨白的战士,他们全是白得像死人;他们叫道——'没有慈

Thee hath in thrall!'

"I saw their starved lips in the gloam¹
With horrid warning gaped wide.
And I awoke and found me here
On the cold hill's side.

"And this is why I sojourn here
Alone and palely loitering,
Though the sedge is wither'd from the Lake
And no birds sing."

On the Grasshopper and Cricket

The poetry of earth is never dead:
When all the birds are faint with the hot sun,
And hide in cooling trees, a voice will run
From hedge to hedge about the new-mown mead.
That is the grasshopper's — he takes the lead
In summer luxury, — he has never done
With his delights, for when tired out with fun,

心的美姑娘迷着你了!'

"我在阴暗中看到他们的饿吻,张大说出可怕的警言,我醒来看到独自在这凄冷的山旁。

"这是我所以迟留这里,独自憔悴地徜徉,虽然芦苇枯死在湖里,鸟儿也早已不歌唱。"

蚱蜢同蟋蟀

地上的歌声是绝不会灭亡:当群鸟都被烈日晒得晕昏,躲在荫凉的树下,在新割的草场旁,将有巡着篱笆的低吟。那是蚱蜢的吟声——他是夏天乐事的先锋——他的欣欢同他是永不相离,当他玩得

---

1 in the gloam: gloaming.

He rests at ease beneath some pleasant weed.

The poetry of earth is ceasing never:
On a lone winter evening, when the frost
Has wrought a silence, from the stove there shrills
The cricket's song, in warmth increasing ever,
And seems to one in drowsiness half-lost,
The grasshopper's among some grassy hills.

Thomas Hood

(1798—1845)

The Bridge of Sighs[1]

One more unfortunate[2]
Weary of breath,
Rashly importunate
Gone to her death!

Take her up tenderly,
Lift her with care;
Fashion'd so slenderly,

累了,他就舒服地躺在快乐的草下。

地上的歌声是绝不会停的:在孤寂的冬晚,当严霜做成了静默,从炉旁发出蟋蟀的尖利歌声,在暖气中愈鸣愈响,对着半入睡乡的人们,这真像绿草如茵的山中的蚱蜢声音。

悲 叹 之 桥

又是一个不幸的人儿,厌倦于生活了,迫切得不顾一切,自己找到了死途!

好好地把她拖上,小心地将她举起;她是长得

---

1 即伦敦的 Waterloo Bridge,在往时,没水自杀的事情常在那儿发生,遂被称为"The Bridge of Sighs"。
2 unfortunate:指卖笑为生的不幸女子。

Young, and so fair!

Look at her garments
Clinging like cerements;
Whilst the wave constantly
Drips from her clothing;
Take her up instantly,
Loving, not loathing. —

Touch her not scornfully;
Think of her mournfully,
Gently and humanly;
Not of the stains of her,
All that remains of her,
Now is pure womanly.

Make no deep scrutiny
Into her mutiny[1]
Rash and undutiful:
Past all dishonour
Death has left on her
Only the beautiful.

这么苗条,这样年青,这般美丽!

看她的衣服罢,紧黏住好似寿衣;河水不断地从她的衣上滴下;立刻把她拖上罢,爱怜着,别要嫌憎。——

不要藐视地抚她;悲哀地,温和地,仁慈地想着她罢;别想到她的污点,现在她所剩下的只是纯洁的女性。

不要深深地去审察她那鲁莽的,不尽本分的胡为:一切可耻的事全不算了,死神留下来的却只有美貌。

---

1 mutiny:违叛法律,因为法律禁止自杀。

Still, for all slips of hers,
One of Eve's family —
Wipe those poor lips of hers
Oozing so clammily.

Loop up her tresses
Escaped from the comb,
Her fair auburn tresses;
Whilst wonderment guesses
Where was her home?

Who was her father?
Who was her mother?
Had she a sister?
Had she a brother?
Or was there a dearer one
Still, and a nearer one
Yet, than all other?

Alas! for the rarity
Of Christian charity
Under the sun!
Oh! it was pitiful!
Near a whole city full,

不管她有多少失足的错事,她仍然是夏娃的一个家人——揩净她这可怜的嘴唇罢,那正在如胶地泄出污水。

扎起她的鬈发罢,那些从头梳下滑出,她那美丽金黄的鬈发;人们纳罕地猜那里是她的家庭?

谁是她的父亲?谁是她的母亲?她有个姊妹吗?她有个兄弟吗?或者还有个更亲爱的又是比一切更接近的人儿吗?

吓呀!在太阳底下,基督教的慈悲是这么稀少呀!呵,这真是可怜!几乎满城的人,她却是

Home she had none!

Sisterly, brotherly,
Fatherly, motherly,
Feelings had changed;
Love, by harsh evidence,
Thrown from its eminence;
Even God's providence
Seeming estranged.

Where the lamps quiver
So far in the river,
With many a light
From window and casement,
From garret to basement,
She stood, with amazement,
Houseless by night.

The bleak wind of March
Made her tremble and shiver;
But not the dark arch,
Or the black flowing river:

无家可归!

姊妹兄弟之爱,父母之爱都已改变了;分明地爱神是从高座上被人们掷下;甚至于上帝好像也不关心。

河里远远地灯光震动,窗里橱中,从顶楼直到地下都有许多的光芒,她却惊奇地站着,深夜里无屋可栖。

三月里凄风使她浑身抖战;但是黑暗的穹窿同墨黑的流水,她却不怕!

Mad from life's history,
Glad to death's mystery,
Swift to be hurl'd —
Anywhere, anywhere,
Out of the world!

In she plunged boldly,
No matter how coldly
The rough river ran, —
Over the brink of it,
Picture it — think of it,
Dissolute man!
Lave in it, drink of it.
Then, if you can!

Take her up tenderly.
Lift he with care;
Fashion'd so slenderly,
Young, and so fair!

Ere her limbs frigidly
Stiffen too rigidly,
Decently, kindly,
Smoothe and compose them:

一生困苦，弄得发狂，高兴去探一探死的神秘；迅速地抛身下河——任去何处都好，只要走出了这个世界！

她勇敢地跳进水中——粗暴的河流多么冰冷，都是无妨——你们走到河边，描想出那时情境——细想一回，放纵的人们！你还能在里面沐浴，再喝那河水吗！

好好地把她拖上，小心地将她举起；她是长得这么苗条，这样年青，这般美丽！

在她的四肢僵化得太硬之前，适当地，好心地将它们放平，将它们舒展罢：她的眼睛，把它们闭

And her eyes, close them,
Staring so blindly!

Dreadfully staring
Thro' muddy impurity,
As when with the daring
Last look of despairing,
Fix'd ⟨on⟩ futurity.

Perishing gloomily,
Spurr'd by contumely,
Cold inhumanity,
Burning insanity,
Into her rest¹.—
Cross her hands humbly,
As if praying dumbly,
Over her breast!

Owning her weakness,
Her evil behaviour,
And leaving, with meekness,
Her sins to her Saviour!

住,别让它们这样盲目地凝视!

在泥泞的污秽里这么可怕地凝视,好像含有失望的最后勇敢眼神,看着将来。

阴惨地死了,被凌辱,冷酷的残忍和热烈的疯狂所催迫,去找到她的长眠——把她双手谦虚地叉在胸前罢,好像她是无声地祷告!

承认,她的弱点,她的恶行,谦卑地让她的"救世主"来理她的罪恶罢!

---

1 into her rest 是接着 spurred 来的。

The Victorian Age

Elizabeth Barrett Browning
(1806—1861)

The Mask

I have a smiling face, she said,
I have a jest for all I meet,
I have a garland for my head
And all its flowers are sweet, —
And so you call me gay, she said.

Grief taught to me this smile, she said,
And Wrong did teach this jesting bold;
These flowers were pluck'd from garden-bed
While a death-chime was toll'd.
And what now will you say? — she said.

Behind no prison-grate, she said,
Which slurs the sunshine half a mile,
Live captives so uncomforted

假　面　具

　　我有一付笑容，她说，我碰着人们，都有一句戏言，我头上戴有花冠，冠上的花儿全有馨芬，——因此你们说我是快乐，她说。

　　悲哀教我装出这付笑容，她说，委屈的确教我这些大胆的戏言；丧钟响时，我从花床上采到这丛芳花。你们现在要怎样说呢？——她说。

　　监狱里的铁窗，她说，半里内阳光不明，窗里的囚犯没有一个像笑脸下的灵魂那么不宁，让我们求上

As souls behind a smile,
God's pity let us pray, she said.

I know my face is bright, she said, —
Such brightness dying suns diffuse;
I bear upon my forehead shed
The sign of what I lose, —
The ending of my day, she said.

If I dared leave this smile, she said,
And take a moan upon my mouth,
And tie a cypress round my head,
And let my tears run smooth, —
It were the happier way, she said.

And since that must not be, she said,
I fain your bitter world would leave.[1]
How calmly, calmly smile the Dead,
Who do not, therefore, grieve!
The yea of Heaven is yea, she said.

---

1 I fain your bitter world would leave: I fain would leave your bitter world.

帝的哀矜罢,她说。

我知道我的脸儿是明朗,她说,——那是落照散出的光辉;我额上挂着我的损失的标记,——我生命的告终,她说。

若使我敢放下这付笑容,她说,嘴上发出微喟,用一枝扁柏来围着头顶,让我的泪珠轻滑地畅流,——那是更幸福得多,她说。

这既是万万不可,她说,我真愿离开你们这酸苦的世界。死人们是多么安逸地,安逸地微笑,所以他们是没有悲伤!天堂的欣欢才是真正的欣欢,她说。

But in your bitter world, she said,
Face-joy's a costly mask to wear.
'Tis bought with pangs long nourished,
And rounded to despair.
Grief's earnest makes life's play, she said.

Ye weep for those who weep? She said —
Ah fools! I bid you pass them by.
Go, weep for those whose hearts have bled
What time their eyes were dry.
Whom sadder can I say? She said.

Grief

I tell you, hopeless grief is passionless;
That only men incredulous of despair,
Half-taught in anguish, through the midnight air,
Beat upward to God's throne in loud access
Of shrieking and reproach. Full desertness
In souls as countries lieth silent-bare

但是在你这酸苦的世界,她说,皮笑是代价不轻的假面。那是用久蕴心头的剧痛和最终难逃的失望买来。悲哀的真实做成了人生的活剧,她说。

你们为着流泪的人儿而流泪吗?她说——唉,蠢货!我叫你们别理他们。去为着那班眼睛已干,流着心血的人们而流泪罢。我能指出谁是更有哀愁?她说。

悲　　哀

我告诉你,没有希望的悲哀是冰冷的;只有那班不信世间有绝望,不大懂得悲痛的人们才会在午夜里大声地呼号责骂,声音直打到上帝的座前。灵魂的十分荒凉同旷野一样静寂地空空地躺着,无限

Under the blanching, vertical eye-glare
Of the absolute Heavens. Deep-hearted man express
Grief for thy Dead in silence like to death —
Most like a monumental statue set
In everlasting watch and moveless woe
Till itself crumble to the dust beneath.
Touch it; the marble eyelids are not wet:
If it could weep, it could arise and go.

If thou must love me, let it be for nought
Except for love's sake only. Do not say,
"I love her for her smile — her look — her way
Of speaking gently, — for a trick of thought
That falls in well with mine, and certes[1] brought
A sense of pleasant ease on such a day" —
For these things in themselves, Beloved, may
Be changed, or change for thee — and love, so wrought,
May be unwrought so. Neither love me for

---

1 certes: assuredly.

的青天在顶上睁着眼睛,把一切全化成白色。深心的人们用死一般的静默来表示对于你自己的心死的沉痛罢——那种沉痛真好像一面庞大的雕像,放在那里永久注视着,痴痴地悲伤,等到它自己也碎如微尘。摸着它;大理石的眼皮是不湿的:若使它能流泪,它早已站起走开。

☆ ☆ ☆

若使你一定要爱我,那么就只为爱的缘故而爱我罢,千万不要为着别的。不要说"我爱她是爱她的微笑……她的丰神……她的低声软语……她那怪想头刚和我的相称,某天里的确使我感到欣慰"——因为这些东西,亲爱的,本身也许会变,或者在你的眼里是变了,——因此而成的爱情也就因此而散。

Thine own dear pity's wiping my cheeks dry:
A creature might forget to weep, who bore
Thy comfort long, and lose thy love thereby!
But love me for love's sake, that evermore
Thou mayst love on, through love's eternity.

Edward Fitzgerald

(1809—1849)[1]

The Three Arrows

Of all the shafts to Cupid's bow,
The first is tipp'd with fire:
All bare their bosoms to the blow
And call the wound Desire.

Love's second is a poison'd dart,
And Jealousy is named:
Which carries poison to the heart
Desire had first inflamed.

  这是 Mrs. Browning 的 *Sonnets From Portuguese* 里十四首。全集共有四十四首的十四行诗,都是歌咏她和 Browning 爱情的经过,柔情似水,很可以和莎翁的十四行诗集媲美。

也不要因为你的怀着怜惜心肠,拭干我的双颊而爱我:一个久得你的殷勤的人儿也许会忘却流泪,因此失丢了你的爱情!却只是为着爱情而爱我,那么你可以常常爱着,永爱无休。

三　条　箭

爱神弓上的各种箭,第一条是火染着尖端:人们全露出胸膛来挨射,把那创伤就叫做"欲望"。

爱神的第二条箭是含了毒药,那是名做"嫉妒":它带着恶毒直到那先被"欲望"所燃烧着的心儿。

---

1 其卒年应为1883年。——编者注

The last of Cupid's arrows all
With heavy lead is set:
That vainly weeping lovers call
Repentance, or Regret.

Come, fill the Cup, and in the Fire of Spring
Your Winter-garment of Repentance fling:
The Bird of Time has but a little way
To flutter — and the Bird is on the Wing.

Whether at Naishápúr[1] or Babylon,
Whether the Cup with sweet or bitter run,
The Wine of Life keeps oozing drop by drop,
The Leaves of Life keep falling one by one.

Each Morn a thousand Roses brings, you say:
Yes, but where leaves the Rose of Yesterday?

---

1 波斯地名

爱神最后的一条箭是镶着重铅：徒然流泪的爱人们叫它做"追悔"或者"惋惜"。

☆ ☆ ☆

来，斟满杯儿，将你这"忏悔"的"冬衣"投在"春天"的烈火里去罢："时间的鸟"只能够翱翔些时——这鸟儿现已在飞。

无论是在 Naishápúr 或是 Babylon，无论杯里盛的是苦汁还是甘露，"生命的酒"老是涓涓不断地慢流，"生命的叶"也是一一凋零。

每天都新开有千朵蔷薇，你说：不错，但是那

And this first Summer month that brings the Rose
Shall take Jamshyd and Kaikobád[1] away.

Alfred Tennyson, Lord Tennyson
(1809—1892)

The Miller's Daughter

It is the miller's daughter,
And she is grown so dear, so dear,
That I would be the jewel
That trembles at her ear:
For hid in ringlets day and night,
I'd touch her neck so warm and white.

And I would be the girdle
About her dainty dainty waist,
And her heart would beat against me
In sorrow and in rest:
And I should know if it beat right,
I'd clasp it round so close and tight.

里能找到昨日的蔷薇?带来这些蔷薇的初夏也带着Jamshyd同Kaikobád去长眠。

磨坊主人的女儿

磨坊主人的女儿,她是长得这么可爱,这么可爱,我愿做一颗明珠,颤跳在她的耳旁:因为朝朝夜夜藏在她的鬈发里面,我会触着她的那么温暖,那么洁白的颈项。

我愿做圈着她的细腰的围带,那么在悲哀时,在安息时,她的心都会向我频击;我也会晓得它跳得有错没有,我要这么逼近地紧紧地绕抱。

---

1 都是波斯王的名字。Fitzgerald译波斯诗人Omar Khayyam的四行诗(*Rubaiyat*)一百余首,上面是里面的三首,因为意思可以连贯起来,所以就把它们当作一首。

And I would be the necklace,
And all day long to fall and rise
Upon her balmy bosom,
With her laughter or her sighs,
And I would lie so light, so light,
I scarce should be unclasp'd at night.

Edward Gray

Sweet Emma Moreland of yonder town
Met me walking on yonder way,
"And have you lost your heart?" she said;
"And are you married yet, Edward Gray?"

Sweet Emma Moreland spoke to me,
Bitterly weeping I turn'd away:
"Sweet Emma Moreland, love no more
Can touch the heart of Edward Gray.

"Ellen Adair she loved me well,
Against her father's and mother's will;
To-day I sat for an hour and wept,

我愿做一个颈环,整天在她的香胸上,随着她的欢笑同叹息而起落,我将这么轻轻地躺在那里,在晚上我也不用解下。

Edward Gray

那个可爱的 Emma Moreland 碰着我在那路上行走,"你被谁迷着了没有?"她问,"你结婚未曾,Edward Gray?"

可爱的 Emma Moreland 向我说着,我痛哭而走开:"可爱的 Emma Moreland,爱情再也不能感动了 Edward Gray 的心儿。

"Ellen Adair,她深深地爱我,违了她父母的意旨;今天我坐着哭了整个钟头,在 Ellen 的墓旁,烈

By Ellen's grave, on the windy hill.

"Shy she was, and I thought her cold —
Thought her proud, and fled over the sea;
Fill'd was with folly and spite,
When Ellen Adair was dying for me.

"Cruel, cruel the words I said!
Cruelly came they back to-day:
'You're too slight and fickle,' I said,
'To trouble the heart of Edward Gray.'

"There I put my face in the grass —
Whisper'd listen to my despair;
I repent me of all I did:
'Speak a little, Ellen Adair!'

"Then I took a pencil, and wrote
On the mossy stone, as I lay
'Here lies the body of Ellen Adair;
And here the heart of Edward Gray!'

风吹着的山上。

"她生来害羞,我却以为是无情——我想她是骄傲,我远遁海外;我心中满怀的傻想同轻蔑当 Ellen Adair 为我憔悴将死。

"我的话是多么残忍!这些话今天残忍地回返我的心头,你是太'无聊,易变',我说,'值不得撩乱 Edward Gray 的胸怀。'

"在那里我面亲青草——低声地说,听我的失望罢;我追悔了我过去的一切:'讲一些话罢,Ellen Adair!'

"然后,我躺着用铅笔,写在苔侵的碑上,'这里头长眠有 Ellen Adair 的躯体;这里头长眠有 Edward Gray 的心儿!'

"Love may come, and love may go,
And fly, like a bird, from tree to tree;
But I will love no more, no more,
Till Ellen Adair come back to me.

"Bitterly wept I over the stone,
Bitterly weeping I turn'd away;
There lies the body of Ellen Adair!
And there the heart of Edward Gray."

The Eagle

He clasps the crag with hooked hands;
Close to the sun in lonely lands,
Ring'd with the azure world, he stands.

The wrinkled sea beneath him crawls;
He watches from his mountain walls,
And like a thunderbolt he falls.

"爱情来来去去,像鸟儿一样缘着——的树木投栖;但是我再也不钟情,再也不,要等到 Ellen Adair 重到我的当前。

"我俯着石碑痛哭,痛哭而走开;在那里长眠有 Ellen Adair 的躯体!在那里长眠有 Edward Gray 的心儿。"

鹰 鸟

他用他有钩的双爪抓着悬岩;在荒凉的境里与太阳为邻,苍天绕在四旁,他就这么站着。

有皱纹的大海在他底下慢爬;他从他这山墙俯视,像雷电一样他陡飞下来。

A Farewell

Flow down, cold rivulet, to the sea,
Thy tribute wave deliver:
No more by thee my steps shall be,
For ever and for ever.

Flow, softly flow, by lawn and lea,
A rivulet then a river:
No where by thee my steps shall be,
For ever and for ever.

But here will sigh thine alder tree,
And here thine aspen shiver;
And here by thee will hum the bee,
For ever and for ever.

A thousand suns will stream on thee,
A thousand moons will quiver;
But not by thee my steps shall be,
For ever and for ever.

别 矣

流下到大海去,清凉的小河,去呈出你所贡献的波浪:我的足迹却再不在你的旁边踯躅,永不,永不。

流着,漪涟地流着,缘着草地同牧场,从小河渐变做大河:我的足迹却不在你的旁边踯躅,永不,永不。

但是在这里你的赤杨将常常叹息,在这里你的白杨将常常颤战;在这里伴着你将有蜂的营营,永久,永久。

千个的太阳将射下光辉到你的身上,千个的月儿将在上摇动;但是我的足迹不会在你的旁边踯躅,永久,永久。

As thro' the land at eve we went,
And pluck'd the ripen'd ears,
We fell out[1], my wife and I,
O we fell out I know not why,
And kiss'd again with tears.

For when we came where lies the child
We lost in other years,
There above the little grave,
O there above the little grave,
We kiss'd again with tears.

Tears, idle tears, I know not what they mean,
Tears from the depth of some divine despair

---

1 fell out: quarrelled.
此首同下面两首见 Tennyson 长篇诗 *Princess* 中。

☆ ☆ ☆

傍晚时我们走过平原,摘着那已熟的麦穗,我们吵嘴起来,我的妻子同我,啊,不晓得怎的,我们吵嘴起来,一会儿又是含着眼泪相吻。

因为当我们走到前几年我们所失掉的小孩的长眠之处,在那小小的墓上,啊,在那小小的墓上,我们又是含着眼泪相吻。

☆ ☆ ☆

眼泪,无谓的眼泪,我不知道它们含有什么意思,那些眼泪是从神圣悲哀的深渊里涌上心头,凑

Rise in the heart, and gather to the eyes,
In looking on the happy Autumn-fields,
And thinking of the days that are no more.

Fresh as the first beam glittering on a sail,
That brings our friends up from the underworld[1],
Sad as the last which reddens over one
That sinks with all we love below the verge;
So sad, so fresh, the days that are no more.

Ah, sad and strange as in dark summer dawns,
The earliest pipe of half-awaken'd birds
To dying ears, when unto dying eyes
The casement slowly grows a glimmering square;[2]
So sad, so strange, the days that are no more.

Dear as remember'd kisses after death,
And sweet as those by hopeless feign'd
On lips that are for others; deep as love,

---

1 underworld: antipodes.
2 意谓 the outline of the window becomes visible as daylight appears。

到眼角,当看到快乐的秋之田野,想到永不回来的过去流光。

新鲜得像帆上闪烁的旭日光辉,当她从水平线下带来我们的朋友,悲哀得像帆上腥〔猩〕红的残照余辉,当她连着我们所爱的一切同沉到水平线下;这么悲哀,这么新鲜,是永不回来的过去流光。

呵,凄恻同奇异好似在漆黑的夏朝,半醒的鸟儿向着将死人的耳朵所发的早吟,当对着将死人的眼睛,窗格慢慢地现出一片朦胧的方形;这么凄恻,这么奇异是永不回来的过去流光。

可爱得像已经去世人的亲吻的回忆,甜蜜得像绝望的人,在想像里给与已属他人的朱唇的那些热吻;

Deep as first love, and wild with all regret;
O Death in Life, the days that are no more!

Home they brought her warrior dead;
She nor swoon'd, nor utter'd cry.
All her maidens, watching said,
"She must weep or she will die."

Then they praised him, soft and low,
Call'd him worthy to be loved,
Truest friend and noblest foe;
Yet she neither spoke nor moved.

Stole a maiden from her place,
Lightly to the warrior stept,
Took the face-cloth from the face;
Yet she neither moved nor wept.

像爱情那么深沉,像初恋那么深沉,又是惆怅得发狂;啊,生命里的死亡,这永不回来的过去流光!

☆　☆　☆

他们把她已死的战士带回家来;她既不晕倒,也不发出哀啼。她的使女们站在一旁,大家说"她必定要哭出声来,否则她将死去。"

他们就曼声地轻轻地赞美他,说他是值得人爱,称他是最真心的朋友,称他是最大量的敌人;可是她还是不说不动。

一个使女偷偷地走开本来站的地方,轻轻地走到战士的尸旁,从脸上翻去盖布;可是她还是不动不哭。

Rose a nurse of ninety years,
Set his child upon her knee —
Like summer tempest came her tears —
"Sweet my child, I live for thee."

I

Oh let the solid ground
Not fail beneath my feet
Before my life has found
What some have found so sweet;
Then let come what come may,
What matter if I go mad,
I shall have had my day.

II

Let the sweet heavens endure,
Not close and darken above me
Before I am quite, quite sure

一位九十岁的老乳媪站起,将她的小孩放她膝上——她眼泪有如夏天的狂风雨——"我可爱的小孩,我现在为你活着。"

☆ ☆ ☆

呵,坚实的大地别要从我的脚下消去,在我找到了人们所觉得那么甜蜜的快乐之前;然后,将来怎样都是可以,我就疯了,也是何妨,我将已有了我得意的佳辰。

美丽的青天别要不存,也不要闭起变成了黑漆一团,在我真真晓得世上有个爱我的人儿之前;然

此首见Tennyson长篇诗 *Maud* 中。

That there is one to love me;
Then let come what come may
To a life that has been so sad,
I shall have had my day.

Crossing the Bar

Sunset and evening star,
And one clear call for me!
And may there be no moaning of the bar,
When I put out to sea.

But such a tide as moving seems asleep,
Too full for sound and foam,
When that which drew from out the boundless deep
Turns again home.

Twilight and evening bell,
And after that the dark!
And may there be no sadness of farewell,
When I embark.

后，对着如是凄凉的一个生涯，怎样的将来都是可以，我将已有了得意的佳辰。

渡过沙洲

上面是落照同太白星，海外来个唤我的清澈呼声！愿沙洲不发出哀吟，当我驶出去海外。

愿只有虽然动着，却好似沉睡的退潮，那是因为太涨满了，反见得无声无沫，当从无边大海里来的潮水再返到故家。

四围是黄昏同晚钟的逸响，过些时就是漆黑的昏夜！愿没有离别的凄苦，当我上船走进大洋。

For tho' from out our bourne of Time and Place
The flood may bear me far,
I hope to see my Pilot[1] face to face
When I have crost the bar.

Robert Browning

(1812—1889)

The year's at the spring;
And day's at the morn;
Morning's at seven;
The hill-side's dew-pearled;
The lark's on the wing;
The snail's on the thorn;
God's in his heaven —
All's right with the world!

Meeting at Night

The grey sea and the long black land;
And the yellow half-moon large and low;
And the startled little waves that leap

因为虽然这大水会带我远离我们"时""空"的小河,我希望与向导者会面,当我渡过了沙洲。

☆ ☆ ☆

岁在阳春;时在清晨;晨在七时;山边满洒着露珠;天鹨在飞;蜗牛在荆棘;上帝在上——万物各得其所!

夜　　会

灰色的大海同悠长的黑地;黄色的上弦月很大个低照在天边;惊醒的小浪从睡眠里跳出,个个是

---

1 指看不见的神圣天使

这首诗是 Tennyson 八十一岁时做的,他在逝世前几日吩咐他的儿子,"将这首诗放在我诗集的末叶里。"这诗代表 Tennyson 对于死所持的态度。

In fiery ringlets from their sleep,
As I gain the cove with pushing prow,
And quench its speed in the slushy sand.

Then a mile of warm sea-scented beach;
Three fields to cross till a farm appears;
A tap at the pane, the quick sharp scratch
And blue spurt of a lighted match,
And a voice less loud, thro' its joys and fears,
Than the two hearts beating each to each!

Home-Thoughts, from Abroad

Oh, to be in England
Now that April's there,
And whoever wakes in England
Sees, some morning, unaware[1],
That the lowest boughs and the brush-wood sheaf
Round the elm-tree bole[2] are in tiny leaf,
While the chaffinch sings on the orchard bough

---

1 unexpectedly

凶猛的小圈,当我驶着直前的船头走近了小湾,当在软泥的沙滩上,我减低它(指船)的速度。

然后,一里带着海味的温暖海岸;走过三片田地,就看见一座农场;玻璃窗上的一声轻敲,接着有急促的,尖锐的推窗声音同着火的洋火的蓝焰,还有一个人声音,比两人互击的心儿还要低声,因为那是含有喜乐同恐惧!

在国外时的乡愁

呵,此时能在英国是多么好呀,现在那里正是初春四月,英国的住民有时醒来,会出惊地看到榆干四周的最低树枝同小丛林发出了小叶,当金丝雀

---

2 trunk

In England — now!

And after April, when May follows,
And the white throat builds, and all the swallows!
Hark! where my blossomed pear-tree in the hedge
Leans to the field and scatters on the clover,
Blossoms and dewdrops — at the bent spray's edge[1]—
That's the wise thrush; he sings each song twice over,
Lest you should think he never could recapture
The first fine careless rapture!
And though the fields look rough with hoary dew,
All will be gay when noontide wakes anew
The buttercups, the little children's dower
— For brighter than this gandy melon-flower!

Home-Thoughts, from the Sea

Nobly, nobly Cape Saint Vincent to the North-West died away,
Sunset ran, one glorious blood-red, reeking into Cadiz Bay;

---

1 画眉压着树枝，所以散下有花朵同露珠。

正栖在英国园里的枝上歌唱。

四月过后，五月接着来了，那时白喉雀和所有的燕子全筑起巢来！听呀，我篱边盛开的梨树向田野斜倾，散下花朵同露珠在金花菜上，——在被压的枝头，正是那聪明的画眉；他每个调子都唱了两遍，怕的是你会想他绝不能再抓住开头随意的狂欢妙调！虽然田野是被白露洒得不齐，一切会全现出喜悦的颜色，当中天的皎日重唤醒了金凤花朵，那是小孩们的恩物——比这里虚华的瓜花要漂亮得多！

海 中 乡 思

Cape Saint Vincent 巍巍地渐消失在西北，落照，一片光荣的血红，如烟地西沉到 Cadiz Bay 里去；在

Bluish 'mid the burning water, full in face Trafalgar lay;
In the dimmest North-East distance dawned Gibraltar grand and gray;
"Here and here did England help me; how can I help England?"— say,
Whose turns as I, this evening, turn to God to praise and pray,
While jove's planet rises yonder, silent over Africa.

Life in a Love

Escape me?
Never —
Beloved!
While I am I, and you are you,
So long as the world contains us both,
Me the loving and you the loath,
While the one eludes, must the other pursue,
My life is a fault at last, I fear:
It seems too much like a fate, indeed!
Though I do my best I shall scarce succeed.

这火光也似的水里，浅蓝的Trafalgar躺在当前；极模糊的东北远处，隐隐地现出伟大灰色的Gibraltar。谁在这里像我这样向上帝去赞美同祈祷，都会说，"在此处，在那处，英国曾经助我；我要怎样子助英国呢？"当月儿从那边上升，静静地笼着Africa。

整整一生花在向一女人求婚里面

逃着我了？绝不能——亲爱的！当我还是我，你还是你，只要我们同住在世上，我爱恋着，你嫌恶着，当你躲避，我总得追逐。我怕，我的一生终是一个大错：这真是太像前定的厄运！虽然尽了我力，我几乎总不能成功。但是若使我在这里失败了，

十八世纪末叶英国在Gibraltar打败法国西班牙联军，在一八〇五年Nelson在Trafalgar战胜法国舰队，这些地方是既与英国的光荣相连，所以Browning触景生情，爱国的念头油然而生。

But what if I fail of my purpose here?
It is but to keep the nerves at strain,
To dry one's eyes and laugh at a fall,
And baffled get up and begin again, —
So the chace[1] takes up one's life, that's all.
While, look but once from your farthest bound
At me so deep in the dust and dark,
No sooner the old hope goes to ground
Than a new one, straight to the selfsame mark
I shape me —
Ever
Removed![2]

Apparitions

Such a starved bank of moss
Till, that May-morn,
Blue ran the flash across:
Violets were born!

Sky — what a scowl of cloud
Till, near and far,

那又如何？那也不过是神经老是紧张，揩干眼泪；笑一笑这回的失败，受了挫折，站起来，重新赶去，——所以这个追逐是要花了一生的光阴，也不过如是而已。当你从那最远的地方一回头看到深陷在尘土同黑暗里的我，我看着我的旧希望一落地下，立刻有个新希望出来，一直朝着我自己所定的同一鹄的——而这个新希望接着又离我而去。

出 现

一个这么瘠瘦的苔岸，等到那天五月的清早，忽然蓝遍池边：紫罗兰生出来了！

天空——暗云这么样的一个怒容，等到远远近近，

---

1 chase
2 and the new one in turn always retires before me.

Ray on ray split the shroud:
Splendid, a star!

World — how it walled about
Life with disgrace,
Till God's own smile came out:
That was thy face!

Epilogue

At the midnight in the silence of the sleep-time,
When you set your fancies free,
Will they pass to where — by death, fools think imprisoned —
Low he lies who once so loved you, whom you loved so,
— Pity me?

Oh to love so, be so loved, yet so mistaken!
What had I on earth to do
With the slothful, with the mawkish, the unmanly?
Like the aimless, helpless, hopeless, did I drivel
— Being — Who?

一丝丝的光线劈开这面尸布：壮丽地来了一颗星儿！

世界——他是怎样地用耻辱围着人生，等到上帝的笑容现出：那是你的庞儿！

尾　声

午夜里在睡时的静寂之中，当你让你的幻想任意飞奔，这些幻想走到墓旁——愚人们以为他是被死关在里面了——在那里低躺着曾那样爱你，那样被你爱着的他（指自己）——你会怜我吗？

啊这么爱过你，这么被你爱，可是有这样的误会！我从前在地上时[1]同懒惰的，可厌的，懦弱的东西有过什么相干？我是什么人？曾经像无目的，无法自助，无希望的人们那样发傻过吗？

1　"on earth"应译作"究竟"而非"在地上时"。——编者注

One who never turned his back but marched breast
  forward,
Never doubted clouds would break,
Never dreamed, though right mere worsted, wrong would
  triumph,
Held we fall to rise, are baffled to fight better,
Sleep to wake.

No, at noonday in the bustle of man's work-time
Greet the unseen with a cheer!
Bid him forward, breast and back as either should be, [1]
"Strive and thrive!" cry "Speed, — fight on, fare ever
There as here!"

Matthew Arnold

(1822—1888)

Self-Dependence

Weary of myself, and sick of asking
What I am, and what I ought to be,

---

1 breast and back as either should be 就是胸向前，背朝后而望〔往〕前进不可转过身来脱逃的意思。

我是从来没有转身而逃,却老是挺着胸膛前进,老是相信云雾是会散的,虽然正义处着最坏的逆境,简直没有想过不义是会胜利,我主张我们摔下当再爬起来,受了挫折,就要更勇地奋斗,睡去还要醒来。

不要怜我,在人们工作匆忙的正午时候,你向着不见的我欢呼罢!叫他前进,挺起胸膛,别去转身,你高呼,"奋斗,再奋斗!快些,——向前努力,在那里同在这里一样!"

自　　助

对于自己,感到了厌倦,也不奈烦再去问我是什么,同我应当是怎样,我站在这船头,他带我前

Browning 自强不息的哲学在这自白里痛快地表现出来,这和 Tennyson 的 "Crossing the Bar" 的情调绝不相同,由此可见两人思想的差异。

At this vessel's prow I stand, which bears me
Forwards, forwards, o'er the starlit sea.

And a look of passionate desire
O'er the sea and to the stars I send:
"Ye who from my childhood up have calm'd me,
Calm me, ah, compose me to the end!

"Ah, once more, " I cried, "Ye stars, ye waters,
On my heart your mighty charm renew;
Still, still let me, as I gaze upon you,
Feel my soul becoming vast like you!"

From the intense, clear, star-sown vault of heaven,
Over the lit sea's unquiet way,
In the rustling night-air came the answer:
"Wouldst thou be as these are? Live as they.

"Unaffrighted by the silence round them,
Undistracted by the sights they see,
These demand not that the things without them
Yield them love, amusement, sympathy.

进，渡过星光底下的大海。

我向着大海同星空发出个热烈希望的神色："你们自从我的稚年就常常安慰我的心儿，安慰我呀，给我以宁静的心境到底罢！你这星儿，你这海水，"我叫道，"你重新将你那伟大的魔力施在我心上一回罢；当我钉〔盯〕视你们时候，还让我觉得我的灵魂化成同你们一样庞大！"

从那热烈的，明澈的，种着星儿的天穹，在明亮大海的不静道路之上，沿着沙沙的夜风，来了一个答词："你想同他们一样吗？那么就像他们那样地生活。

"不怕他们四周的静寂，不为他们听见的东西而分心，他们也不要身外的东西给他们以爱情，娱乐和同情。

"And with joy the stars perform their shining,
And the sea its long moon-silver'd roll;
For self-poised they live, nor pine with noting
All the fever of some differing soul.

"Bounded by themselves, and unregardful
In what state God's other works may be,
In their own tasks all their powers pouring,
These attain the mighty life you see."

O air-born voiced! long since, severely clear,
A cry like thine in mine own heart I hear:
"Resolve to be thyself; and know, that he
Who finds himself, loses his misery!"

Requiescat[1]

Strew on her roses, roses,
And never a spray of yew!
In quiet she reposes:

---

[1] May she rest.

"星儿愉快地照耀下界,大海愉快地掀起月色染白的长波;他们不倚不靠地活着,也没有看到别个不同的灵魂的一切热狂而自伤。

"范围在自己之内,也不管上帝别的创造物是处在什么情形,他们把一切能力全倾注在自己的工作里去,他们达到你所看见的伟大生涯。"

呵,空中生出的声音!此后在我自己的心里我好久听到同你一样的清彻呼声:"决心立定脚跟罢;要知道找到自己的人是去掉了他的悲哀!"

安灵祈祷

撒下蔷薇在她的身上罢,绝不要杂些紫杉的小

Ah, would that I did too!

Her mirth the world required;
She bathed it in smiles of glee.
But her heart was tired, tired,
And now they let her be.

Her life was turning, turning,
In mazes of heat and sound.
But for peace her soul was yearning,
And now peace laps[1] her round.

Her cabin'd, ample spirit,
It flutter'd and fail'd for breath.
To-night it doth inherit
The vasty hall of Death.

---

1 laps: wraps.

枝！她沉静地安卧着：呵，多么希望我也如此！

世界从前需要她的欢声；它浴在她的快乐笑容之中。但是她的心是已倦，已倦，现在他们也让她自如。

她的一生是在热闹的纷纷里旋转。但是她的灵魂是渴望安宁，现在她躺在安宁的怀中。

她那被关住的宽大灵魂，从前鼓翼欲飞，却感到窒息。今晚她却住在"死神"的大厅。

Dante Gabriel Rossetti

(1828—1882)

Sudden Light[1]

I have been here before,
But when or how I cannot tell:
I know the grass beyond the door,
The sweet keen smell,
The sighing sound, the lights around the shore.

You have been mine before, —
How long ago I may not know:
But just when at that swallow's soar
Your neck turned so,
So veil did fall, — I know it all of yore.

Then, now, — perchance again!...
O round mine eyes your tresses shake!
Shall we not lie as we have lain
Thus for Love's sake,
And sleep, and wake, yet never break the chain?

顿　　悟

　　我从前曾经走到这里,但是何时同怎样走来,我却不能说出;我知道那户外的青草,刺鼻的香味,叹息着的风声同围着河岸的灯火。

　　你从前曾经属于我的,——是多久以前,我却不知;但是当燕子高飞,你的颈项那么转过时节,有些面罩坠下来了,——这个脸孔我古时曾经熟识。

　　从前有过,现在重现——或者将来还会发生罢!……呵,你的鬈发围着我的眼睛而颤动!我们不是要像从前那样同眠,为着爱情的缘故,睡着,醒来,却绝不打断那长链?

---

1 当爱人们相聚时候,他们有时会有一种极微妙的感觉,仿佛他们前生曾经在一块儿过,这不过是续前世之缘。这话真实与否,我个人无法证明。

Three Shadows

I looked and saw your eyes in the shadow of your hair,
As a traveller sees the stream in the shadow of the wood; —
And I said, "My faint heart sighs, ah me! to linger there,
To drink deep and to dream in that sweet solitude."

I looked and saw your heart in the shadow of your eyes,
As a seeker sees the gold in the shadow of the stream;
And I said, "Ah, me! what art should win the immortal prize,
Whose want must make life cold and Heaven a hollow dream?"

I looked and saw your love in the shadow of your heart,
As a diver sees the pearl in the shadow of the sea;
And I murmured, not above my breath, but all apart, —
"Ah! you can love, true girl, and is your love for me?"

三　　影

　　我望着，在你发影中看到你的双眸，好似行客在树影里看到江流；——我说，"我这虚弱的心儿叹息着，我呀，留连在这里，在这甜蜜的幽处深深地喝了一口这恬静的空气，做出些好梦。"

　　我望着，在你眼影中，看到你的心儿，好似一个寻金者在江流的波影里看到黄金；我说，"我呀！有什么法术能够得到这不朽的至宝，没有它，生命是冰冷的，天堂是一场空梦？"

　　我望着，在你的心影中，看到你的爱情，好似潜水的人在海中的涛影里看到真珠；我喃喃地说道，声音比呼吸还低，是用另外的细细低声，——"呵你能够爱恋人，诚实的女郎，你的爱情是对着我吗？"

Christina Rossetti

(1830—1894)

When I am dead, my dearest,
Sing no sad songs for me;
Plant thou no roses at my head,
Nor shady cypress tree:
Be the green grass above me
With showers and dewdrops wet[1];
And if thou wilt, remember,
And if thou wilt, forget.

I shall not see the shadows,
I shall not feel the rain;
I shall not hear the nightingale
Sing on, as if in pain;
And dreaming through the twilight
That doth not rise nor set,
Haply I may remember,
And haply may forget.

☆ ☆ ☆

当我死后,我的亲亲,别要为我唱出哀歌;你不用在我头上栽了蔷薇,也不用什么浓荫的柏树:让我上面的青草沾着雨露;若使你想记着我,那么就记着罢,若使你想忘却了我,那么也就忘却罢。

我将看不见影子,我将感不着霖雨;我将听不到夜莺好像是沉痛地歌唱;在那不升不降的蒙胧界中的梦里,也许我会记着,也许我已忘却。

---

1 with showers and dewdrops wet: wet with showers and dewdrops.(wet 形容 grass)

Remember

Remember me when I am gone away,
Gone far away into the silent land;
When you can no more hold me by the hand,
Nor I half turn to go yet turning stay.
Remember me when no more day by day,
You tell me of our future that you planned:
Only remember me; you understand
It will be late to counsel then or pray.
Yet if you should forget me for a while
And afterwards remember, do not grieve:
For if the darkness and corruption leave
A vestige of the thoughts that once I had,
Better by far[1] you should forget and smile
Than that you should remember and be sad.

---

1 better by far: much better.

忆

请你记念着我,当我瞑目远去,远去到寂默的国土;当你再不能拉着我手我也不能一半转身,将去而又停。请你记念着我,当你再不能天天告诉我以你所筹划的将来:只请你记念着我罢;你晓得到那时劝告同祈祷都是太迟。可是若使你暂时忘却了我,以后又记念起来,请你别要伤心,因为若使墓里的黑暗同腐烂在我从前的思想上加下污点,你还是忘却我而现出笑脸好得多了,别要记念着我而悲哀。

Up-Hill

Does the road wind up-hill all the way?
Yes, to the very end.
Will the day's journey take the whole long day?
From morn to night, my friend.

But is there for the night a resting-place?
A roof for when the slow dark hours begin.
May not the darkness hide it from my face?
You cannot miss that inn.

Shall I meet other wayfarers at night?
Those who have gone before.
Then must I knock, or call when just in sight?
They will not keep you standing at that door.

Shall I find comfort, travel-sore[1] and weak?

---

1 travel-sore 这是两字铸成一字，等于 sore with travel。这首诗自然也是死的冥想，上山的路就是人的一生。

上　山

这条路老是蜿蜒上登吗？是的，一直到路底。这天的路程要走整天吗？从清早走到黄昏，我的朋友。

但是晚上有个休息的场所吗？有一间屋子，当迟慢的黑夜开始时候。黑暗会使我看不见这屋子吗？你绝不会错过了这座旅舍。

晚上我会遇到那个行人吗？会遇到动身在前的人们。那么我要叩门，或者一看见时就叫喊吗？他们不会使你在门外久候。

我在征途苦辛，四肢无力之后，会得到舒服吗？

Of labour you shall find the sum.
Will there be beds for me and all who seek?
Yea, beds for all who come.

Last Prayer

Before the beginning thou hast foreknown the end,
Before the birthday the death-bed was seen of thee:
Cleanse what I cannot cleanse, mend what I cannot mend,
O Lord All-Merciful, be merciful to me.

While the end is drawing near I know not mine end;
Birth I recall not, my death I cannot foresee:
O God, arise to defend, arise to befriend,
O Lord All-Merciful, be merciful to me.

  Christina Rossetti是个非常虔敬的诗人，她这种对于死的态度，很可以拿来同前面Tennyson，Browning的二首歌咏死的诗相比较。

你将得到你一切劳苦的收成。那里有床铺给我同到那里的一切人们吗?是的,来的人们都可得到了床铺。

最后的祷告

在我出世之前,"你"已早晓得这个终局,在我降生之前,"你"已看到我这弥留之床:洗净我自己所不能洗净的罢,修补我自己所不能修补的罢,呵,慈云普照的上帝,仁慈地对待我罢。

当终局快到时候,我不晓得自己的终局;降生,我是记不清的,死亡,我也不能预知;呵,上帝,起来回护我罢,起来做我的朋友罢,呵,慈云普照的上帝,仁慈地对待我罢。

William Morris

(1834—1896)

Love is enough: though the World be a-waning[1],
And the woods have no voice but the voice of complaining,
Though the sky be too dark for dim eyes to discover
The gold-cups and daisies fair blooming thereunder,
Though the hills be held shadows, and the sea a dark wonder,
And this day draw a veil over all deeds pass'd over,
Yet their hands shall not tremble, their feet shall not falter;
The void shall not weary, the fear shall not alter
These lips and these eyes of the loved and the lover.

Error and Loss

Upon an eve I sat me down and wept,
Because the world to me seemed nowise good;
Still autumn was it, and the meadows slept,

---

1 a-waning: on waning。普通在 gerund 前面加个 a 字，这个 a 字都是作 on 解。

☆　☆　☆

有了爱情就够了,虽然宇宙是日渐消沉,林中只有哀怨的声音,虽然天空是太暗了,蒙钝的眼睛因此看不见下面正在盛开的毛茛同雏菊,虽然我们把小山看做影子,将大海当做黑暗的怪物,今日放下一层薄幕盖着了过去一切的事情,然而他们的手不颤摇,他们的足不会战栗;虚空不会倦了,恐惧不会变了,爱人俩的唇眼。

错误同丧失

有一晚我坐下流泪,因为世界对我好像是一无好处;那是恬静的秋天,草场睡着,雾中的小山梦着,

The misty hills dreamed, and the silent wood
Seemed listening to the sorrow of my mood:
I knew not if the earth with me did grieve,
Or if it mocked my grief that bitter eve.

Then 'twixt my tears a maiden did I see,
Who drew anigh me on the leaf-strewn grass,
Then stood and gazed upon me pitifully
With grief-worn eyes, until my woe did pass
From me to her, and tearless now I was,
And she mid tears was asking me of one
She long had sought unaided and alone,

I know not of him, and she turned away
Into the dark wood, and my own great pain
Still held me there, till dark had slain the day,
And perished at the grey dawn's hand again;
Then from the wood a voice cried: "Ah in vain,
In vain I seek thee, O thou bitter-sweet!
In what lone land are set thy longed-for feet?"

默默的森林好似在听我心境的凄凉；我不晓得世界是伴我悲伤，还是在这辛酸的夜里讥笑我的浓愁。

从泪眼中我看到一位姑娘，她踏着落叶缤纷的草上前来；然后她站住，悲哀得无光的双眸矜怜地望着我，等到我的悲怀离我而去，投到她的心里，现在我是无泪地站住，她在泪中问我以她寻找已久的人儿的消息，她一向是无助地孤单找着。

我不晓得他，她转身到黑林里去了，我自己的悲哀还留我在那儿，黑夜杀死了白天；自己又死在灰色的晨曦手上；然后从森林中来了叫喊的声音："呵徒然地我去找你，呵，你是又甜又苦！我所想见的你的双脚是踏在什么寂寞的国土里？"

Then I looked up, and lo, a man there came
From midst the trees, and stood regarding me
Until my tears were dried for very shame;
Then he cried out: "O mourner, where is she
Whom I have sought o'er every land and sea?
I love her and she loveth me, and still
We meet no more than green hill meeteth hill."

With that he passed on sadly, and I knew
That these had met and missed in the dark night,
Blinded by blindness of the world untrue,
That hideth love and maketh wrong of right.
Then midst my pity for their lost delight,
Yet more with barren longing I grew weak,
Yet move I mourned that I had none to seek.

Algernon Charles Swinburne

(1837—1909)

The Garden of Proserpine[1]

Here, where the world is quiet;

我抬起头一瞧,看哪,从林中来了个男人,站着尽望我,弄得我的眼泪因为害羞而干;他喊道:"呵伤心的人,我走尽海角天涯所找的她到底是在那儿?我爱她,她也爱我,可是我们不能相会如有青山的无从相逢。"

说了这些他悲哀地走开,我知道他们在黑夜是碰到,而错过了,被这不真世界的盲目所盲,这世界将爱情藏起,使正义好像是罪过。然后我既是怜惜他们快乐的失掉,可是我也因为空空的希望而精神更见衰弱,可是我更悲哀我的无人可找。

Proserpine 的园地

在这里,世界是恬静的;在这里一切的纷扰都

---

1 Proserpine 是 Ceres（地上果壳女神）的女儿,被阎罗王（Pluto）夺去做王后,普天下的教堂坟地都算是她的园地。

Here, where all trouble seems
Dead winds' and spent waves' riot
In doubtful dreams of dreams;
I watch the green field growing
For reaping folk and sowing,
For harvest-time and mowing,
A sleepy world of streams.

I am tired of tears and laughter,
And men that laugh and weep;
Of what may come hereafter,
For men that sow to reap;
I am weary of days and hours,
Blown buds of barren flowers,
Desires and dreams and powers,
And everything but sleep.

Here life has death for neighbour,
And far from eye or ear
Wan waves and wet winds labour,
Weak ships and spirits steer;
They drive adrift, and whither
They wot not who make thither;

像是可疑的梦中的梦里面死风逝水的骚动；我瞧青青的田地正在生成，给人们来刈禾下种，来收获割稻，这真是满布江流的睡乡。

我是倦于清泪同狂笑，以及啼笑的人们；我是倦于下种收获的人们的将来；朝朝，刻刻，枯花的残蕾，希望，梦儿，权力以及一切的东西，我全厌倦，只除开了睡眠。

在这里生命是与死为邻，无色无声地惨淡的小波同潮湿的微风动摇着，柔弱的船只同精灵慢驶着；到匆忙的世界里去的人们是随狂风乱飘，他们自己

此首诗每行中常有同一consonant开头的字数个，如第一行的where, world，第四行的doubtful dreams of dreams，第十四行的blown buds of barren flowers等皆是，这样子念起来自然有一种轻柔的声调，因此增加了诗中哀惋〔婉〕暗淡的风韵。

But no such winds blow hither;
And no such things grow here.

No growth of moor or coppice,
No heather-flower or vine,
But bloomless buds of poppies,
Green grapes of Proserpine,
Pale buds of blowing rushes,
Where no leaf blooms or blushes
Save this whereout she crushes
For dead men deadly wine.

Pale, without name or number,
In fruitless fields of corn
They bow themselves and slumber
All night till light is born;
And like a soul belated,
In hell and heaven unmated,
By cloud and mist abated
Comes out of darkness morn.

Though one were strong as seven,
He too with death shall dwell,

也不晓得是到何方；但是没有这样的风吹到此间，没有这样的事情发生在这里。

这里没有泽地的野草，矮小的树林，没有野花，没有蔓茎，却只有罂粟的无花枝芽同 Proserpine 的葡萄以及吐萼的灯心草的苍白花床，这里没有叶子招展或者现出绯红，除非是她从罂粟的头上榨出鸦片来做死人的毒酒。

苍白的没有名字，没有数目，在没有收成的稻田里，这群树林，弯着腰肢，睡了整晚，一直到天明；清晨好似是迟到的灵魂，在地狱与天堂里俱感到无侣，被云雾所勾留慢腾腾地从黑暗里出来。

虽然一人的力量大得可敌过七人，他也要与死同

Nor wake with wings in heaven,
Nor weep for pains in hell;
Though one were fair as roses,
His beauty clouds and closes;
And well though love reposes,
In the end it is not well.

Pale, beyond porch and portal,
Crowned with calm leaves, she[1] stands
Who gathers all things mortal
With cold immortal hands;
Her languid lips are sweeter
Than Love's, who fears to greet her,
To men that mix and meet her
From many times and lands.

She waits for each and other,
She waits for all men born;
Forgets the earth her mother,
The life of fruits and corn;
And spring and seed and swallow
Take wing for her and follow
Where summer song rings hollow

居,既不能振着天翼而醒,也不能为着地狱的苦痛而哭;虽然一人是鲜丽如蔷薇,他的美貌也阴沉消歇;虽然爱情是好好地休憩,最终也只落得个不好。

苍白的她站在门廊同大门之外,载着恬静的枝叶,她用不灭的冷手收拾了一切会死的东西;她那无精打采〔采〕的嘴唇对着从一切时代,一切地方来和她同居相会的人们,是比爱情的唇还要甜蜜,爱情却是怕和她相见。

她等候个个的人们,她等候世上所有的生人;她忘却了大地,那是她的母亲,她忘却了果壳的生涯;春天,种子同燕子都鼓翼而来到她的住所,追

---

1 指 Proserpine。

And flowers are put to scorn.

There go the loves that wither,
The old loves with wearier wings;
And all dead years draw thither,
And all disastrous things;
Dead dreams of days forsaken,
Blind buds that snows have shaken,
Wild leaves that winds have taken,
Red strays of ruined springs.

We are not sure of sorrow,
And joy was never sure;
To-day will die to-morrow;
Time stoops to no man's lure;
And Love, grown faint and fretful,
With lips but half regretful
Sighs, and with eyes forgetful
Weeps that no loves endure.

From too much love of living,
From hope and fear set free,
We thank, with brief thanksgiving
Whatever gods may be,

随到夏歌声哑,花儿枯萎的地方。

凋谢的爱情也到那里,已老的爱情也乘着倦翼飞来;已去的流年同诸般的厄运全来那里;被弃的时日的旧梦,霜雪摇下的未开花蕾,狂风吹散的狂叶,残春剩下的无主落红。

我们料不定悲哀,快乐老是没有准的;"今日"是将在"明日"死去;时光不肯俯受谁的钩饵;爱情变为颓唐同烦躁;用了含怨的双唇,发出微叹,用了易忘的眼睛,哭着没有爱情能够久留。

我们从生的迷恋里,我们从希望恐惧里解放出来,我们用简短的谢词,向着任何的天神,谢谢没

That no life lives forever;
That dead men rise up never;
That even the weariest river
Winds somewhere safe to sea.

Then star nor sun shall waken,
Nor any change of light;
Nor sound of waters shaken,
Nor any sound or sight;
Nor wintry leaves nor vernal,
Nor days nor things diurnal;
Only the sleep eternal
In an eternal night.

有生命是可长生;死者是绝不能复活;就是最疲累的小河湾〔弯〕来转去,也总会安然地投入大海。

然后也没有星儿或者太阳来唤醒,也没有明暗的交迭;没有流水震动的声音,真可是无声无色;没有冬天白枯叶,也没有阳春的茂叶,无昼无日夜;却只有一个不灭的黑夜里的不断的长眠。

Modern Poetry

Austin Dobson
(1840—1921)

The Child-Musician

He had played for his lordship's levee,
He had played for her ladyship's whim,
Till the poor little head was heavy,
And the poor little brain would swim.

And the face grew peeked[1] and eerie,
And the large eyes strange and bright,
And they said — too late — "He is weary!
He shall rest for, at least, to-night!"

But at dawn, when the birds were waking,
As they watched in the silent room,
With the sound of a strained cord breaking,
A something snapped in the gloom.

---

1 应为 peaked，原书误。——编者注

稚年的音乐家

他为爵士大人天天的朝会奏乐,他为爵士夫人一时的兴致奏乐,弄得那可怜的小头觉得沉重,可怜的小脑感到晕眩。

他的脸呈出眯视怪诞的样子,他的大眼睛渐渐变成奇异而光亮,他们说——太迟了——"他是疲倦了,最少今晚上他该休息!"

但是破晓时,当鸟儿正醒来,他们在静室里看护,有如一条过紧弦索的中断,暗中发出尖锐的声音。

'Twas the string of his violoncello,
And they heard him stir in his bed: —
"Make room for a tired little fellow,
Kind God!" — was the last that he said.

Robert Bridges

(1844—   )[1]

Winter Nightfall

The day begins to droop, —
Its course is done:
But nothing tells the place
Of the setting sun.

The hazy darkness deepens,
And up the lane
You may hear, but cannot see,
The homing wain.

An engine pants and hums
In the farm hard by:

那是四弦低音大提琴的弦索,他们听他在床上转动:——"腾一块地方给疲倦的小孩罢,仁慈的上帝!"——这是他最后的一句话。

冬天的薄暮

白天渐渐地消沉——它的行程是已走完;但是没有东西指出日落的地方。

朦胧的黑暗刻刻加深,你可听到,却不能看见,回家的货车望〔往〕着小径走去。

一座汽机在邻近的农场里喘气,发出含糊的声

---

1 其卒年为1930年。——编者注

Its lowering smoke is lost
In the lowering sky.

The soaking branches drip,
And all night through
The dropping will not cease
In the avenue.

A tall man there in the house
Must keep his chair:
He knows he will never again
Breathe the spring air.

His heart is worn with work;
He is giddy and sick
If he rise to go as far
As the nearest rick.

He think of his morn of life,
His hale, strong years;
And braves as he may the night
Of darkness and tears.

音：它那惨淡的乌烟是消失在惨淡的天里。

浸透的小枝滴沥着,整夜里在树荫的路中,这种点滴是没有停时。

屋里一个高汉子不得不守着他的靠椅:他晓得他绝不能再吸春天的空气。

他的心是被劳工所磨损;若使他起来只走到最近的禾堆,他也会头晕心里作恶。

他回想他此生的清晨,那是他健全强壮的年时;他只得尽力来抵抗这昏暗多泪的黑夜。

Nightingales

Beautiful must be the mountains whence ye come,
And bright in the fruitful valleys the streams wherefrom
Ye learn your song:
Where are those starry woods? O might I wander there,
Among the flowers, which in that heavenly air
Bloom the year long!

Nay, barren are those mountains and spent the streams:
Our song is the voice of desire, that haunts our dreams,
A throe of the heart,
Whose pining visions dim, forbidden hopes profound,
No dying cadence nor long sigh can sound,
For all our art.

Alone, aloud in the raptured ear of men
We pour our dark nocturnal secret; and then,
As night is withdrawn

夜　莺

你所从来的深山必是美艳绝伦，教你歌唱的河流必定是在果实繁多的谷里照耀：那些辉煌的森林是在那里？我多么想能够到那里漫游，在天堂般的空气中，四时不凋的花里！

不，那些高山是不毛的，那些河流是无力的：我们的歌是希望的呼声，这些希望回荡在我们的梦中，那是心中的极痛，那种悲伤模糊的幻想，深远违禁的希望是任何飘渺的音调同深长的浩叹所不能宣，不管我们有多么微妙的艺术。

孤单地，在人们听得销魂的耳朵里响着我们所吐出黑夜的秘密；然后，良夜离着这馨香的草场同

From these sweet-springing meads and bursting boughs of
　　May,
Dream, while the innumerable choir of day
Welcome the dawn.

Elegy

The wood is bare; a river-mist is steeping
The trees that winter's chill of life bereaves[1]:
Only their stiffened boughs break silence, weeping
Over their fallen leaves;

That lie upon the dank earth brown and rotten,
Miry and matted[2] in the soaking wet:
Forgotten with the spring, that is forgotten
By them that can forget.

Yet it was here we walked when ferns were springing,
And through the mossy bank shot bud and blade; —
Here found in summer, when the birds were singing,
A green and pleasant shade.

---

　　1 that winter's chill of life bereaves 一句，若使照本来文法次序是 winter's chill bereaves（that）of life。

五月的吐萼繁枝而去，我们就做起梦来，当无数的白天歌鸟向着朝暾送出欢声。

挽　　歌

森林是凋落了；一阵河雾浸着那被冬天的苦冷剥夺去生气的树林：只有它们已僵的枝干打破了这寂寞，在他们的落叶上悲啼；棕色的，腐烂的落叶躺在潮湿的地上，化为泥土，缠结在透彻的泥泞之中：这些落叶是同春天一样地被人忘却，春天是被那班能忘却的人们所忘。

可是我们是在这里散步，当羊齿丛生，花蕾小叶布满了苔岸的时候；——在夏天里，当众鸟歌唱的时候，我们在此处得到青青可喜的凉荫。

2　matted: brought into a thickly tangled state.

'Twas here we loved in sunnier days and greener;
And now, in this disconsolate decay,
I come to see her where I most have seen her,
And touch the happier day.

For on this path, at every turn and corner,
The fancy of her figure on me falls;
Yet walks she with the slow step of a mourner,
Nor hears my voice that calls.

So through my heart there winds a track of feeling,
A path of memory, that is all her own:
Whereto her phantom beauty ever stealing
Haunts the sad spot alone.

About her steps the trunks are bare, the branches
Drip heavy tears upon her downcast head;
And bleed from unseen wounds that no sun stanches,
For the year's sun is dead.

当那幸运同年青的日子,我们是在此处互相爱恋,现在当此凄凉的衰残时期,我到我从前最常看她的地方再来看她,抚一抚我快乐的前尘。

因为这条径里,每个转湾〔弯〕,每个基角,她的倩影会来到我的心中;但是她是像一个送葬人那样慢步,也没有听到我的呼声。

所以有一条情感的线路盘旋我的心中,一条记忆的路途,那是全属于她的:她那虚幻的美貌老是偷偷地走着,独自逗遛在这悲哀的处所。

她走过的路旁的枝干是凋零的,枯枝滴下厚泪到她低俯的头上;这些血是从隐痛处流下,也没有太阳来医,因为今年的太阳已经死去。

And dead leaves wrap the fruits that summer planted:
And birds that love the South have taken wing.
The wanderer, loitering o'er the scene enchanted,
Weeps, and despairs of spring.

William Ernest Henley

(1849—1903)

Unconquerable[1]

Out of the night that covers me,
Black as the pit from pole to pole,
I thank whatever gods may be
For my unconquerable soul.

In the fell clutch of circumstance
I have not winced nor cried aloud.
Under the bludgeonings of chance
My head is bloody, but unbow'd.

---

1 原诗题为 Invictus，是拉丁词，意指 unconquerable。——编者注

死叶包起夏天种下的树木的果子：喜欢南方的鸟儿早已振翼南飞。流荡者逗遛在这有魔力的境内，哭着，晓得春天是再也不回来。

刚 强 不 屈

从这遮盖着我的黑夜，那是蔽住了大地，黑得像深渊，我谢谢任何的天神，谢他给我以这个刚强不屈的灵魂。

在环境的残忍掌握之中，我从不退缩，从不痛呼。受了命运的鞭打，我的头是血淋淋，但是我不低头。

Beyond this place of wrath and tears
Looms but the Horror of the shade,
And yet the menace of the years
Finds and shall find me unafraid.

It matters not how strait the gate,
How charged with punishments the scroll,
I am the master of my fate,
I am the captain of my soul.

The full sea rolls and thunders
In glory and in glee.
O, bury me not in the senseless earth
But in the living sea!

Ay, bury me where it surges
A thousand miles from shore,
And in its brotherly unrest
I'll range for evermore.

这个受罚流泪的人世之后，隐隐地现出地府的"恐怖"，然而这多年的威吓不能使我恐惧，再过了多少年也是不能。

这是全不碍事的，不管到天堂的门是多么狭窄，不管天上的卷册写有多少的责罚，我总是我自己命运的主人，我总是我灵魂的司令。

☆　☆　☆

澎湃的大海光荣地快乐地怒卷雷鸣。阿，别葬我在毫无生气的大地，要葬我在这生气勃勃的海里！

葬我在远离海岸，怒涛汹涌的地方，在它那与我同气的不宁里，我将永久地漫游。

The Blackbird

The nightingale has a lyre of gold,
The lark's is a clarion call,
And the blackbird play but a boxwood flute,
But I love him best of all.

For his song is all of the joy of life,
And we in the mad, spring weather,
We two have listened till he sang
Our hearts and lips together.

The Passing

A late lark twitters from the quiet skies;
And from the west,
Where the sun, his day's work ended,
Lingers as in content,
There falls on the old, gray city
An influence luminous and serene,

乌　　鸦

夜莺有一张黄金的七弦琴，天鹨的声调是喇叭的呜呜，乌鸦只弄一把黄杨木的笛子，但是我却最喜欢他。

因为他的歌声说出人生的一切欣欢，我俩在疯狂的春天里听着，等到他唱得我们的心儿唇儿对对相连。

去　　世

一只迟留未去的天鹨在静寂的天上啭鸣；太阳做完了他这一天的工作，满意地淹留在西方，从那里降下一段光明安恬的气象，一种白亮的和平空气

A shining peace.

The smoke ascends
In a rosy-and-golden haze. The spires
Shine, and are changed. In the valley
Shadows rise. The lark sings on. The sun,
Closing his benediction,
Sinks, and the darkening air
Thrills with a sense of the triumphing night —
Night with her train of stars
And her great gift of sleep.

So be my passing!
My task accomplished and the long day done.
My wages taken, and in my heart
Some late lark singing,
Let me be gathered to the quiet west,
The sundown splendid and serene,
Death.

到这灰色的古城。

烟雾上升，那个一阵玫瑰色杂着黄金的烟雾。空中的许多尖塔被夕照照着发出艳光，一忽儿又变了颜色。山谷里阴影一一现出。天鹦还是唱着，太阳完结了他的祝福而下沉，朦胧转暗的光景忽然跳动，它感到了良夜的得胜——良夜带着星群同它伟大的礼物，睡眠。

我的去世也就这样罢！我的工作做成，悠长的时日过去。我的工钱拿了，在我心里有一个迟留未去的天鹦唱着，让我这样子归到恬静的西方罢，那是个光荣寂然的落日，那就是死。

Robert Louis Stevenson

(1850—1894)

Rain

The rain is raining all around,
It falls on field and tree,
It rains on the umbrellas here,
And on the ships at sea.

The Wind

I saw you toss the kites on high
And blow the birds about the sky;
And all around I heard you pass,
Like ladies' skirts across the grass —
O wind, a-blowing all day long,
O wind, that sings so loud a song!

I saw the different things you did,
But always you yourself you hid.
I felt you push, I heard you call,

雨

这雨是落到四方,它落到田里,落到树间,它落到这里的伞上,它又落到海上的船中。

风

我看你吹着纸鸢高飞,我看你吹着鸟儿四散在天中;四面我听你走过,像贵妇的裙子曳过青草的声音——呵,风呀,你整天地吹着,呵,风呵,你唱出一曲这么大声的歌调!

我看见你做各种不同的事情,但是你总是隐起了自己。我觉得你在后面推着,我听到你在呼唤,

I could not see yourself at all —
O wind, a-blowing all day long,
O wind, that sings so loud a song!

O you that are so strong and cold,
O blower, are you young or old?
Are you a beast of field and tree,
Or just a stronger child than me?
O wind, a-blowing all day long,
O wind, that sings so loud a song!

Young Night Thought

All night long and every night,
When my mama puts out the light,
I see the people marching by,
As plain as day, before my eye.

Armies and emperors and kings,
All carrying different kinds of things,

我却总不能够看得见你——呵风呀,你整天地吹着,呵风呀,你唱出一曲这么大声的歌调!

呵你是这么强壮寒冷,呵,吹者,你是年青还是年老?你是田野里树林间的一个走兽,还是不过一个比我强壮点的小孩?呵风呀,你整天地吹着,呵风呀,你唱出一曲这么大声的歌调!

小孩子晚上的梦想

整晚里,每晚里,当妈妈熄灯时候,我看见人们列队游行,同白天一样地分明,经过我的眼前。

军队,皇帝同国王,大家拿着不同的东西,这

And marching in so grand a way,
You never saw the like by day.

So fine a show was never seen
At the great circus on the green;
For every kind of beast and man
Is marching in that caravan.

At first they move a little slow,
But still the faster on they go, [1]
And still beside them close I keep
Until we reach the town of Sleep.

Alice Meynell

(1850—1923)[2]

The Shepherdess

She walks — the lady of my delight —
A shepherdess of sheep:
Her flocks are thoughts, she keeps them white;
She guards them from the steep;

么好看地游行,你在白天是绝没有看见。

这么有趣的赛会,你在草地里大马戏场中也没有看到;因为种种的兽和人都在这队里游行。

起先他们走得慢点,但是他们越走越快,我却是老站在近旁,一直等我们到了"睡乡"。

牧 羊 女 郎

她走着——我所喜欢的姑娘——一个牧羊的女郎:思想是她的羊群,她使他们老是洁白;她保护他们免得坠下悬岩;她驱他们就草在芳芬的高地,

---

1 But they go on still the faster.
2 其生卒年又作1847—1922年。——编者注

She feeds them from on the fragrant height,
And folds them in for sleep.

She roams maternal hills and bright,
Dark valleys safe and deep;
Into that tender breast at night
The chastest stars may peep.
She walks — the lady of my delight —
A shepherdess of sheep.

She holds her little thoughts in sight,
Though gay they run and leap,
She is so circumspect and right;
She has her soul to keep.
She walks — the lady of my delight —
A shepherdess of sheep.

At Night

Home, home from the horizon far and clear,
Hither the soft wings sweep;
Flocks of the memories of the day draw near

她晚上把他们关到栏里去安眠。

她漫游于光明慈爱的小山冈,以及安全幽深的阴谷;她那慈悲的心胸配得上夜间最纯洁星儿的窥视。她走着——我所喜欢的姑娘——一个牧羊的女郎。

她不让她轻轻的思想离开眼前,虽然她的思想是欣欢地跳跑,她是这么小心翼翼,这么守礼不乱;她好好地保着她的灵魂。她走着——我所喜欢的姑娘——一个牧羊的女郎。

夜　　间

从清澈悠远的天外回到家来,这群柔软的轻翼疾飞回来;这是白日里的一群记忆飞近"睡眠"的

The dovecote doors of sleep.

Oh, which are they that come through sweetest light
Of all these homing birds?
Which with the straightest and the swiftest flight?
Your words to me, your words!

Francis Thompson

(1857—1907)

Daisy

Where the thistle lifts a purple crown
Six foot out of the turf,
And the harebell shakes on the windy hill —
O the breath of the distant surf! —

The hills look over on the South,
And southward dreams the sea;
And, with the sea-breeze hand in hand,
Came innocence and she[1].

鸽舍门前。

啊，这些归鸟里那个是穿过最美的光景前来？那个是飞得最直最快？是你对我的细语，你的细语！

雏　　菊

在那里蓟树举起一个紫色的小冠，离开地面有六呎，钟形花也在山上临风招展——啊，那是远浪的气息！——

小山朝着南面，海也是望南长梦；"天真"和她与海风携手同来。

---

1 指雏菊。

Where 'mid the gorse the raspberry
Red for the gatherer springs,
Two children did we stray and talk
Wise, idle, childish things.

She listened with big-lipped surprise,
Breast-deep 'mid flower and spine:
Her skin was like a grape, whose veins
Run snow instead of wine.

She knew not those sweet words she spoke,
Nor knew her own sweet way,
But there's never a bird so sweet a song
Thronged in whose throat that day!

Oh, there were flowers in Storrington
On the turf and on the spray,
But the sweetest flower on Sussex hills
Was the Daisy-flower that day!

Her beauty smoothed earth's furrowed face!
She gave me tokens three: —

覆盆子抽红在金雀花丛中，等那采花的人们，在那里，我们这两个小孩慢游着，谈些聪明的，无所谓的，小孩气的话儿。

她露出嘴唇惊奇地聆着，花棘围到她的胸前：她的皮好似葡萄，血管里流着白雪，替了那甘酒。

她不晓她所说的甜蜜的话儿，她也不知她自己可爱的态度，但是那天里没有一只鸟儿歌喉里有这么可耳的歌儿！

啊，Storrington的泥上枝头有不少的鲜花，但是雏菊是Sussex小山里那天最可爱的花儿。

她的美丽铺平了有皱纹的地面！她给我以三件

A look, a word of her winsome mouth,
And a wild raspberry.

A berry red, a guileless look,
A still word, — strings of sand!
And yet they made my wild, wild heart
Fly down to her little hand.

For, standing artless as the air,
And candid as the skies,
She took the berries with her hand,
And the love with her sweet eyes.

The fairest things have fleetest end:
Their scent survives their close;
But the rose's scent is bitterness
To him that loved the rose!

She looked a little wistfully,
Then went her sunshine way; —

的纪念物：——一寸秋波，她那可人的口里一句话儿，同一粒的覆盆子。

一粒红红的浆果，一下无害的盼视，一声细细的话句，——这真是有如一串土砂！但是它们使我这狂热的心儿丢到她的手里。

她站着烂漫如风，坦白好似青天，她用她的手得到了浆果，她用她的美眸赢来了爱情。

最美的东西是最快灭亡：它们死了，它们的香气犹存；但是玫瑰死后剩下的芬芳是苦的，对着爱惜玫瑰的人们！

她现出微有所思的神气，然后顺她那阳光照着

The sea's eye had a mist on it,
And the leaves fell from the day.

She went her unremembering way,
She went, and left in me
The pang of all the partings gone,
And partings yet to be.

She left me marvelling why my soul
Was sad that she was glad;
At all the sadness in the sweet,
The sweetness in the sad.

Still, still I seemed to see her, still
Look up, with soft replies,
And take the berries with her hand,
And the love with her lovely eyes.

Nothing begins, and nothing ends,
That is not paid with moan;
For we are born in other's pain,
And perish in our own.

的道路而逝；——海的眼睛因此带了雾气，从那天起叶子也渐渐纷落。

她顺着她那踪迹不留的道路而逝，她去了，留下给我的是古往今来一切离别的悲伤。

她使我纳罕为甚我的心儿哀愁，当她欢乐的时候，以及纳罕一切欢乐里的愁思同一切悲愁里的乐绪。

我还是好像看到她，她还是含着柔软的回答望着，还是用她的手得到了浆果，还是用她的美眸赢来了爱情。

万物的始终都是用呻吟换来的！我们是从他人的苦痛里降世，我们自己又是苦痛地死去。

William Watson

（1858— ）[1]

Invention

I envy not the Lark his song divine,
Nor thee, O Maid, thy beauty's faultless mould.
Perhaps the chief felicity is mine,
Who hearken and behold.

The joy of the Artificer Unknown[2]
Whose genins could devise the Lark and thee —
This, or a kindred rapture, let me own.
I covet ceaselessly!

Leavetaking

Pass, thou wild light,
Wild light on peaks that so

---

1 其卒年为1935年。——编者注

发　　明

我不羡慕天鹨有他的神圣歌调，也不妒忌你，呵姑娘有你这样美丽无疵的身材。也许顶大的幸福是属于我的，这个听着看着的我。

"不知的大匠"的欣欢，他的英才能够创做出天鹨同你——让我说出真话罢，我是不停地想得到他的欣欢或者同类的大悦！

告　　别

消灭罢，你这狂热的阳光，你迟留在山颠，这

---

2 指"造物"。

Grieve to let go
The day.
Lovely thy tarrying, lovely too is night:
Pass thou away.

Pass, thou wild heart,
Wild heart of youth that still
Hast half a will
To stay.
I grow too old a comrade, let us part:
Pass thou away.

Alfred Edward Housman

(1859—   )[1]

When I was one-and-twenty
I heard a wise man say,
"Give crowns and pounds and guineas
But not your heart away;
Give pearls away and rubies
But keep your fancy free."
But I was one-and-twenty,
No use to talk to me.

样悲哀地不愿让白天走去。你这逗遛是可爱的,静夜却也是可爱的:你消灭罢。

消灭罢,你这狂热的心儿,青春的狂热心儿还是有些迟留不走的意思。我太老了,不好再同你结伴,我们还是分手罢:你消灭罢。

☆ ☆ ☆

当我是二十一岁,我听到一位聪明人说道,"尽可把金子银子给人,可是别送丢你的心儿;尽可以把真珠宝石给人,可是要留下了个自由的心儿。"但是我只是二十一岁,同我说是没有用的。

---

1 其卒年为1936年。——编者注

When I was one-and-twenty
I heard him say again,
"The heart out of the bosom
Was never given in vain;
'Tis paid with sighs a plenty
And sold for endless rue."
And I am two-and-twenty,
And oh, 'tis true, 'tis true.

Arthur Symons

(1865—   )[1]

Love in Dreams

I lie on my pallet bed,
And I hear the drip of the rain,
The rain on my garret roof is falling,
And I am cold and in pain.

I lie on my pallet bed,
And my heart is wild with delight;
I hear her voice through the midnight calling,
As I lie awake in the night.[2]

当我是二十一岁,我又听到他说,"心儿从胸里拿出给人是绝不会白送的;它换来无数的叹息,它市来不尽的悲伤。"我现在是二十二岁,呵,这话是真的,这话是真的。

梦里的爱情

我躺在我的草铺上面,我听到滴沥的声音,雨是落在我顶楼的屋顶,我冷着又感到了苦痛。

我躺在我的草铺上面,我的心里欣喜得发狂:午夜里我听她的声音正在呼唤,当夜里我清醒地躺着。

---

1 其卒年为1945年。——编者注
2 这时他已经有些离了现实,走到睡乡,下段的甜梦做成功了。

I lie on my pallet bed,
And I see her bright eyes gleam;
She smiles, she speakes, and the world is ended,
And made again in a dream.

Rain on the Down

Night, and the down by the sea,
And the veil of rain on the down;
And she came through the mist and the rain to me
From the safe warm lights of the town.

The rain shone in her hair,
And her face gleam'd in the rain;
And only the night and the rain were there
As she came to me out of the rain.

我躺在我的草铺上面,我看见她的双眸发出光辉;她笑了,她说话了,世界就消灭了,在梦中重新做过。

沙堤上的雨

夜里海边的沙堤,堤上雨下如帘;她从城中安全温暖的灯光里,穿雾穿雨来到我的跟前。

雨水在她发中发光,她的庞儿在雨里闪烁;外面只有黑夜同蒙雨,当她从雨里来到我的跟前。

William Butler Yeats

(1865—   )[1]

The Lake Isle of Innisfree

I will arise and go now, and go to Innisfree,
And a small cabin build there, of clay and wattles made;
Nine bean rows will I have there, a hive for the honey-bee,
And live alone in the bee-loud glade.

And I shall have some peace there, for peace comes dropping slow,
Dropping from the veils of the morning to where the cricket sings;
There midnight's all a glimmer, and noon a purple glow,
And evening full of the linnet's wings.

I will arise and go now, for always night and day
I hear lake water lapping with low sounds by the shore;
While I stand on the roadway, or on the pavements gray,

---

1 其卒年为1939年。——编者注

湖中的小岛 Innisfree

我要站起,现在要走了,走到 Innisfree 去,在那里盖起一间小茅屋,那是泥土同树枝做的;我要种九排菽豆,筑一个蜂巢给蜜蜂儿,就孤寂地住在那蜂声营营的林中荫地。

在那里我将得到宁静的境界,因为宁静是慢慢地滴滴流下,从晨曦的薄雾滴到蟋蟀细吟的所在;在那里午夜是一片微光,中午是紫红如火,黄昏就满是红雀的飞翼。

我要站起,现在要走了,因为朝朝夜夜我老是听到河水拍岸的低声;当我站在路上,或者灰

I hear it in the deep heart's core.

Ernest Dowson

(1867—1900)

> They are not long the weeping and the laughter,
> Love and desire and hate:
> I think they have no portion in us after
> We pass the gate.
>
> They are not long, the days of wine and roses:
> Out of a misty dream
> Our path emerges for a while, then closes
> Within a dream.

A. E. (George William Russell)

(1867—   )[1]

Frolic

> The children were shouting together
> And racing along the sands,

色的侧道，我也在自己心中的深处听到河水拍岸的低声。

☆ ☆ ☆

哭，笑，爱，欲，憎，它们都是不长久的：我想它们与我们会无纠葛，当我们走过了死门。

美酒蔷薇的日子，也是不长久的：我们的路是从模糊的梦里暂时现出，然后又隐到一场梦中去了。

行　　乐

小孩们结群欢呼，缘着沙岸飞奔，只见一瞥的

---

1 其卒年为1935年。——编者注

A glimmer of dancing shadows.
A dovelike flutter of hands.

The stars were shouting in heaven,
The sun was chasing the moon:
The game was the same as the children's,
They danced to the self-same tune.

The whole of the world was merry.
One joy from the vale to the height,
Where the blue woods of twilight encircled
The lovely lawns of the light.

Stephen Phillips

(1868—1915)

My dead Love came to me, and said:
"God gives me one hour's rest,
To spend upon the earth with thee:
How shall we spend it best?"

"Why, as of old, " I said, and so

舞影。小手乱摇，好似鸽子的鼓翼。

星群在天上欢呼，太阳追赶月亮：它们的游戏正同小孩一样，他们是照着同一的调儿舞蹈。

全宇宙都觉快乐。一种的欣欢从深谷直到苍穹，在那里暮霭中的蓝树围着可爱的光明空地。

☆ ☆ ☆

我已死的爱人来对我说："上帝给我一点钟的休息，到地上和你相聚，我们要怎样地好好用这时光呢？"

"当然是照旧过活，"我说，于是我们照旧吵

We quarrelled as of old.
But when I turned to make my peace,
That one short hour was told.

New "De Profundis" [1]

Out from the mist, the mist, I cry;
Let not my soul of numbness die!
My life is furled in every limb,
And my existence groweth dim.
My senses all like weapons rust,
And lie disused in endless dust.
I may not love, I may not hate;
Slowly I feel my life abate.

O would there were a heaven to hear!
O would there were a hell to fear!
Ah, welcome fire, eternal fire,
To burn for ever and not tire!
Better Ixion's[2] whirling wheel,

1　out of the deeps 从（心的）深处出（意指悲哀的呼声）。

嘴。但是当我转身来向她说和,那短短的一点钟却已过去。

新时代的悲哀

从阴霾里,从阴霾里,我大声叫喊:别让我的灵魂麻木死去!我的精力是四肢卷起,我的生存是渐归暗澹。我的感官全像武器那样生锈,躺着无用在无边的尘里。我不会爱人,我不会憎人,慢慢地我觉到我的生命销沉。

呵,真希望有个上帝来听我的祈祷!呵,真希望有个地狱来使我害怕!呀,欢迎烈火的来临,不灭的烈火,永久烧着,而不使我厌闷!还是尝受地

---

2 希腊神话中Ixion被罚在地狱中老是跟着一个旋轮旋转。

And still at any cost to feel!
Dear Son of God, in mercy give
My soul to flame, but let me live.

I am discouraged by the street,
The pacing of monotonous feet;
Faces of all emotion purged;
From nothing unto nothing urged;
The living men that shadows go,
A vain procession to and fro.
The earth an unreal course doth run,
Haunted by a phantasmal sun.

Thou didst create me keen and bright,
Of hearing exquisite and sight.
Look on thy creature, muffled, furled,
That has no glory in thy world,
In odours that like arrows dart,
Beauty that overwhelms the heart.
I neither hear, nor smell, nor see;
But only glide perpetually.

府旋轮的苦痛罢,不管化了多大代价,总得做到感官不死!亲爱的上帝之子,大慈大悲地把我的灵魂投到烈火里去罢,可是让我生气勃勃地活着。

我走上街上真觉得气馁,为着单调的脚步往来;为着那情感完全丧失的脸孔;他们被驱从虚空去追捉虚空;活人却像影子来来往往的无聊一队人们。地球走个空幻的道路,一个虚幻的太阳老在纠缠。

上帝造我锐敏又光明,耳目都也伶俐。现在看你所做的生物罢,聪明尽丧,简直不感到你的世界的光荣,在尖利如飞箭的香里,在醉人心儿的美里。我是无闻无嗅又无视;却只是不歇地寂然潜行。

I seem to feel upon my soul
The slow approach, the gradual roll
Of Darkness older than the light,
Of blackness gaining on the bright.
O wasted is that wine like blood,
Wasted the flesh that was our food!
If in the dimness without strife
I perish, life, O give me life!

William Henry Davies

(1870—)[1]

The Moon

Thy beauty haunts me heart and soul,
Oh thou fair Moon, so close and bright;
Thy beauty makes me like the child,
That cries aloud to own thy light:
The little child that lifts each arm
To press thee to her bosom warm.

Though there are birds that sing this night

我好像觉得光明以前的黑暗同侵占光明的漆黑渐渐地卷地前来，慢慢地走到我灵魂上面。呵，如血的酒是白花了，我们所食的肉也是白花了！若使我毫无奋斗地消灭在朦胧之中，生命，呵，给我以生命罢！

月

你的清辉萦着我的心灵，呵你这好月，这么近人，这么光明；你的美丽使我喜欢那高声索求，想得你光的小孩：那小孩接连地举起他的左右臂，想将你拥在她温暖的胸怀。

虽然今晚有鸟歌唱，你的白光横着它们的咽喉，

---

1 其生卒年又作1871—1940年。——编者注

With thy white beams across their throats,
Let my deep silence speak for me
More than for them their sweetest notes:
Who worships thee till music fails
Is greater than thy nightingales.

Leisure

What is this life if full of care,
We have no time to stand and stare?

No time to stand beneath the boughs
And stare as long as sheep or cows.

No time to see, when woods we pass,
Where squirrels hide their nuts in grass.

No time to see in broad daylight,
Streams full of stars, like skies at night.

让我这深沉的静默说出我的赞美,更胜于它们最悦耳的歌声吐出它们的胸臆:崇拜你到音乐不足以达热忱的人,他的积悃是更强于你的夜莺。

闲　　暇

这是一种什么生活,若使满腹忧愁,我们没有时间站着闲眺?

没有时间站在树枝底下像牛羊那样长久地闲眺。

没有时间去看松鼠在那处将它们的坚果藏在草里,当我们走过森林的一旁。

没有时间在光天化日之下去看溪流里满是星群,有如夜里的天空;

No time to turn at Beauty's glance,
And watch her feet, how they can dance.

No time to wait till her mouth can
Enrich that smile her eyes began.

A poor life this if, full of care,
We have no time to stand and stare.

Truly Great

My walls outside must have some flowers,
My walls within must have some books,
A house that's small; a garden large,
And in it leafy nooks.

A little gold that's sure each week;
That comes not from my living kind,
But from a dead man in his grave,
Who cannot change his mind.

没有时间为着美人的一顾而回首,去看她的双脚,瞧它们会怎样地舞着。

没有时间去等候她的口完成她双眼所发的笑颜。

那真是一种可怜的生活,若使满腹忧愁,我们没有时间站着闲望。

真正的伟大

我的墙外一定要几树花,我的墙内一定要几本书,一间小小的屋子;一所宽阔的花园,里面有绿荫深闭的僻处。

一点每星期准会来的金钱;那不是从我们的活人得到,却是得自墓中不会变心的一位死人。

A lovely wife, and gentle too;
Contented that no eyes but mine
Can see her many charms, nor voice
To call her beauty fine.

Where she would in that stone cage live,
A self-made prisoner, with me;
While many a wild bird sang around,
On gate, on bush, on tree.

And she sometimes to answer them,
In her far sweeter voice than all;
Till birds, that loved to look on leaves,
Will doat on a stone wall.

With this small house, this garden large,
This little gold, this lovely mate,
With health in body, peace at heart —
Show me a man more great.

一位温柔可爱的妻子,她情愿只有我的眼睛看见她的许多风韵,也没有别人来赞美她的姿容。

她也愿在这石笼里与我同住,一个甘心自囚的人儿;当许多野鸟叫唤于四围,在门上,在枝头,在树间。

有时她回答它们,用她那远胜众音的妙喉;等到爱瞧绿叶的鸟儿也喜欢了这一片石墙。

有了这一所小屋,这块大园,这点金钱,这位良伴,身健又心宁——你能指出一个更伟大的人吗。

Walter de la Mare

(1873—)[1]

The Stranger

Half-hidden in a graveyard,
In the blackness of a yew,
Where never living creature stirs,
Nor sunbeam pierces through.

Is a tomb, lichened and crooked—
Its faded legend gone—
With but one rain-worn cherub's head
Of mouldering stone.

There, when the dusk is falling,
Silence broods so deep,
It seems that every wind that breathes
Blows from the fields of sleep.

Day breaks in headless beauty,

生　人

半隐在坟地之中，深藏于扁柏黑影之下，那里绝无生物走动，太阳光也穿不过。

有一座满是青苔的颓废古坟——它模糊的题语早已消失——只有一个小天使的头部，那也被雨蚀得只剩一块烂石。

在那里当暮色渐浓，静默是这么深深地居在那里，好似每阵吹来的微风都是从睡国吹来。

日出灿烂，却无人注意，朝暾燃着滴滴的露珠。

1　其卒年为1956年。——编者注

Kindling each drop of dew,
But unforsaking shadow dwells
Beneath this lonely yew.

And, all else lost and faded,
Only this listening head
Keeps with a strange, unanswering smile
Its secret with the dead.

An Epitaph

Here lies a most beautiful lady,
Light of step and heart was she;
I think she was the most beautiful lady
That ever was in the West Country.
But beauty vanishes; beauty passes;
However rare — rare it be;
And when I crumble, who will remember
This lady of the West Country?

但是这寂寞的扁柏树下却住有永不他去的阴影。

别的一切全消失了,模糊了,只有这个倾耳静聆的头像呈出一种奇怪的,沉默的微笑,和死人一起守着它的秘密。

墓　　铭

这里躺有一个最标致的姑娘,她的脚步轻盈,她的心儿快乐;我想"西乡"里从没有过这么美丽的姑娘。但是美丽云烟般消失了;美丽成为过去了;不管那是多么难得——多么难得;当我死后,谁还记得"西乡"里这位姑娘?

Silver

Slowly, silently, now the moon
Walks the night in her silver shoon;
This way, and that, she peers, and sees
Silver fruit upon silver trees;
One by one the casements catch
Her beams beneath the silvery thatch;
Couched in his kennel, like a log,
With paws of silver sleeps the dog;
From their shadowy cote the white breasts peep
Of doves in a silver-feathered sleep;
A harvest mouse goes scampering by,
With silver claws, and silver eye;
And moveless fish in the water gleam,
By silver reeds in a silver stream.

银　　色

　　慢慢地，寂寂地，现在月亮穿她银色的鞋子，走过良夜；向这边又向那边窥视，看到银色的树长有银色的果子；银色的茅草底下的窗扉一一得到她的光芒；卧在狗舍里像一块木头，一只狗睡着蹲在他银色的四跖；从阴暗的鸽棚，鸽子的白胸露出，它们睡着，两翅白得如银，一个秋收时的耗子奔窜过去，带着银色的脚爪同银色的眼睛；不动的鱼在水里发光，依在一个银色的水里的银色芦苇之傍〔旁〕。

Wilfrid Wilson Gibson

(1878—　)[1]

The Messages

"I cannot quite remember, ... There were five
Dropt dead beside me me in the trench — and three
Whispered their dying messages to me..."

Back from the trenches, more dead than alive,
Stone-deaf and dazed, and with a broken knee,
He hobbled slowly, muttering vacantly:

"I cannot quite remember, ...There were five
Dropt dead beside me in the trench — and three
Whispered their dying messages to me...

"Their friends are waiting, wondering how they thrive —
Waiting a word in silence patiently...
But what they said, or who their friends may be

---

[1] 其卒年为1962年。——编者注

遗　　言

"我不能十分记得……在战壕里我身边有五个倒下死去——三个向我低声说出他们临终的遗言……"

从战壕回来，不像活人像死人，完全聋了，并且晕眩，拖着已折的膝头，他慢慢地跛行，胡里胡涂地喃喃道：

"我不能十分记得……在战壕里我身边有五个倒下死去——三个向我低声说出他们临终的遗言……

"他们的朋友们等着，正在纳罕他们是怎样好好地过活——静静地耐心等候他们的一言……但是他们说了什么，同他们的朋友们是谁，我却不能十分

> "I cannot quite remember... There were five
> Dropt dead beside me in the trench — and three
> Whispered their dying messages to me..."

John Masefield

(1878—   )[1]

Sea-Fever

I must go down to the seas again, to the lonely sea and the sky,
And all I ask is a tall ship and a star to steer her by,
And the wheel's kick and the wind's song, and the White sail's shaking,
And a grey mist on the sea's face, and the grey dawn breaking.

I must go down to the seas again, for the call of the running tide
Is a wild call and a clear call that may not be denied;
And all I ask is a windy day with the white clouds flying,
And the flung spray and the blown spume, and the

记得……在战壕里我身边有五个倒下死去——三个向我说出他们临终的遗言……"

航海的热狂

我必定要再到大海里去,去那寂寞的大海同海上的青天,我所需的只是一只高大的海船同一颗指示方向的星儿,舵轮的跳动,海风的狂啸同白帆的震荡,海面一片的灰雾和破晓时的灰色晨光。

我必定要再到大海里去,因为怒潮的呼唤是一种狂野的呼唤,一种清澈的呼唤,那是不能蔑视;我所需的只是狂风的日子,白云高飞,浪花,飞沫

---

1 其卒年为1967年。——编者注

seagull's crying.

I must go down to the seas again, to the vagrant gypsy life,
To the gull's way and the whale's way, where the wind's like a whetted knife,
And all I ask is a merry yarn from a laughing fellow-rover,
And a quiet sleep and a sweet dream when the long trick's over.

The Seekers

Friends and loves we have none, nor wealth nor blessed abode,
But the hope, the burning hope, and the road, the open road.

Not for us are content, and quiet and peace of mind,
For we go seeking cities that we shall never find.

同海鸥的哀泪。

我必定要再到大海里去，去过流浪的游民生涯，走上海鸥鲸鱼的道路，那里风是像磨过的利刀，我所需的只是一个哈哈笑的流浪伴侣，信口说的一篇快乐故事，以及恬静的睡眠同甜蜜的好梦，当这长久的把戏已作过去。

探 寻 者

我们没有朋友和爱人，也没有财富同安居，却只有希望，火一般热的希望，和道路，通行的大路。

满足，平静同心宁这全是与我们无分的，因为我们是去找那我们将永找不到的城廓。

There is no solace on earth for us — for such as we —
Who search for the hidden beauty that eyes may never see.

Only the road and the dawn, the sun, the wind, and the rain,
And the watch fire under the stars, and sleep, and the road again.

We seek the city of God, and the haunt where beauty dwells,
And we find the noisy mart and the sound of burial bells.

Never the golden city, where radiant people meet,
But the dolorous town where mourners are going about the street.

We travel the dusty road, till the light of the day is dim,
And sunset shows us spires away on the world's rim.

We travel from dawn to dusk, till the day is past and by,
Seeking the holy city beyond the rim of the sky.

世上不能给我们什么安慰——对于像我们这样的人们——我们是探求也许永不瞧见的隐晦美丽。

我们所有的只是大路和清晨，太阳，风风同雨雨，星群底下守夜的警火，睡觉，醒后重走上大路。

我们探求上帝的都城，"美丽"的去处，我们所遇的却只是喧哗的市场同葬钟的声音。

我们绝没有碰到灿烂的人们所会聚的黄金城廓，却只是悲哀的市镇，在那里伤心的人们来往街上。

我们走着尘埃四起的道路，等到白天的光线化为暗淡，夕阳却照出世界边端以外的尖塔。

我们从清早走到黄昏，等到白天过去了，我们老是寻找天边以外的圣城。

Friends and loves we have none, nor wealth nor blessed abode,
But the hope, the burning hope, and the road, the open road.

James Stephens

(1882—   )[1]

Hate

My enemy came nigh,
And I
Stared fiercely in his face,
My lips went writhing back in a grimace,
And stern I watched him with a narrow eye,
Then, as I turned away, my enemy,
That bitter heart and savage, said to me:
"Some day, when this is past,
When all the arrows that we have are cast,
We may ask one another why we hate,
And fail to find a story to relate.
It may seem to us then a mystery

我们没有朋友和爱人,也没有财富同安居,却只有希望,火一般热的希望和道路,通行的大路。

恨

我的敌人走近,我就凶狠地睁着眼睛望他的脸孔,我的双唇反卷进去,存在一付鬼脸之中,我用缩成一线的眼睛,严厉地注视着他。当我将转身走去,我的敌人,那个狠心,那个野人,对我说道:"有一天,当这些事过去了,当我们所有的箭矢全射完了,我们也许会相问为什么我们相恨,而不能说出一个缘由。那时我们也许觉得这简直是个神秘,

---

1 其卒年为1950年。——编者注

That we could hate each other."

Thus said he,

And did not turn away,

Waiting to hear what I might have to say;

But I fled quickly, fearing if I stayed

I might have kissed him as I would a maid.

我们当初会那样互恨。"他这么说着,却不走开,等着听我有什么话说;但是我赶快跑开,怕的是若使我滞着,我会吻他,好似我吻一位姑娘。

Madrigal

情　歌

（英汉对照）

梁遇春　译注

"英文小丛书"之一，上海北新书局，1931年10月付排，1931年11月初版

CONTENTS

目　　次

Elizabethan Love Songs by Unknown Authors

Madrigal

情歌 …………………………………………………… 460

Love Me...

爱我…… ………………………………………………… 460

The Wakening

睡醒 …………………………………………………… 462

Chloris in the Snow

雪中的 Chloris ………………………………………… 464

Sir Philip Sidney(1554—1586)

Wooing Stuff

求婚的资料 …………………………………………… 466

Michael Drayton(1563—1618)

The Parting

分别 ·· 470

William Shakespeare(1564—1616)

(缺目) ·· 472

Thomas Campion(1567—1619)

(缺目) ·· 474

John Donne(1573—1631)

The Ecstasy

狂欢 ·· 478

Robert Herrick(1591—1674)

To Electra

呈 Electra ·· 482

The Primrose

莲馨花 ·· 482

The Bracelet: To Julia

手镯：呈 Julia ·· 484

To Daisies

致雏菊 ·· 486

Robert Burns(1759—1796)

Mary Morison

Mary Morison ·· 488

Bonnie Lesley

美丽的 Lesley ·· 490

Highland Mary

山地的 Mary ·· 494

Samuel Taylor Coleridge(1772—1834)

Recollections of Love

爱之回忆 ·· 498

Water Ballad

水调 ·· 500

To Lesbia

致 Lesbia ··· 502

（缺目）··· 504

Leigh Hunt(1784—1859)

（缺目）··· 506

George Gordon Byron (1788—1824)

（缺目）··· 508

Percy Bysshe Shelley(1792—1822)

（缺目）··· 510

John Keats(1795—1821)

（缺目）··· 512

Alfred Tennyson(1809—1892)

（缺目）··· 514

Robert Browning(1812—1889)

（缺目） ·· 516

Christina Georgina Rossetti(1830—1894)

A Birthday
诞生之辰 ·· 518

Echo
回声 ·· 520

The Poor Ghost
可怜的鬼 ·· 522

Thomas Hardy(1840—1928)

Without Ceremony
不拘礼 ·· 526

The Haunter
缠绕身旁的幽灵 ·· 528

A Dream or No
梦耶非耶 ·· 532

After a Journey
旅途之后 ·· 534

Beeny Cliff
Beeny峭壁 ··· 538

The Phantom Horsewoman
骑马女子的魅影 ·· 542

Her Father
她的爸爸 ················· 546
At Waking
醒时 ················· 550

Laurence Hope

The Net of Memory
记忆的网子 ················· 552
Song of Ramesram Temple Girl
Ramesram 庙里少女之歌 ················· 554
On Pilgrimage
参诣圣地的途中 ················· 558
Disappointment
失望 ················· 560

跋 ················· 570

Elizabethan Love Songs by Unknown Authors

Madrigal

My Love[1] in her attire doth show her wit,
It doth so well become her;
For every season she hath dressings fit,
For Winter, Spring and Summer.

No beauty she doth miss
When all her robes are on[2]:
But Beauty's self[3] she is,
When all her robes are gone.

Love Me...

Love me not for comely grace,

---

1 Love: sweetheart; lover 爱人；情人。
2 on: attached to a body 着在身上。

情　歌

我的爱人在她衣服上显出她的聪明，那跟她是这么相称；每季里她都有适当的衣裳，不论是春夏或冬天。

当她盛装的时候，人间的美丽她全具有了；但是脱尽了身上的衣裳，她却是"美丽"的化身。

爱我……

爱我，不要为着温婉的姿容，不要为着我这悦

---

3 Beauty's self: 把"美丽"当作是一个人，这种办法在修辞学里叫做personification，"活喻"或"拟人法"，这样用时，常把那个字的第一个字母拿来大写。

For my pleasing eye or face,
Nor for any outward part,
No, nor for my constant heart, —
For those may fail or turn to ill,
So thou and I shall sever.

Keep therefore a true woman's eye,
And love me still[1], but know not why —
So hast thou the same reason still
To doat upon me ever!

The Wakening

On a time the amorous Silvy
Said to her shepherd, "Sweet[2], how do ye?
Kiss me this once and then God be with ye,
My sweetest dear!
Kiss me this once and then God be with ye,
For now the morning draweth near."

---

1 still: always 老是；永远。
2 sweet: sweetheart 爱人儿。

人的眼睛或者庞儿，不要为着我的外表，不，也不要为着我的忠心，——因为这些会失效了，或者变坏了，那么你我就得分离。

所以请留个真正女人的眼睛，老是爱我，却不知道为着什么——那么，你可以老有个同一的理由，来永远向我钟情！

睡　　醒

有一回，多情的 Silvy 向她的牧羊郎说："爱人儿，你睡得好吗？吻我这一下，愿上帝保佑你，我最甜蜜的爱人呀！吻我这一下，愿上帝保佑你，因为现在清晨已将来临。"

With that, her fairest bosom showing,
Op'ning her lips, rich perfumes blowing,
She said, "Now kiss me and be going,
My sweetest dear!
Kiss me this once and then be going,
For now the morning draweth near."

With that the shepherd waked from sleeping,
And spying where the day was peeping,
He said, "Now take my soul in keeping,
My sweetest dear!
Kiss me and take my soul in keeping.
Since I must go, now day is near."

Chloris in the Snow

I saw fair Chloris walk alone,
When feather'd rain[1] came softly down,
As Jove[2] descending from his Tower

---

1 指雪花。

于是，露出她艳丽的胸膛，展开双唇，吹出馥郁的香气，她说："请就吻我，走开罢，我最甜蜜的爱人！吻我这一下，然后走开，因为现在清晨已将来临。"

于是，牧羊郎从睡里醒来，眯着眼看清晨已在那儿窥视，他说："现在请将我的灵魂保存起来，我最甜蜜的爱人！吻我，将我的灵魂保存起来。因为我是必得走开，现在清晨快来了。"

雪中的 Chloris

我看见标致的 Chloris 独自走着，当毛羽般的雨花轻微地飞来，那是天帝从他的塔上降落人间，在

---

2 Jove：希腊神话里的"天帝"可是不像我们的"玉皇"那么规矩却极喜欢人世的浪漫情事，做出了许多蕴藉的勾当，有时也遭他老婆的妒忌。希腊人说到天神，还要叫他具有人间性，于此也可以看出他们的精神是多么"人的"，真是迷醉于人生了，绝对地忠于"地之母"的。

To court her in a silver shower:
The wanton snow flew to her breast,
Like pretty birds into their nest,
But, overcome with whiteness there,
For grief it thaw'd into a tear,
Thence falling on her garments' hem,
To deck her, froze into a gem.

Sir Philip Sidney

(1554—1586)

Wooing Stuff

Faint Amorist[1], what! dost thou think
To taste love's honey, and not drink
One dram of gall? Or to devour
A world of sweet and taste no sour?
Dost thou ever think to enter
The Elysian[2] fields, that dar'st not venture
In Charon's[3] barge? A lover's mind
Must use[4] to sail with every wind.

银丝的急雨里向她献出殷勤：贪欢的雪花飞到她怀里，有如艳鸟的入巢，但是不比她酥胸的洁白，它悲哀得化成一滴清泪，然后掉到她的衣缘，为着装饰她，冻成为一粒宝石。

求婚的资料

胆小的爱人，怎么，你想尝到爱的甜蜜，不喝一滴苦水吗？或者狼吞无限的甘味，不尝一下酸辛吗？你不敢坐着 Charon 的船冒险倒会打算进乐园去吗？一个爱人的心应当是遇什么风都能受下。爱着，

---

1 amorist: a gallant 情人，风流自喜者。
2 Elysian: of Elysium（abode of the blessed after death 死后上天堂的人们所住的地方）。
3 Charon: ferryman taking souls to Hades 渡灵魂到地狱去的船夫。
4 to use: to be accustomed to 惯于。

He that loves, and fears to try,
Learns¹ his mistress to deny.

Doth she chide thee? 'tis to show it
That thy coldness makes her do it.
Is she silent? is she mute?
Silence fully grants thy suit.
Doth she pout, and leave the room?
Then she goes to bid thee come.
Is she sick? Why then be sure
She invites thee to the cure.
Doth she cross thy suit with No?
Tush, she loves to hear thee woo.
Doth she call the faith of man
In question? Nay, she loves thee than²;
And if ere she makes a blot.
She's lost if that thou hit'st her not.
He that after ten denials
Dares attempt no further trials,
Hath no warrant to acquire
The dainties of his chaste desire.

又怕尝试的人简直是教他的爱人来拒绝他。

她骂你吗？那是做出给你看，你的冷淡使她生气。她不说话吗？她默然吗？静默是完全答应了你的请求。她努嘴，走出房子吗？她走去就是叫你来。她病了吗？吓呀，那么她一定要叫你去医她。她用个"不"字来挡住你的请求吗？咄，她喜欢听你求婚的情话。她说出不信男人是有真情吗？不，她那时已爱着你了；在她露出破绽之前，你失掉她了，若使你不乘虚攻击。受到十次的拒绝，就不敢再试一下的人是不配尝到他所诚心渴望的佳味。

---

1 learns: this verb was commonly employed with a personal object in Elizabethan English.
2 than：than这字同前注"learns"的用法现在皆已不通行。

Michael Drayton

(1563—1618)[1]

The Parting

Since there's no help, come, let us kiss and part—
Nay, I have done[2], you get no more of me;
And I am glad, yea, glad with all my heart,
That thus so cleanly I myself can free.
Shake hands for ever[3], cancel all our vows,
And when we meet at any time again,
Be it not seen in either of our brows
That we one jot of former love retain.

Now at the last gasp of Love's latest breath,
When, his pulse failing, Passion[4] speechless lies,
When Faith is kneeling by his bed of death[5],
And Innocence is closing up his eyes[6], —

---

1 其卒年应为1631年。——编者注
2 to have done: to have made an end 了事;已了。
3 for ever: eternally 永远。
4 Passion: 即前行的"Love"。

分　　别

　　既是无可奈何了，来，让我们一吻而别罢——不，我已跟你决绝了，你不能再得我的什么；我很高兴，是的，满心高兴，我能够这么干净地解放自己。握手永诀罢，我们的誓言都付诸东流，当我们此后不论何时重见，我们两人的眉梢不要露出我们还留有一点前情。

　　现在当"爱情"奄奄一息的最后喘气时候，当他的脉消沉，"热情"不则一声地躺着，当"忠心"跪在他死床的一旁，"天真"把他的眼睛闭起，——

5　bed of death：bed on which one dies 有人在上面死去之床。
6　closing up his eyes：指替死人把眼睛闭起。

Now If thou wouldst, when all have given him over[1],
From death to life thou might'st him yet recover.

William Shakespeare

(1564—1616)

When in the chronicle of wasted[2] time
I see descriptions of the fairest wights,
And beauty making beautiful old rime[3],
In praise of ladies dead and lovely knights,
Then, in the blazon[4] of sweet beauty's best,
Of hand, of foot, of lip, of eye, of brow,
I see their antique pen would have express'd
Even such a beauty as you master[5] now.
So all their praises are but prophecies
Of this our time, all you prefiguring;
And, for they look'd but with divining eyes,
They had not skill enough your worth to sing:
For we, which now behold these present days,

---

1 to give over: to conclude lost 认为无希望了。
2 wasted: past 过去的。

现在,若使你愿意,当大家都以为他绝望了,你还可以使他从死里回生。

☆ ☆ ☆

当我在过去的纪录里看见描写出绝代佳人,她的艳丽使古韵增光,当他们赞美已死的贵妇和可爱的骑士;那时看他们描摹个无上的甜蜜人儿,说出她的手脚唇眼和眉,我觉得古人的手是写下你现在所具有的这副姿容。所以他们一切的赞美只是预言我们此刻的时光,全是揣度你们的风度;因为他们只是猜拟,所以他们的才力不足以歌颂你的光荣:我们现在见到你了,

---

3 rime:rhyme 韵。
4 blazon:description 描写。
5 to master:to be the master of 具有。

Have eyes to wonder, but lack tongues to praise.

Thomas Campion

(1567—1619)

I

Blame not my cheeks, though pale with love they be;
The kindly heat unto my heart is flown,
To cherish it that is dismayed by thee,
Who art so cruel and unsteadfast[1] grown:
For Nature, called for[2] by distressed hearts,
Neglects and quite forsakes the outward parts.

II

But they whose cheeks with careless blood are stained,
Nurse not one spark of love within their hearts;
And when they woo, they speak with passion feigned,
For their fat love lies in their outward parts:
But in their breasts, where love his court should hold,

---

1 unsteadfast: not constant 不忠心。
2 called for: demanded 被要求。

只有眼睛出奇地痴望着,却缺乏舌头去赞扬。

☆ ☆ ☆

I

不要责难我的双颊,虽然它们为爱情而惨白了;可喜的热力飞到我的心里,去滋养给你吓住了的心儿,因为你变得这么残酷同无常;"自然"一听到焦急心儿的呼唤,忘却了,全扔下了,外表的光荣。

II

可是颊儿涨着无聊红血的人们,他们心里没有燃起一星的情火;他们求婚,他们说的却是一片假情,因为他们痴肥的爱情都是排在面上:在他们胸中,那是爱情的朝廷,可怜的"爱神"却坐着冻得

Poor Cupid sits and blows his nails for cold.

Sleep, angry beauty[1], sleep, and fear not me.
For who a sleeping lion dares provoke?
It shall suffice me[2] here to sit and see
Those lips shut up, that never kindly spoke.
What sight can more content a lover's mind
Than beauty seeming harmless, if not kind?

My words have charmed her, for secure she sleeps,
Though guilty much of wrong done to my love;
And in her slumber, see! She, close-eyed, weeps!
Dreams often more than waking passions move.
Plead, Sleep, my cause, and make her soft like thee,
That she in peace may wake and pity me.

III

O sweet delight, O more than human bliss,
With her to live that ever loving is;
To hear her speak, whose words are so well placed,

---

1 beauty: beautiful lady 美人。
2 to suffice me: to meet my needs 应我的需要。

呵手取暖。

睡着罢，生气的美人，睡着罢，别要怕我。谁敢惹一只睡狮呢？坐着，看这双绝未曾说过缠绵细语的嘴唇闭紧，这于我已经够了。什么东西更能满足一个爱人的心，比起美人好像是无害的，虽然并不殷勤？

我的话对于她施展出魔力了，因为她伏贴贴地睡着，虽然很得罪了我的爱情；在她睡里，你看，她闭着眼睛呜咽！梦常比醒时更易动情。睡神，替我说话罢，把她弄得同你一样的温柔，那么她会在恬静之中醒来，对我感到怜悯。

Ⅲ

啊，甜蜜的快乐，超过人世的幸福，跟她住在一起，她总是这么亲爱；听她的谈吐，她的话是这

That she by them, as they in her are graced:
Those looks to view, that feast the viewer's eye,
How blest is he that may so live and die!

Such love as this the golden times did know,
When all did reap, yet none took care to sow;
Such love as this an endless summer makes,
And all distaste from frail affection takes.
So loved, so blessed, in my beloved am I,
Which till their eyes ache let iron men envy!

John Donne

(1573—1631)

The Ecstasy

Where, like a pillow on a bed,
A pregnant[1] bank swelled up to rest
The violet's reclining head,
Sat we two, one another's best.

---

1 pregnant: fertile 丰饶。

么巧妙地安排,她同她的话儿真是彼此互增了光辉:看见这样的形容,那使观者的眼睛饱餐秀色,这样活着,这样死去的人是多么有福!

像这样的爱情真是走到黄金时代了,那时都得到收获,谁也用不着去下种;像这样的爱做出永久的夏天,使薄情失掉了一切的滋味。如此被爱着,如此有福,是我于我的情人,让铁石人嫉妒得眼睛疼痛罢!

狂　　欢

那里,像床上的枕头,有丰满的山坡隆起,让紫罗兰斜倚着的花冠休息,就在那儿,我俩坐着,都是彼此心里最得意的人儿。

Our hands were firmly cemented
By a fast balm which thence did spring;
Our eye-beams twisted, and did thread
Our eyes upon one double string.

So to engraft our hands, as yet
Was all the means to make us one;
And pictures in our eyes to get
Was all our propagation.

As 'twixt two equal armies, Fate
Suspends uncertain victory,
Our Souls — which to advance their state
Were gone out — hung 'twixt her and me.

And whilst our souls negotiate there,
We like sepulchral[1] statues lay;
All day the same our postures were,
And we said nothing all the day.

---

1 sepulchral: of the grave 坟墓的。

我们的手是坚牢地黏着,它们紧握时所生的香油把它们胶住;我们的眼线编织,用一条双行的线把我们的眼睛缝在一起。

所以,使我俩更成为一人的惟一媒介还只是我们的手枝枝相接;我们惟一的生产品是我们眼睛里的欢乐画图。

好像在旗鼓相当的车队之中,"命运之神"还未决那难定的优胜,我们的灵魂——那已为着自己的好处走出去了——悬挂在她与我之中。

当我们的灵魂在那儿交涉,我们躺着,寂然好像墓上的石像;整天我们的姿势老是那样;我们也没有吐一个字,从清早一直到黄昏。

Robert Herrick

(1591—1674)

To Electra

I dare not ask a kiss,
I dare not beg a smile,
Lest having that, or this,
I might grow proud the while.

No, no, the utmost share
Of my desire shall be
Only to kiss that air
That lately kissed thee.

The Primrose

Ask me why I send you here
This sweet Infanta[1] of the year?
Ask me why I send to you
This primrose, thus bepearl'd[2] with dew?

呈 Electra

我不敢请你给我一吻，我不敢妄求给我一笑，

怕的是有了那个或这个，我当时会骄傲起来。

不，不，我希望的极颠只是吻那最近吻过你的

空气。

莲 馨 花

问我为什么这儿送你这个今年的甜蜜公主？问

我为什么送你这样子满洒着露珠的这朵莲馨花？我

---

1 Infanta：daughter of a king or queen of Spain or Portugal 西班牙或葡萄牙公主的称呼。

2 bepearled：covered with pearls 满是珠盖着。

I will whisper to your ears: —
The sweets of love are mix'd with tears.

Ask me why this flower does show
So yellow-green, and sickly too?
Ask me why the stalk is weak
And bending (yet it doth not break)?
I will answer: — These discover
What fainting hopes are in a lover.

The Bracelet: To Julia

Why I tie about thy wrist,
Julia[1], this silken twist;
For what other reason is 't
But to show thee how, in part,
Thou my pretty captive art?
But thy bond-slave is my heart:
'Tis but silk that bindeth thee,
Knap the thread and thou art free;
But 'tis otherwise with me:

将靠近你的耳朵低声说语道：——爱情的甜蜜是杂着泪珠。

问我为什么这朵花现出这么惨绿枯黄的颜色，又是这样满脸病容？问我为什么花梗这样柔弱下弯（却没有中断）呢？我一定答道——这些都指出爱人心里的希望是多么微弱。

手镯：呈Julia

为什么我将这些丝线缚在你的手腕；只是要让你看你一部分也是我可爱的俘虏，此外还会有什么别的理由呢？然而，我的心是你的奴隶：束缚你的只是丝线，啮断它，你就自由了；但是我却不是这

---

1 Julia这个称呼译文中未体现。——编者注

—I am bound and fast bound, so
That from thee I cannot go;
If I could, I would not so.

To Daisies

Shut not so soon; the dull-eyed night
Has not as yet begun
To make a seizure on the light,
Or to seal up the sun.

No marigolds yet closed are,
No shadows great appear;
Nor doth the early shepherd's star
Shine like a spangle here.

Stay but till my Julia close
Her life-begetting eye,
And let the whole world then dispose
Itself to live or die.

样：——我是束缚住了,这么紧地束缚住了,以致我无法离开;就说能够罢,我自己也不愿意。

致 雏 菊

不要这么快就萎谢了;睡眼惺忪的夜还没有开始去攫阳光,或者将太阳封起。

还没有金盏花闭了,还没有大影子出现;最早涌现的牧羊人的星也还未在那里像小金片地发光。

等着罢,只要我 Julia 闭起她那赋人以生命的眼睛,那时整个世界的生死都可随它。

Robert Burns

(1759—1796)

Mary Morison

O Mary, at thy window be,
It is the wish'd, the trysted[1] hour!
Those smiles and glances let me see
That make the miser's treasure poor:
How blythely[2] wad[3] I bide[4] the stoure[5],
A weary slave frae[6] sun to sun,
Could I the rich reward secure,
The lovely Mary Morison.

Yestreen[7], when to the trembling string
The dance gaed[8] thro' the lighted ha'[9],
To thee my fancy took its wing,
I sat, but neither heard nor saw:

---

1 trysted: appointed for meeting 约定好的。
2 blythely: happily 快乐地。
3 wad: would.

Mary Morison

啊，Mary，请站在你的窗旁，此刻是所希望的幽会时光！让我看那些微笑同美盼，那使守财奴的藏宝不值一钱：我会多么快乐地忍受风尘，天天在太阳底下当个疲倦的奴才，若使我能得到这个值钱的奖品，这位美丽的 Mary Morison。

昨夜，华灯高张的大厅里，大家按着颤动的繁弦慢舞，我的心却飞到你那里，我坐着，却听不到

---

4 to bide：to endure 忍受。
5 stoure：dust 风尘。
6 frae: from.
7 yestreen：last night 昨夜。
8 gaed: went.
9 ha'：hall 大厅。

Tho' this was fair, and that was braw¹,
And yon the toast² of a' the town,
I sigh'd, and said amang³ them a'
"Ye are na⁴ Mary Morison."

O Mary, canst thou wreck his peace
Wha for thy sake wad gladly dee⁵?
Or canst thou break that heart of his,
Whase⁶ only faut⁷ is loving thee?
If love for love thou wilt na gie⁸,
At least be pity to me shown:
A thought ungentle canna be
The thought o' Mary Morison.

Bonnie⁹ Lesley

O saw ye bonnie Lesley
As she gaed o'er the border?

---

1 braw: handsome 漂亮。
2 toast: person whose health is drunk 受人祝饮健康的人。
3 amang: among.

什么,看不见什么:虽然这位长得漂亮,那位生得美丽,还有那边的一位是全城倾到〔倒〕的佳人,我坐在她们中间叹气,说道,"你们都不是 Mary Morison。"

啊 Mary,你忍心破坏他心里的安宁吗,那人为着你的情愿死去?你忍心使他心碎吗,那人惟一的错处是爱上了你?若使你不肯以爱还爱,最少也对我露出怜悯:一个不温柔的念头不会是 Mary Morison 的念头。

美丽的 Lesley

啊!你看见美丽的 Lesley 没有,当她走过边界?

---

4 na: not.
5 to dee:to die 死。
6 whase: whose.
7 faut:fault 过失。
8 to gie:to give 给。
9 bonnie:pretty 美丽。

She's gane, like Alexander,
To spread her conquests farther.

To see her is to love her,
And love but her for ever;¹
For Nature made her what she is,
And never made anither².

Thou art a queen, fair Lesley,
Thy subjects we before thee;
Thou art divine, fair Lesley,
The hearts o' men adore thee.

The deil³ he could na scaith⁴ thee,
Or aught that wad belang thee,
He'd look into thy bonnie face,
And say "I canna wrang⁵ thee!"

The Powers aboon⁶ will tent⁷ thee;

---

1 这两句是 Burns 最有名的句子，恐怕没有人不喜欢它们。
2 anither: another.
3 deil: devil.
4 to scaith: to harm.

她去了,像亚历山大,去推广她的征略。

看到她一定会爱她,而且永久只爱着她;因为"自然"做出她这样一个人儿,却没有再做出第二个。

你是个皇后,美丽的Lesley,我们都是你治下的臣民;你是神圣的,美丽的Lesley,人们的心都崇拜你。

魔鬼不能损你,和一切属于你的东西,他一看到你可爱的庞儿,会说道,"我不能伤害你!"

上天的威力会保护你;灾患不会困恼你;你

---

5 to wrang:to wrong 伤害,虐待。
6 aboon:above.
7 to tent:to protect 保护。

Misfortune sha'na steer[1] thee;
Thou'rt like themselves sae lovely,
That ill they'll ne'er let near thee.

Return again, fair Lesley,
Return to Caledonie!
That we may brag we hae a lass
There's nane again sae bonnie.

Highland Mary

Ye banks and braes[2] and streams around
The castle o' Montgomery,
Green be your woods, and fair your flowers,
Your waters never drumlie[3]!
There simmer first unfauld[4] her robes,
And there the langest tarry;
For there I took the last fareweel[5]

---

1 to steer: to molest 损伤。
2 brae: hill-side.
3 drumlie: muddy 污浊。

是像他们这么可爱,他们绝不让"不幸"走近你的身旁。

回来呀,美丽的 Lesley,回到 Caledonie!那么我们可以夸言我们有个姑娘,天下找不出像她那么美丽。

山地的 Mary

Montgomery 堡边的堤岸,小山同河流,愿你们的森林长绿,你们的花朵艳丽,你们的流水永不浑浊!愿夏天先在那儿展出她的盛装,也在那里带〔待〕得最久;因为在那里我同我甜蜜的山地 Mary 做

---

4 unfauld:unfold 展开。
5 fareweel:farewell 再见。

O' my sweet Highland Mary.

How sweetly bloom'd the gay green birk,
How rich the hawthorn's blossom,
As underneath their fragrant shade
I clasp'd her to my bosom!
The golden hours on angel wings
Flew o'er me and my dearie[1];
For dear to me as light and life
Was my sweet Highland Mary.

Wi' mony a vow and lock'd embrace
Our parting was fu' tender;
And pledging aft[2] to meet again,
We tore oursels asunder;
But, oh! fell Death's untimely frost,
That nipt my flower sae[3] early!
Now green's the sod, and cauld's[4] the clay,
That wraps my Highland Mary!

---

1 dearie: dear加上 ie 表示亲昵之意。
2 aft: often.

最后的诀别。

快乐鲜绿的赤杨花开得多么芬芳,山楂树的花朵又多么灿烂,当在它们甜香的阴下,我把她紧拥在怀中!黄金的时光乘天使的翅膀在我同我亲爱人儿的头上飞去;我这甜蜜的山地姑娘于我真是可爱得有如生命同阳光。

说了许多誓言,锁一样地一连拥抱了许多回数,我们的分离满是柔情;盟约好后来再会,我们勉强把彼此扯开;但是,唉,死神太早的严霜降下,这么快就使我的小花凋零!现在土已青青,泥也冷了,底下包有我的山地Mary!

---

3 sae: so.
4 cauld: cold.

O pale, pale now, those rosy lips,
I aft hae kiss'd sae fondly!
And closed for ay[1] the sparkling glance
That dwelt on me sae kindly;
And mouldering now in silent dust
That heart that lo'ed me dearly!
But still within my bosom's core
Shall live my Highland Mary.

Samuel Taylor Coleridge
(1772—1834)

Recollections of Love[2]

How warm this woodland wild recess!
Love surely hath been breathing here:
And this sweet bed of heath, my dear!
Swells up, then sinks with fair caress,
As if to have you yet more near.

Eight springs have flown since last I lay
On sea-ward Quantock's heathy hills,

那些玫瑰色的嘴唇现在已经变灰白了,那是我常常这么痴情地吻着!那个闪烁的眼色也永远闭起,它曾经这么钟爱地向我凝眸;那样爱着我的心儿现在毁烂于冷灰之下!但是我心坎里还活着我山地的 Mary。

爱 之 回 忆

这里林地的荒芜深处是多么温暖!爱情一定曾在这儿呼吸:这个芬芳的草床,我的爱人呀!隆起,然后又满怀抱着地沉下,好像为的是要你更亲近些。

八个春天已飞去了,自从我前一次躺在面海的,

---

1 for ay: for ever, eternally 永久。
2 这首是一个爱人旧地重游,回忆起八年前一段春风,不胜惆怅时的默想和希冀。

Where quiet sounds from hidden rills
Float here and there, like things astray,
And high o'er head the skylark shrills.

No voice as yet had made the air
Be music with your name; yet why
That asking look? That yearning sigh?
That sense of promise every where?
Beloved! Flew your spirit by?

Water Ballad

Come hither, gently rowing,
Come, bear me quickly o'er
This stream so brightly flowing
To yonder woodland shore.
But vain were my endeavour
To pay thee, courteous guide;
Row on, row on, for ever
I'd have thee by my side.

乱草蔓生的 Quantock 小山，那里现在有幽隐小河的低微声音四处流散，好像迷路的东西，高高地在我们头上有天鹨尖声叫喊。

还没有声音说出你的名字，使空气变为音乐；但是四围为什么有这么一种追问的神情？这样伫望的叹息？到处这个允诺的感觉呢？亲爱的人儿！是你的灵魂飞过去吗？

水　　调

到这儿来，轻轻地划罢，来，快把我渡过这个清流，到彼岸的林地；但是我无法报酬你的辛苦，温文的引导者；望〔往〕前划，望前划，我将要你老在我身旁。

"Good boatman, prithee haste thee,
I seek my father-land." —
"Say, when I there have place thee?
Dare I demand thy hand'?"
"A maiden's head can never
So hard a point decide;
Row on, row on, for ever,
I'd have thee by my side."

The happy bridal over
The wanderer ceased to roam,
For, seated by her lover,
The boat became her home.
And still they sang together
As steering o'er the tide:
"Row on through wind and weather
For ever by my side."

To Lesbia

My Lesbia, let us love and live,
And to the winds, my Lesbia, give

"好船夫,请你赶快些,我是回到我的祖国。"

"请你说,当我把你放在那儿,我敢向你求婚吗?"

"一个姑娘的头脑永不能解决这么麻烦的问题;望〔往〕前划,望前划,我将要你老在我的身旁。"

快乐的婚礼行了,漂泊者不再漫游了,因为坐在她爱人身旁,小船就是她的家了。当他们乘潮驶着,他们还是同声唱道:"不辞风雨望〔往〕前划,永远在我的身旁。"

致 Lesbia

我的 Lesbia,让我们恋爱,快乐地过活罢!冷淡的拘束,老年的隐忧同她一切严酷的套话,我的 Lesbia,

---

1 to demand one's hand: to ask the hand 求婚。

Each cold restraint, each boding fear
Of age and all her saws[1] severe.
Yon sun now posting[2] to the main
Will set, — but 'tis to rise again; —
But we, when once our mortal light
Is set, must sleep in endless night.
Then come, with whom alone I'll live,
A thousand kisses take and give!
Another thousand!— to the store
Add hundreds — then a thousand more!
And when they to a million mount,
Let confusion take the account, —
That you, the number never knowing,
May continue still bestowing —
That I for joys may never pine,
Which never can again be mine!

When thou to my true-love com'st
Greet her from me kindly;

让我都把它们付之东风。那边的太阳驱驰到海上，不久将落山，——但是，那会再升；——我们，当我们有限的光辉一歇，却必得睡在这不尽的长夜。那么，来罢，我只愿与你独自住在一起，受我同给我一千的热吻罢！再来一千！——为着要积蓄，再加上几百——然后，再来一千！当他们凑成百万之数，让做成个糊涂账罢，——那么你不知道了确数，会不断地继续给我——那么，我也不至于怅望那永不能再得的欣欢！

☆　☆　☆

当你看到我的真心爱人，替我向她殷勤问好；

1　saws：maxims 格言。
2　posting：hastening 赶快，就是我们所谓"速如置邮"的意思。欧洲从前传递紧急的信件，也是用每站换马的办法。

When she asks thee how I fare?
Say, folks in Heaven fare finely.

When she asks, "What! Is he sick?"
Say, dead!— and when for sorrow
She begins to sob and cry,
Say, I come to-morrow.

Leigh Hunt

(1784—1859)

Jenny kiss'd me when we met,
Jumping from the chair she sat in;
Time, you thief, who love to get
Sweet into your list, put that in![1]

Say I'm weary, say I'm sad
Say that health and wealth have miss'd me,
Say I'm growing old, but add
Jenny kiss'd me.

---

1 这是说乐事转瞬即逝，已成陈迹，好像给"时光老人"偷去一样。

当她问你我过活如何？你说，在天上的人们，日子过得很好。

当她问，"怎么！他病了吗？"说，死了！——当她悲哀得呜咽痛哭起来，说，我明天会来。

☆ ☆ ☆

我们相遇时，Jenny吻着我，她从她坐的椅子里跳下；"时光老人"，你这个小偷，爱把一切喜事放在你那过去的纪录里，也将这事记进去罢！

说我疲劳，说我悲哀，说健康和财富与我无分，说我渐渐老了，但是请加上去，Jenny曾吻过我。

George Gordon Byron

(1788—1824)

So, we'll go no more a-roving
So late into the night.
Though the heart be still as loving,
And the moon be still as bright.

For the sword outwears[1] its sheath,
And the soul wears out[2] the breast
And the heart must pause to breathe,
And love itself have rest.

Though the night was made for loving,
And the day returns too soon,
Yet we'll go no more a-roving
By the light of the moon.

---

1 to outwear: to consume by wearing 磨损。
2 to wear out: to outwear.

☆　☆　☆

那么，我们不再出去漫游一直到夜深时分了。虽然心儿还是那样挚爱，月亮还是那样光明。

因为剑会磨损它的鞘，灵魂也会使胸中感到疲劳，心儿总得歇一下出一口气，爱情本身也得有个休息。

虽然，夜是为爱而做的，白天又回来得太快，然而我们不再去漫游在那月光之下。

Percy Bysshe Shelley

(1792—1822)

True Love in this differs from gold and clay,
That to divide is not to take away[1].
Love is like understanding, that grows bright,
Gazing on many truths; 'tis like thy light,
Imagination! which from earth and sky,
And from the depths of human fantasy,
As from a thousand prisms and mirrors, fills
The Universe with glorious beams, and kills
Error, the worm, with many a sun-like arrow
Of its reverberated lightning. Narrow[2]
The heart that loves, the brain that contemplates.
The life that wears, the spirit that creates
One object, and one form and builds thereby
A sepulchre for its eternity.

---

1 Shelley主张精神之爱，所谓"柏拉图式的爱情"（Platonic love），所以认为一个人可以同时爱许多人，而对于每个人的爱并不因此而减少，正和只爱一个人时一样。他跟许多女子有这种精神上的恋爱如 Contessina

☆　☆　☆

真实的爱，跟黄金和泥土不同，虽然分散却没有减少。爱情是像智识，看到许多真理，会更见光明；那又像你的光辉，"想像"呀！从上天下地，从人们心里的深处，有如从千面的结晶同镜子，反映出来，使世界充满荣光，用它那反射出万千的阳光利箭，杀死错误，那是只"害虫"。心儿只爱，脑子只想着，生命只销磨于，精神只创造出——一个对象，一个形态，而在那上面建起永久的坟墓，这是多么狭窄呀。

Emilia Viviani，Jane（Mrs. Williams）等，他写出几首极真纯飘渺的诗赞颂她们。

2 narrow: narrow（is）the heart...the brain...the life...the spirit.

John Keats

(1795—1821)

Bright star, would I were steadfast as thou art —
Not in lone splendour hung aloft the night,
And watching, with eternal lids apart,
Like nature's patient, sleepless Eremite[1],
The moving waters at their priestlike task
Of pure ablution round earth's human shores,
Or gazing on the new soft-fallen mask
Of snow upon the mountains and the moors —
No — yet still steadfast, still unchangeable,
Pillow'd upon my fair love's ripening breast,
To feel for ever its soft fall and swell,
Awake for ever in a sweet unrest,
Still, still to hear her tender-taken breath,
And so live ever — or else swoon to death.

---

1 Eremite: hermit 隐士。

☆ ☆ ☆

明星，多么希望我是像你那么固定——并不是要如你那样孤光高照于夜的中天，永远开眼，好似"大自然"的，有耐心的，不眠的隐士，注目流动的水正在干它神甫般的工作，净洗地球上人居的海岸，或者凝视新降的雪片，替高山旷野盖上一个面具——不——可是仍是固定，还是不变，枕于我美丽爱人成熟的胸中，永远感到它温柔的涨落，永远在个甜蜜的不安里醒着，永远听到她细微呼吸的气息，这么永远活着——否则愿就如此晕死。

Alfred Tennyson

(1809—1892)

Ask me no more: the moon may draw the sea;
The cloud may stoop from heaven and take the shape,
With fold to fold, of mountain or of cape;
But O too fond[1], when have I answer'd thee?
Ask me no more.

Ask me no more: what answer should I give?
I love not hollow cheek or faded eye;
Yet, O my friend, I will not have thee die!
Ask me no more, lest I shall bid thee live;
Ask me no more.

Ask me no more: thy fate and mine are seal'd;
I strove against the stream and all in vain;
Let the great river take me to the main:
No more: dear love, for at a touch I yield;
Ask me no more.

---

1 fond: foolish 愚蠢，诗里面当作此义解。

☆　☆　☆

不要再问我：月亮可以吸引海水；云团可以从上天下降，围着高山同海角，显出它们的奇形；但是太傻了，我那时答应过你？不要再问我罢。

不要再问我：我将说出什么答话呢？我并不爱瘦削的脸颊或者失神的眼睛；然而，啊，我的朋友吓，我绝不肯让你死去！不要再问我，怕的是我会叫你活着；不要再问我罢。

不要再问我：你的命运和我的命运是定了；我一向抵抗这狂潮，总是枉然；让大河带我到海里去罢：不要再说，亲亲的爱人，因为一触我就会顺从；不要再问我罢。

Robert Browning
（1812—1889）

You'll love me yet!— and I can tarry
Your love's protracted growing:
June rear'd that bunch of flowers you carry,
From seeds of April's sowing.

I plant a heartful now: some seed
At least is sure to strike[1],
And yield — what you'll not pluck indeed,
Not love, but, may be, like.

You'll look at least on love's remains.
A grave's one violet[2]:
Your look? — That pays a thousand pains.
What's death? You'll love me yet!

---

1 to strike：to thrust in its roots 生根。
2 因为"爱情"是这么美丽的东西，所以因情而死，埋在坟墓里面时，这座墓也可以当做一朵轻朵的紫罗兰看。

☆　☆　☆

你总有一天会爱我！——我也能够迟候你爱情慢慢的生长：你手上捧的花是六月培植出来的，它的下种却在四月中。

现在我播下满心的种：最少有几粒会发芽，生出——那的确是你所不采的，也不能爱恋着，然而也许会喜欢。

你最少会一顾爱的残留，一座坟也是一朵紫罗兰：你的一顾？——这补偿了千般哀怨。死有什么要紧？你总有一天会爱我！

Christina Georgina Rossetti

(1830—1894)

A Birthday

My heart is like a singing bird
Whose nest is in a watered shoot[1];
My heart is like an apple-tree
Whose boughs are bent with thickset[2] fruit;
My heart is like a rainbow shell
That paddles in a halcyon[3] sea;
My heart is gladder than all these
Because my love is come to me.

Raise me a dais[4] of silk and down;
Hang it with vair[5] and purple dyes;
Carve it in doves, and pomegranates,
And peacocks with a hundred eyes;
Work it in gold and silver grapes,

---

1 a watered shoot: the rocks fringing a waterfall 瀑布旁边的岩石。

诞 生 之 辰

  我的心是像一只歌鸟,它的巢筑在泉边的悬岩;我的心是像一颗苹果树,它的枝子被密生的果子压得下弯;我的心是像一粒虹色的介壳,在平静的海军〔中〕漂游;我的心是比这一切都快乐,因为我的爱人来到我这儿。

  为我盖起一座丝缎同绒毛做的平台上的座位;挂上栗鼠皮和紫色的绸料;雕出鸽子,石榴同百目的孔雀;镶进金银葡萄,树叶同银白的鸢尾花;

---

2 thickset: set closely together 密簇的。
3 halcyon: calm 平静。
4 dais: a seat on a platform at the end of a hall 大厅顶端平台上的坐位。
5 vair: a fine fur used for lining robes 镶衣边用的一种皮。

In leaves, and silver fleurs-de-lys;
Because the birthday of my life
Is come, my love is come to me.

Echo

Come to me in the silence of the night;
Come in the speaking silence of a dream;
Come with soft rounded cheeks and eyes as bright
As sunlight on a stream;
Come back in tears,
O memory, hope, love of finished years.

Oh dream how sweet, too sweet, too bitter sweet,
Whose wakening should have been in Paradise,
Where souls brimful of love abide and meet;
Where thirsting longing eyes
Watch the slow door [1]
That opening, letting in, lets out no more.

---

1 指天国的门。

因为我生命的诞生日子到了,现在我的爱人来到我这儿。

回　声

在夜的寂静里回到我这儿来罢;在一场梦中,含意无穷的寂静里来罢;来时请带一双柔软丰满的脸颊,再带来溪上日光一样地光明的眼睛;满眼清泪地回来罢,啊,已去年华里的记忆,希望和爱情。

多么甜蜜的梦呀,太甜蜜了,甜蜜得变成太酸苦了,从这场梦醒来,我们该在天国,充满了爱的人儿就住在那里,朝朝相会;渴望地等候着的眼睛在那里守着那迟缓的门户,它开后,让人进来,永不让再出去了。

Yet come to me in dreams, that I may live
My very life again though cold in death;
Come back to me in dreams, that I may give
Pulse for pulse, breath for breath:
Speak low, lean low,
As long ago, my love, how long ago!

The Poor Ghost

"Oh whence do you come, my dear friend, to me,
With your golden hair all fallen below your knee,
And your face as white as snowdrops on the lea,
And your voice as hollow as the hollow sea?"

"From the other world I come back to you,
My locks are uncurled with dripping drenching dew,
You know the old, whilst I know the new:
But to-morrow you shall know this too."

"Oh not to-morrow into the dark, I pray;
Oh not to-morrow, too soon to go away:

可是在梦里到我这儿来罢,那么我可以再尝生活的滋味,虽然冰冷冷地死了;在梦里到我这儿来罢,那么我可以和你脉脉相应,息息相呼:低声说,低低地挨靠着,跟从前一样,我的爱人,那是多么久的事了!

可怜的鬼

"啊,你从什么地方到我这里来呢,我亲爱的朋友,你金黄的头发全垂到膝下,你的脸白得像草场上的雪花,你的声音空洞得像空洞的大海?"

"从另个世界,我回来找你,我的卷发被点滴浸濡的露水弄垂直了,你知道旧的世界,我却晓得新的世界;但是明天你会了解这个情形。"

"啊,不要说明天就到黑暗里去,我求你;啊,不

Here I feel warm and well-content and gay;
Give me another year, another day."

"Am I so changed in a day and a night
That mine own only love shrinks from me with fright,
Is fain to turn away to left or right
And cover up his eyes from the sight?"

"Indeed I loved you; my chosen friend,
I loved you for life[1], but life has an end;
Through sickness I was ready to tend;
But death mars all, which we cannot mend.

"Indeed I loved you; I love you yet,
If you will stay where your bed is set,
Where I have planted a violet,
Which the wind waves, which the dew makes wet."

"Life is gone, then love too is gone,
It was a reed that I leant upon:

---

1 for life: for the period of earthly existence 终身。

要说是明天,那未免太早离开了:在这儿我觉温暖,满足同快乐;多给我一年的时光,一天的时光罢。"

"一天一夜我就变得这么厉害,以至我亲亲惟一的爱人见到我都吓得退缩,想向左右躲避,向我遮住眼睛吗?"

"我从前的确爱你;我的意中人,我一生都在爱你,然而生命也有个止期;你病时我很愿伺候,但是死却毁坏了一切,那是我们无法挽回。

"我真是爱你;我还是爱你,若使你肯滞在你床铺安好的地方,那里我栽有一株紫罗兰,风儿吹着,露珠湿着。"

"生命没有了,爱情也就没有了,我依靠的原来

Never doubt I will leave you alone
And not wake you rattling bone with bone.

"I go home alone to my bed,
Dug deep at the foot and deep at the head,
Roofed in with a load of lead,
Warm enough for the forgotten dead.

"But why did your tears soak through the clay,
And why did your sobs wake me where I lay?
I was away, far enough away:
Let me sleep now till the Judgment Day."

Thomas Hardy

(1840—1928)

Without Ceremony

It was your way, my dear,
To vanish without a word
When callers, friends, or kin
Had left, and I hastened in
To rejoin you, as I inferred.

是一根芦苇：请相信，我会让你独自在人间，绝不会再骨头碰得响辚辚地来把你喊醒。

"我独自回到我的家里，我的床头脚都深掘在地中，正面有沉重的铅压着，对于被人忘却的死人已够暖和。

"但是为什么你的眼泪渗透过泥土，为什么你的呜咽把我从躺的地方惊醒？我已走很远了，一个够远的地方；现在请让我一直睡到末日的审判。"

不 拘 礼

亲爱的，你素来是如此，一声不响地离开；当客人，朋友或者亲戚走去了，我以为你在里面，赶紧进去找你的时候。

And when you'd a mind to career
Off anywhere — say[1] to town —
You were all on a sudden[2] gone
Before I had thought thereon,
Or noticed your trunks were down.

So, now that you disappear
For ever in that swift style,
Your meaning seems to me
Just as it used to be:
"Good-bye is not worth while!"

The Haunter

He does not think that I haunt here nightly:
How shall I let him know
That whither his fancy sets him wandering,
I, too, alertly go? —
Hover and hover a few feet from him
Just as I used to do,
But cannot answer the words he lifts me —
Only listen thereto!

当你打算到那里去玩——比如说到城市去——你是一下子就走了,那时我还没有想到,也没有瞧见你的皮箱拿下来。

所以,你现在也就这样飞快地同我永诀,据我看来,你的意思正同往常一样,是"握别是用不着的!"

缠绕身旁的幽灵

他没有想到我夜夜常来这里;我怎么能够使他知道,他随便想到何方漫游,我立刻也到那里?——徜徉着,徜徉着,跟他相隔几尺,正同往常一样,但是不能回答他向我说的话——只能倾耳聆着!

---

1 say: select as example 比如说。
2 all on a sudden: suddenly 突然。

When I could answer he did not say them:
When I could let him know
How I would like to join in his journeys
Seldom he wished to go.
Now that he goes and wants me with him
More than he used to do,
Never he sees my faithful phantom
Though he speaks thereto.

Yes, I companion him to places
Only dreamers know,
Where the shy hares print long paces,
Where the night rooks go;
Into old aisles where the Past is all to him,
Close as his shade can do,
Always lacking the power to call to him,
Near as I reach thereto!

What a good haunter I am, O tell him!
Quickly make him know
If he but sigh since my loss befell him
Straight to his side I go.
Tell him a faithful one is doing

当我能够回答,他却不说这些话:当我能够使他知道我多么愿意同他一起旅行,他却不大想出游。现在他出去,比往常更欲我同他一块,他却绝没有看见我忠实的鬼影,虽然他向它说出话来。

是的,我陪他到只有梦里人才知道的地方,那里害羞的兔子印下长距离的足迹,那里夜鸟飞着;随他到教堂里的古廊,那里"过去"是他的一切,我紧随着他,他的影子也只能如是,总差个喊他的力气,无论我多么近他!

我是个多么有本领的缠绕他身旁的人,啊,告诉他罢!快使他知道,自从丧失了我使他伤神,只要他一叹息,我就一直到他身旁。告诉他一个忠实的人干了他所能干的一切工作,他的路也许还值得

All that love can do,
Still that his path may be worth pursuing,
And to bring peace thereto.

A Dream or No

Why go to Saint-Juliot? What's Juliot to me?
Some strange necromancy
But charmed me to fancy
That much of my life claims the spot as its key.

Yes, I have had dreams of that place in the West,
And a maiden abiding;
Thereat as in hiding
Fair-eyed and white-shouldered, broad-browed and brown-tressed.

And of how, coastward bound on a night long ago,
There lonely I found her,
The sea-birds around her,
And other than nigh things uncaring to know.

追踪，使那里有个安宁。

梦耶非耶

为什么到Saint-Juliot去？Juliot同我有什么相关？一些奇怪的魔术把我迷了，使我相信我生命的大部分认那地方做它的中心。

是的，我曾梦过西边那个地方，同一位姑娘住在那儿，好像躲着；艳丽眼睛的，雪白肩膀的，宽眉棕发的。

还梦见许多年以前的一夜，向海滨走去，我怎样独自遇到她，她的四围有海鸟，其它不太近她的东西，我也不想去细看。

So sweet her life there (in my thought has it seemed)
That quickly she drew me
To take her unto me,
And lodge her long years with me.
Such have I dreamed.

But nought of that maid from Saint-Juliot I see;
Can she ever have been here,
And shed her life's sheen here,
The woman I thought a long housemate with me?

Does there even a place like Saint-Juliot exist?
Or a Valency Valley
With stream and leafed alley,
Or Beeny, or Bos with its flounce flinging mist?

After a Journey

Hereto I come to view a voiceless ghost;
Whither, O whither will its whim now draw me?
Up the cliff, down, till I'm lonely, lost,

她在那里的生活是这么甜蜜（在我思想里仿佛如此），她很快就吸引我，把她拉来给我自己，跟她同住了许多年头。我做了这样一场梦。

但是我现在看不见从Juliot来的姑娘的踪迹了；她曾经到这里来过吗，在这里散下她的光辉吗，这个女人，我以为跟我同居了这许多年头？

世上真有像Saint-Juliot这么一个地方吗？或者有清流贯着，里面有个绿叶丛生的小巷的Valency谷吗，或者Beeny高峰，或者在飞驰着的谷皱密雾下的Bos河吗？

旅 途 之 后

我到这里来看一个没有声音的幽灵；啊，它此刻的兴致要带我到那里去呢，到那里去呢？爬上峻

And the unseen waters' ejaculations awe me.
Where you will next be there's no knowing,
Facing round about me everywhere,
With your nut-coloured hair,
And gray eyes, and rose-flush coming and going.

Yes: I have re-entered your olden haunts at last;
Through the years, though the dead scenes I have tracked you.
What have you now found to say of our past —
Scanned across the dark space wherein I have lacked you?
Summer gave us sweets, but autumn wrought division?
Things were not lastly as firstly well
With us twain, you tell?
But all's closed now, despite Time's derision.

I see what you are doing: you are leading me on
To the spots we knew when we haunted here together,
The waterfall, above which the mist-bow shone
At the then fair hour in the then fair weather,
And the cave just under, with a voice still so hollow

岩,又走下来一直到我独自在这里迷路了,瞧不见的泉水的潺潺使我心惊。你会再到什么地方去,是无法可猜,处处总是脸朝着我,带着你那栗色的头发,灰色的眼睛,同忽来忽去玫瑰色的红潮。

是的,我最后又走进你从前常游之地;我追迹你,经过许多年头,经过那已死的情景。你现在对于我们的过去有什么可说吗——你细看我失丢你后所度的漆黑空虚吗?你想起夏天与我们以甜蜜,秋天做成这个分离吗?你说我俩后来情形大不如前吗?但是现在一切都过去了,不管"时光"怎样嘲笑。

我看出你干的是什么:你是带我到我们都知道的地方,当从前我们同来这儿游玩时候,这里有瀑布,上面有雾照着,在那个晴朗天气里晴朗时光之中,下面有穴,里头的声音还是那么空洞,好像是

That it seems to call out to me from forty years ago
When you were all aglow,
And not the thin ghost that I now frailly follow!

Ignorant of what there is flitting here to see,
The waked birds preen and the seals flop lazily,
Soon you will have, Dear, to vanish from me,
For the stars close their shutters and the dawn whitens hazily.
Trust me, I mind not, though Life lours[1],
The bringing me here; nay, bring me here again!
I am just the same as when
Our days were a joy, and our paths through flowers.

Beeny Cliff

March 1870 — March 1913

I

O the opal and the sapphire of that wandering western sea,

---

1 to lour: to lower 降低。

从四十年前向我叫喊,那时你整个人是光辉,不像我现在微弱地跟着的一个瘦鬼!

不知道跑来这里东瞧西望的是什么东西,已醒的鸟就去修拾它的毛羽,海豹懒洋洋地拍扑着,一会见,亲爱的,你会隐去,我会看不见你了,因为星儿将闭起它们的窗子,清晨模糊地发出白光。请你相信,虽然生活消沉,我没有不高兴你带我到这里;不,请你再带我到这里!我正同从前一样,那时我们的日子全是欣欢,我们的路也铺着芳花。

Beeny 峭壁

一八七〇年三月——一九一三年三月

一

啊,那边浮荡的西海是珠光和碧翠交辉,那个

And the woman riding high above with bright hair flapping free—
The woman whom I loved so, and who loyally loved me.

II

The pale mews[1] plained below us, and the waves seemed far away
In a nether sky, engrossed in saying their ceaseless babbling say,
As we laughed light-heartedly aloft on that clear-sunned March day.

III

A little cloud then cloaked us, and there flew an irised rain.
And the Atlantic dyed its levels with a dull misfeatured stain,
And then the sun burst out again, and purples prinked the main.

---

1 mew: gulls 鸥。

女子骑马高山上光亮的头发如羽翼地乱飞——那个女子，我是这么爱着，她也这么忠实地爱我。

二

灰白色的海鸥在我们底下呻吟，浪花好像还远在那里无色的天边，专心一志去说出它们不断喋喋的话儿，当我们在那个晴和的三月天里居高处心旷神怡地大笑。

三

一阵小云把我们包住，飞来了虹色的微雨。大西洋染它的平面以一块乱七八糟的污点，然后太阳又冲出，大海披上绛红色的新装。

IV

— Still in all its chasmal[1] beauty bulks old Beeny to the sky.
And shall she and I not go there once again now March is nigh,
And the sweet things said in that March say anew there by and by[2]?

V

What if still in chasmal beauty looms that wild weird western shore.
The woman now is — elsewhere — whom the ambling pony bore.
And nor knows nor cares for Beeny, and will laugh there nevermore.

The Phantom Horsewoman

I

Queer are the ways of a man I know:

---

1 chasmal: of chasm 空洞的；裂隙的。

四

——老Beeny还是空灵地矗立中天。她同我不再到那里去吗,现在三月又近了,那个三月里所唱的歌声又渐渐在那儿唱起来了?

五

吓,那个荒凉古怪的西岸还是空灵地涌现在那里。那个女人——溜蹄的马所载的——已到别地方去了。不知,也不理Beeny了,更不会再在那里大笑。

骑马女子的魅影

一

我知道一个人,他的举动真怪:他来这里,

---

2 by and by:gradually 渐渐。

He comes and stands
In a careworn craze.
And looks at the sands
And the seaward haze
With moveless hands
And face and gaze,
Then turns to go...
And what does he see when he gazes so?

II

They say he sees as an instant thing
More clear than to-day,
A sweet soft scene
That once was in play,
By that bring green;
Yes, notes alway
Warm, real and keen,
What his back years bring —
A phantom of his own figuring.

III

Of this vision of his they might say more:
Not only there

忧愁得昏迷地站着。看岸上的沙和海上的雾气,手是不动的,脸孔是不动的,凝眸也是不动的,然后转身走开……他看的是什么呢,当他这样瞪着眼睛尽望?

二

他们说,他看见一段温柔旖旎的情景,那曾演于这块海滨绿波之旁,此刻一下子现在他眼前,比当日的东西更来得分明;那是个永远温暖的,永远真实的,永远亲切的情调,是他过去年华所带回来的——他自己臆想的一个魅影。

三

关于他这个幻像,他们还可以说许多:不单

Does he see this sight,
But everywhere
In his brain — day, night,
As if on the air
It were drawn rose bright —
Yea, far from that shore
Does he carry this vision of heretofore.

IV

A ghost-girl-rider. And though, toil-tried,
He withers daily,
Time touches her not,
But she still rides gaily
In his rapt thought
On that shagged and shaly
Atlantic spot,
And as when first eyed
Draws rein and sings to the swing of the tide.

Her Father

I met her, as we had privily planned,
Where passing feet beat busily:

是在这里,他看见这幅图画,到处这都在他脑子里——白天,晚上,玫瑰色鲜明地画在空中——是的,他一向把这个幻像带到远离这海岸的地方:那是一个骑马女子的魅影。

四

虽然挨着苦难,他天天憔悴,时光却不能损害她,在他那迷惑的脑子里,她还是快乐地骑马飞驰过粗糙鳞动的大西洋之滨,正同第一次看见那样,拉着缰,向潮的涨落高歌。

她 的 爸 爸

我与她相遇,像我们从前私下定好的,在过路人脚步忙乱践踏的地方:她低声说:"爸爸在旁边!

She whispered: "Father is at hand!
He wished to walk with me."

His presence as he joined us there
Banished our words of warmth away;
We felt, with cloudings of despair,
What Love must lose that day.

Her crimson lips remained unkissed,
Our fingers kept no tender hold,
His lack of feeling made the tryst
Embarrassed, stiff, and cold.

A cynic ghost then rose and said
"But is his love for her so small
That, nigh to yours, it may be read[1]
As of no worth at all?"

"You love her for her pink and white;
But what when their fresh splendours close?

---

1 read: counted 认为，算做。

他想同我一起散步。"

当他加入我们里面,我们热情的话全远遁了;在失望的密云之中,我们感到爱情那天一定有个多么大的损失。

她娇红的嘴唇仍原是没有被吻,我们的手指也没有温柔地交叉,他的漠然无情使我们的幽期变成烦恼的,硬板的,冰冷的。

一个刻薄的精灵那时起来说道:"他对于她的情是这么微弱吗,一碰到你的,他的情就可算做不值一提吗?"

"你为她的脸红是红,白是白而爱她,当它们新

His love will last her in despite
Of Time, and wrack, and foes."

At Waking

When night was lifting,
And dawn had crept under its shade,
Amid cold clouds drifting
Dead-white as a corpse outlaid,
With a sudden scare
I seemed to behold
My Love in bare
Hard lines unfold.

Yea, in a moment,
An insight that would not die
Killed her old endowment
Of charm that had capped all night,
Which vanished to none
Like the gilt of a cloud
And showed her but one
Of the common crowd.

鲜的光荣消失了,你又怎样呢?他对于她的情会永远继续下去,不管时光,患难同敌人。"

醒　　时

当夜幕揭开了,朝暾偷跑到它的影里,在飘游着,白得像躺着的死尸的冷云之中,吓了一跳,我好像看见我爱人裸露的写实轮廓。

是的,一刹那中,一个永不会忘记的灼见杀死她从前的娇媚,那占了整个晚上,现在却消失得无影无踪,像云团的黄金边子,指出她不过是普通人们里的一个。

She seemed but a sample
Of earth's poor average kind,
Lit up by no ample
Enrichments of mien or mind.
I covered my eyes
As to cover the thought,
And unrecognize
What the morn had taught.

O vision appalling
When the one believed-in thing
Is seen falling, falling.
Off: it is not true;
For it cannot be
That the prize I drew
Is a blank to me!

Laurence Hope[1]

The Net of Memory

I cast the Net of Memory,
Man's torment and delight,
Over the level Sands of Youth

她好像只是地球上可怜的平凡人们的榜样,并没有被心身的美照着。我掩起眼睛,为的是要掩起这个念头,不去认早上所告诉的实情。

呵,可怕的启示,当看见我们惟一相信的东西也堕落了,堕落了,连同希望所能抓到的一切。滚去:这绝不是真的;因为我所抽的好奖绝不至于变做一张没有中彩的空票!

记忆的网子

过去的"青春"有如一片平沙,恬静光明地铺着,我向它抛下记忆的网子,那些记忆是人们的苦

---

1 其生卒年为1865—1904年。——编者注

That lay serenely bright,
Their tranquil gold at times submerged
In the Spring Tides of Love's Delight.

The Net brought up, in silver gleams,
Forgotten truth and fancies fair:
Like opal shells, small happy facts
Within the Net entangled were
With the red coral of his lips,
The waving seaweed of his hair.

We were so young; he was so fair.

Song of Ramesram Temple Girl

Now is the season of my youth,
Not thus shall I always be,
Listen, dear Lord, thou too art young,
Take thy pleasure with me.
My hair is straight as the falling rain
And fine as morning mist,
I am a rose awaiting thee
That none have touched or kissed.

楚和欣欢,平沙上安详的金黄沙子有时沉浸在爱之欣欢的春潮之中。

网子捞起已忘的真理和美丽的想头,个个都闪出银光:网里可喜的小事情跟骊珠的壳子一样,是同他那珊瑚的双唇和他那飘扬海草的头发缠在一起。

那时我们是这么年青;他又是那么漂亮。

Ramesram 庙里少女之歌

现在是我青春的季候,我不会永远是这样,听啊,亲爱的主子,你也正年青,来跟我恣情为欢罢。我的头发垂下,像正落着的雨丝,又精细得像晓雾,我是一朵未经人们触过或吻过的玫瑰花。

Do as thou wilt with mine and me,
Beloved, I only pray,
Follow the promptings of thy youth,
Let there be no delay!

A leaf that flutters upon bough,
A moment, and it is gone, —
A bubble amid the fountain spray, —
Ah, pause and think thereon;
For such is youth and its passing bloom
That wait for thee this hour,
If aught in thy heart incline to me
Ah, stoop and pluck thy flower!

Come, my Lord, to the temple shade,
Where cooling fountains play,
If aught in thy heart incline to love
Let there be no delay!

Many shall faint with love of me
And I shall shake their thirst,
But Fate has brought thee hither to-day
That thou shouldst be the first.

对于我和我的，请你随意行事，亲爱的，我只求你照你青春的冲动做去，不要白耽搁了大好时光！

枝上临风招舞的叶子，一会儿就落下了，——飞泉浪花中的一粒水泡——啊，请你停住，默想一下这些东西；青春同它倏逝的光荣也正如此，它们此刻都正在等候你，倘然你心里于我有意，呀，弯下腰来，请采你面前这小花！

来，我的主子，到庙里阴影的地方，那儿冰凉的泉水跳动着，倘然你心里有意钟情，不要白耽搁了好时光！

许多人将因为爱着我而晕去，我也将一解他们的狂渴，但是"命运"带你来到这儿，使你得做了他们的先锋。庙墙的年代是这么老了，这么老了，

Old, so old, are the temple-walls,
Love is older than they;
But I am the short-lived temple rose
Blooming for thee to-day.

Thine am I, Prince, and only thine,
What is there more to say?
If aught in thy heart incline to love,
Let there be no delay!

On Pilgrimage

Oh, youthful bearer of my palanquin,
Thy glossy hair lies loosened on thy neck,
The "tears of labour"[1] gem thy velvet skin
Whose even texture knows no other fleck.

Thy slender shoulder strains beneath my weight;
Too fair thou art, for work, sweet slave of mine,
Would that this idle breast, reversing fate,

---

1 tear of labour: 汗珠。

爱情却比它们更老；然而我只是庙里短命的玫瑰，今天为你而开花。

我是你的，主子，我是只属于你的，还有什么可说呢？倘然你心里有意钟情，不要白耽搁了大好时光！

参诣圣地的途中

啊，我的年青轿夫，你光滑的头发松松地垂在颈旁，"劳工的眼泪"如珠宝一样镶在丝绒般的皮肉上面，它那平整的结构绝没有一丝斑纹。

你的细肩给我压得奋力使劲；你是太漂亮了，不宜工作，我这甜蜜可爱的奴才呀，我多么希望，我这个清闲的胸膛能够颠倒命运，当一个愿意的情

A willing serf to love, supported thine!

I smell the savage scent of sunwarmed fur
Close in the jungle, musky, hot and sweet—
The air comes from thy shoulder, even as myrrh,
Would we were as the panthers, free to meet.

The Temple road is steep; I grieve to see
Thy slender ankles bruised among the clods.
Oh, my Beloved, if I might worship thee!
Beauty is greater far than all the Gods.

Disappointment

Oh, come, Beloved, before my beauty fades,
Pity the sorrow of my loneliness.
I am a rosebush that the cypress shades,
No sunbeams find or lighten my distress.

奴,来承受你的胸膛!

我闻到邻近丛莽里太阳晒着皮毛的野香,有如麝香,热腾腾的,甜蜜蜜的。——从你肩上来的气味也正同末药一样,那是多么好吓,若使我们是一双豹子,能够随意合欢。

到庙里去的路是陡的;我真心痛,看到你的细踝给土块碰伤。我亲爱的,若使我能够崇拜你!美的威力是胜过一切的天神。

失　　望

啊,来罢,亲爱的,在我的美丽消逝之前,请可怜我的寂寞,那是多么可伤。我是给松柏遮住了的玫瑰丛,没有太阳看出或者照亮我的悲哀。

Daily I watch the waning of my bloom.
Ah, piteous fading of a thing so fair!
While Fate, remorseless, weaving at her loom, [1]
Twines furtive silver in my twisted hair.

This noon I watched a tremulous fading rose
Rise on the wind to court a butterfly.
"One speck of pollen, ere my petals close,
Bring me one touch of love before I die!"

But the gay butterfly, who had the power
To grant, refused, flew far across the dell,
And, as he fertilised a younger flower,
The petals of the rose, defrauded, fell.

Such was my fate, thou not come to me,
Thine eyes are absent, and thy voice is mute,
Though I am slim, as this papaya tree,
With breasts out-pointing, even as its fruit.

---

1 希腊神话说"命运之神"天天织布,织下人们的命运。

天天我注视我艳容的日趋暗淡。呀，这么美的一件东西的消逝是多么堪怜！而残酷的"命运"纺织时却偷偷地向我的卷发编上银丝。

今天中午我看见一朵将萎的玫瑰花在风中飘荡，去跟一只蝴蝶调情。"给我一粒的花粉罢，在我花蕊紧闭之前，给我一刹那的爱情罢，在我瞑目之前！"

但是快乐的蝴蝶虽然能够赐福，却拒绝了，远渡山谷，当他滋润一朵更年青的花朵时，玫瑰的花瓣因为失恋而凋零。

这样是我的命运，你还不到我这里来，你的眼睛不在这里，你的声音也是寂然，虽然我苗条得有如这颗〔棵〕香瓜树，乳峰外指，也正似它的果实。

Beauty was mine, it brought me no caress,
My lips were red, yet there were none to taste,
I saw my youth consume in loneliness,
And all the fervour of my heart run waste.

While I still hoped that thou would'st come to me,
I and the garden waited for their Lord.
Here He will rest, beneath this champa tree;
Hence, all ye spike-set grasses from the sward!

In this cool rillet I shall bathe his feet,
Come, rounded pebbles, from a smoother shore.
This is the honey that his lips will eat,
Hasten, O bees, enhance the amber store!

Ripen ye, custard apples, round and fair,
Practise your songs, O bulbuls, on the bough,
Surely some sweeter sweetness haunts the air:
Maybe His feet draw near us, even now!

美丽是属于我的,它却没有给我带来爱人的拥抱,我的唇是红的,但是没有人来尝,我眼看我的青春消磨于寂寞里,我满心的热火也归徒然。

当我还希望你会来找,我同花园都等候着它们的主人。他将在这里憩息,这株金香木底下;所以,你们这班有刺的草儿都得滚出花园!

在这个清冷的小河里,我将为他洗脚,细圆的石子,请从更光滑的河岸流来。这是他将尝到的香蜜,快些,啊,蜜蜂儿,加甜那琥珀色的贮藏!

成熟罢,你这番荔枝,又圆又美,练习你的歌声罢,啊,枝上的夜莺,的确有些比往常更甜蜜的甜味萦绕空中:也许他的脚走近我们了,甚至于就是此时!

Disperse, ye fireflies, clustered on the palm,
Love heeds no lamp, he welcomes moonless skies,
Soon shall ye find, O stars, serene and calm,
Your sparkling rivals in my lover's eyes!

Closely I wove my leafy jasmin bowers,
Hoping to hide my pleasure and my shame,
Where the lantana's indecisive flowers
Vary from palest rose to orange flame.

Ay, there were lovely hours, 'neath fern and palm
Almost my aching longing I forgot.
White nights of silence, noons of golden calm,
All past, all wasted, since thou camest not!

Night after night the champa trees distilled
Their cruel sweetness on the careless air.
Noon after noon I watched the bulbuls build,
And saw with hungry eyes the sun-birds pair.

散开罢,你们这班聚在棕榈上的飞萤,爱情不要明灯,他欢迎无月的天空,恬静平和的星群呀,不久你将在我爱人的眼睛里看到你光荣的匹敌!

我把我的亭子用素馨织得密密地,希望的是可以藏起我的欣欢和我的娇羞,那里色相无定的马鞭草花从极浅的玫瑰色到火一般的橘红色样样都齐。

唉,在羊齿同棕榈之下,有真可喜的时候,使我几乎忘却我这剧痛的伫候。白色的静夜,金黄的恬午,全过去了,全白花了,因为你还是没有来临!

夜夜金香木吐出它们残忍的馨香于无情的空中,天天中午时候,我注视夜莺筑巢,用着饿眼看太阳鸟于飞。

None came, and none will come; no use to wait —
Youth's fragrance dies, its tender light dies down.
I will arise, before it grows too late,
And seek the noisy brilliance of the town.

Before many waiting years I longed for gold,
Now must I needs console me with alloy.
Before this beauty fades, this pulse grows cold,
I may not love, I will at least enjoy!

Farewell my solitude of scented flowers,
Across whose glades the emerald parrots gleam.
Haunt of false hope, and home of wasted hours,
I am awake, at last — guard thou the dream!

谁也不来，谁也不会来；等也无用，——青春的芬芳灭了，它的微光也烬了。在时光已太迟之前，我将起来，去追寻城市的喧哗热闹。

这许多年光里，我渴望纯金，现在我必得拿合金来慰情。在这个美丽消失，这个脉搏变冷之前，我也许不能恋爱，我最少总得享乐！

别矣，我这香花的独居，浓绿的鹦鹉在那里草地上闪烁生光。那是骗人的希望之所居，空费的时间之老家，我最后也醒来了——你好好保护那个梦罢！

跋[1]

这里所选的四十三首[2]是代表英国四百年来的情诗。

从开头四首古诗到Thomas Campion都是十六世纪伊利沙伯时代的作品。甜适流利是它们共同的特色，不过有时有夸张太过的地方。可是它们音韵柔美，并且具有初期文艺的新鲜色彩，所以能够不朽。

Donne虽然是属于伊利沙伯时代，他的作风却与他们不同，开了十七世纪用精深巧思入诗的先河。他的诗思想的成分极多，他的诗意就靠着这孪生不已的古怪想头，近代人们厌于滥调，因此对于Donne非常赞美，认为有近代情调的诗人。Herrick同他差不多，不过文字上珠圆玉润，有时免不了伤于纤巧。

十八世纪人们太喜欢讲无聊的道德了，而且爱装腔作势。他们的诗近于散文，拿来骂人到〔倒〕是个工具，献与如花少女是有些不称，所以好情诗很少。十八世纪末期Robert Burns出来用单纯的土话同真挚的情调来唱情歌，写下许多永远有生气的杰作。他的诗豪爽英迈，完全没有当时假古典主义的毛病，的确放一异彩。

---

1 原书该篇无题，题为编者所加。——编者注
2 此数字与《情歌》实际所收情诗数不符，疑为统计有误。——编者注

浪漫派作家（自 Coleridge 到 Keats）把情诗的情调加多，凡是想起来的一切古怪想头都拿来入诗，同时又将诗里的意思弄得很精微玄妙，常拿整首诗浸在梦的境界里，总之 Burns 使情诗的文字得到解放，他们使情诗的内容得到解放。

Tennyson 同 Browning 继浪漫派而起，Tennyson 在文字上下了很深的工夫，颇得古代甜蜜声调的好处，不过又比它们复杂了许多。Browning 的情诗诚恳动人，故意用粗糙的字眼，古怪的句法，因此更见得它的内容是多么诗的。Rossetti 是个含有无限哀怨的女诗人，她的诗极有韵致，又是那么单纯。

我们拿 Hardy 同 Hope 来代表近代情诗。Hardy 颇有 Browning 之风。他诗的主要色彩是 restraint，一点也不放纵，但是个个字好像都是心血凝成的，他的情诗多半是为忆念比他先死的妻子而作，全是极凄凉的悼亡词。Laurence Hope 任情高歌出心中情绪，那种毫不顾虑的热烈同颓唐的心境是我们现代人所常有的，也就是生活苦闷所发的冲动罢。她现在还健在，也许"失望"着。

最后一首诗是《失望》，读者看了这许多情词，何妨尝滴苦水呢？